THE
PRODIGAL
HOUR

THE PRODIGAL HOUR

A Novel

WILL ENTREKIN

For anyone who's only ever wanted another chance.

"It is not unknown to me that many have been and still are of the opinion that the affairs of this world are so under the direction of Fortune and of God that man's prudence cannot control them; in fact that man has no resource against them. For this reason, many think there is no use in sweating much over such matters, but that one might as well let Chance take control."
   -Niccolo Machiavelli,
      The Prince

Part I
Present Fears

"Do I dare
Disturb the universe?
In a minute, there is time
For decisions and revisions which a minute
will reverse."
        -T.S. Eliot, "The Love Song of J. Alfred
Prufrock"

1

C hance Sowin hoped only for a new beginning.
Halloween 2001 found Chance driving the
narrow streets of the development in which he'd
grown up, headed home. Six weeks before, he'd hustled
out the main entrance of the World Trade Center only an
hour before it fell, taking all that business and life, along
with Chance's temp job at a law firm, down with it.

Chance hadn't been sure what to do next. His
father, Dennis, had suggested he come home. "Take
some time," his father had said. "Sort yourself out. All
the time you need."

Chance had been uncertain about it until he'd
realized there was no longer anything keeping him in
Manhattan, and familiar sounded good. Familiar sounded
just about right. And so he'd packed everything he

owned into a compact rental car and taken the Jersey Turnpike south, and now he pulled that car to the curb in front of his childhood home, a long, flat rancher. He squeezed the steering wheel as he took a deep breath, as if to steel himself, though for what he didn't know, and then he got out of the car and stepped up the curb and was struck by déjà vu like sudden density goose-prickling up his neck: *You've been here before.*

Of course he had: he'd grown up here, after all, played stickball at the foot of the cul-de-sac, even tripped and busted his baby teeth on the very same curb he stepped up, but what crawled his skin was not simple familiarity. It was stronger, stranger, and it made the world seem hyper-intense, the October leaves speckling the lawn more vibrant, the afternoon light more glaring. It persisted as Chance crossed his lawn, until he saw the front door: brief space between the edge of the door and its jamb, wood splintered where the deadbolt had broken. Chance felt two simultaneous emotions collide.

First: uncanny familiarity—of infinite broken doors on infinite splintered days, over and over again— followed then, as lightning by thunder, by cold, brutal fear.

Chance eased the door open with his palm. A dead leaf skittered inside, and daylight dazzled the hardwood floor of the foyer beyond golden. Chance's own shadow spindled into the hallway, reaching toward the kitchen, and the walls hid in the dark like they were scared.

You've seen this.

Not just the foyer, the hallway, the kitchen: the slant of light against the grain of wood. He knew these sounds, too—the desiccated scatter of that leaf, the soft whisper of the door's weatherstripped bottom against the floor—but it was not merely familiarity. It was more like a multi-dimensional echo, sounds and sights crossing and re-crossing each other at sharp angles and crazy tangents.

He would have called out to his father except the house seemed too quiet; instead, he eased into through the hallway, and barely restrained from gasping when he saw the living room had been ransacked. Desperate, seemingly searching domestic chaos, the thought of which tightened Chance's stomach into a warm, dense ball of anxiety and violation. Tableaus like the one Chance was staring at were not supposed to occur. Not in the house where he'd grown up, not in the very same living room in which he and his parents had set up the Christmas tree.

Where is safe when home is not?

Chance swallowed, surprised to taste bile. The back of his jaw ached as his mouth watered, and he swallowed again, fought to make it work, keep his gorge down. His breath whooshed out, but as he inhaled he began to troubleshoot, problem solve.

Act.

He flipped open his cell phone to dial 911. A woman answered.

"There's been a break-in. Four five one Bradbury Lane," Chance whispered, his voice low and measured, then hung up while the woman was still talking. The cell's display read 1:57.

Chance held his breath, listening, as he moved farther into the house, until he heard sounds from the basement, just through the kitchen. Chance crept toward the wide-open basement door and descended the stairs on his toes. A voice: his father's, urgent, anxious; another he didn't recognize, more urgent, demanding.

Dusty sunlight fragile as old spiderwebs filtered through windows set high in the basement walls, and a thin slant of light marked the door to Chance's father's office. Chance crossed carefully toward it, then heard the unfamiliar voice: "Where is it?"

Followed by his father's: "I've worked too hard."

You know this.

Before Chance could consider that thought, a glimpse into the office chilled him. A man in a black mask and body suit pointed a gun that looked twice as long as it should have at Chance's father.

In college, Chance had studied martial arts, and his training overtook his perception, then,

slowing the world

as he leapt through the doorway,

toward the gunman,

who rolled even as he fell.

Chance's father lunged forward—

time snapped back to the room and a lot of things happened at once: a sound like rapid-fire sneezes caught; Chance's father cried out in pain, fell; Chance kicked the gunman, who caught Chance's foot and lifted.

Chance fell but twisted to his side, scissoring his legs sideways around the gunman's ankles to yank them backward. The gunman fell hard, and when his gun sneezed again as it hit the ground, the computer monitor popped in a flash of sparks and singed ozone.

The man twisted and fired his gun again, again. Chance dove as finger-sized holes punched into the wall behind him, but then the man smashed the butt of his pistol across Chance's face. He staggered backward, then doubled over when the man hit him in the solar plexus, before white-hot pain seared across his shoulder so hard he spun around and crumpled to his knees.

Two more shots pokked into the carpet, but then the gun's barrel sprung-locked empty. The man pushed it forward like he didn't want it to be empty, then tucked it to his side as he turned.

Pain like a brand flared down Chance's left arm when he tried to put weight on it. The air seemed to gain density, tightening around his head and pressing darkness into his vision. When he heard distant ringing gaining volume, Chance at first mistook it as tinnitus before he realized a siren was approaching.

The gunman sprinted from the room, his footsteps quick across the basement to the stairs. Chance tried to ignore the pain and forced his body forward, but adrenaline-surge and flight-response clouded his perception, and he gagged on white-cold nausea when his shot shoulder bumped the door. Sweat sprang out on his head, and he groaned, blinking back tears. He tried to push off from the jamb, hoping the momentum would carry him across the basement; if he could just get to the stairs he could shake it off, he could make it—

"Chance?" His father's voice.

Chance turned. The room wobbled. The floor threatened to pitch him sideways.

His father lay on the ground. Furious crimson stains had blossomed on his white shirt.

Crossing the room felt like wading through the floor. Chance knelt. The wounds looked worse up close.

"Chancellor."

"Don't talk, dad."

His father swallowed, made a face as if he had tasted something sour. Tiny gagging sounds came from the back of his throat, and he breathed in small spurts. "I—,"but his voice closed on him and nothing more came. He fidgeted a thin silver chain from his shirt collar, twisted it free, then pressed his hand to Chance's, forcing something small and pointed into Chance's palm, closing Chance's fingers so hard around it that it hurt. His father's fingers slacked, and Chance opened his hand: a small, familiar, ring with an ornate filigree design and a large sapphire set behind the crucifix jutting from its crest. What little light made it into the room gleamed around the circumference to twinkle like a tiny star that seemed finally to explode, a hot blast of white light that washed the world away and left Chance to the darkness beyond.

2

Southwark, England. 1606.
The first public performance of Shakespeare's
The Tragedy of Macbeth.

The Globe Theater was exactly as Leonard Kensington had expected: an open-air amphitheatre with three levels of gallery seats looming up and over him. Crushed hazelnut shells on the ground didn't quite mask the body odor of 2,000 people who lived in a society that hadn't yet discovered underarm deodorant.

Onstage, Richard Burbage, as Macbeth, began the fifth act to conclude the play. "Hang out our banners on the outward walls," he pointed out over the audience as if he were seeing Inverness, and so the Globe pretended it was a centuries-old castle in Scotland, the river Thames pretended it was Ness. "The cry is still, 'They come.' Our castle's strength will laugh a siege to scorn. Here let them lie till famine and the ague eat them up. Were they not forced with those that should be ours, we might have met them dareful, beard to beard, and beat them backward home."

The quantum implant in Leonard's temporal lobe began to buzz. He squeezed his earlobe, quietly cleared his throat, which meant: wait. He looked around at the people standing beside him, all of whom were enthralled by that big man on the stage and his words.

Backstage, and so in the bowels of Castle Inverness, several women screamed. Macbeth turned toward the sound. "What is that noise?"

"It is the cry of women, my good lord," Will Shakespeare, playing Macbeth's attendant, Seyton, answered. Shakespeare was a small, pale man with fine features and quick, lively eyes. He hurried offstage to investigate.

As Macbeth turned again to survey his home, Leonard began to ease backward through the yard. Theatergoers glared at him.

The call crackled as it disconnected, but then the implant began to vibrate again. This time he didn't squeeze his ear to answer the call, just continued to strafe and sidestep around the audience members.

Onstage: Seyton reappeared, faltering as if halting from a sprint. Leonard turned, again, to watch. Leonard had enough handwriting samples and discarded play pages, but he thought Will's acting ability better evidence that he had written those plays; the man knew what audiences wanted and how to play to it. Burbage, as Macbeth, was the star of the show, but Will Shakespeare stole every damned scene he was in.

Macbeth turned when Seyton reappeared. "Wherefore was that cry?"

Seyton looked down at his hands, which he'd begun to wring. "The queen, my lord," then, looking again at Macbeth like he expected he might be struck, "is dead."

Leonard had made it to the back of the crowd, almost to the door, and his implant had begun to buzz at a higher frequency, indicating greater urgency, but still he paused. He hadn't ventured back nearly four hundred years to determine whether Shakespeare had written the plays attributed to his hand to miss Burbage's big speech.

Macbeth's eyes widened, his body starting, but then it passed and the mania that had possessed him a moment before returned, and he looked toward the walls of his castle, beyond which the woods were rapidly approaching. "She should have died hereafter. There would have been time for such a word," he said. "Tomorrow and tomorrow and tomorrow creeps at this petty pace from day to day until the last syllable of recorded time, and all our yesterdays have lighted fools the ways to dusty death—."

Leonard ducked through the door. What had smelled bad in the Globe nearly made Leonard gag outside it: tanning hides and sizzling meat, horse manure and body odor.

He tugged his earlobe. "Okay, okay, Race, I'm here," he said in a British accent he'd thought was thick until he'd visited Southwark. Its streets and byways bustled with shoppers and merchants, priests and parishioners, pickpockets and thugs. Leonard hurried to find less populated areas. The leather soles of his boots scritch-scratched over the sand of the path and around the detritus of 17th century life: animal droppings, rotted fruit, cats and dead rats, feathers like mad.

"Why didn't you answer?" Grand Marshall Horatio Atropos—whom everyone called "Race"—asked him. Race oversaw the Operations Center at CIRTN and was the only person who could contact Leonard when Leonard was on a mission.

"I couldn't very well answer a call in the middle of *Macbeth*."

"*Macbeth?*"

"*Macbeth.* Double bubble toil and trouble, out, out damned spot, I'm a crazy king who's going to murder everyone? *Macbeth.*"

"The Shakespeare project."

"Yes, the Shakespeare project," Leonard said. He dodged as someone on a floor above him emptied a bedpan, spilling an evil-smelling, bio-hazard orange onto the street.

"I need you back."

"Is there a problem?" he asked, stepping around a man carting a carcass of unidentifiable origin down the path. Flies buzzed around what hadn't yet been carved for food.

"There's going to be," Race's voice boomed through his cranium. "We've already coordinated the Safe for your return."

Leonard realized that, in his effort to find less populated areas, he had also found less safe areas; several men had paused to give him more attention than he felt comfortable receiving. "I might be detained," Leonard said, even as three men started moving, not approaching him, yet, but following. They wore heavy grey smocks that looked not just lived in but also slept in. One man, his stringy brown hair matted down, his face dirty, his eyes sunken, smiled to reveal a mouth full of rotted teeth.

"If you must," Race said, and then the call disconnected.

Leonard broke into a jog, difficult in his leather and wool clothing, bulky in all the places he'd want tight and constricting in all the places he'd want loose. Three sets of footsteps followed, but Leonard didn't look back as he cut left and right around buildings, struggling to keep footing on simple boots that didn't have much tread. Labyrinthine grey-stone passages and corridors intersected and looped back around each other, and then Leonard skidded around another corner, right into a dead-end alley. The only way out was the way he'd just entered, and he turned just as the three men walked around the corner of the alley.

Leonard abhorred violence. "One chance to turn around and forget you ever saw me."

"Now why would we do that, sir?" One man, his accent thick as tar and smoke, advanced. Scars criss-crossed his cheek, and he licked his cracked lips. "You look a wealthy man burdened by a heavy purse, and we hoped to relieve yo—."

Quick, precise movements—grasp, twist, leverage, chop, stomp—Leonard crumpled the man—who never finished his sentence—to the ground.

Leonard looked at the other two men, who looked uncertainly at each other, then back at Leonard. "Go on," Leonard said. "Run."

They did, leaving Leonard alone in the alley save for the man unconscious on the ground. Leonard pulled his sleeve up.

Around his wrist, Leonard wore a simple watch, silver with a black dial. Because it was anachronistic to the Elizabethan era, Leonard was wearing it with the face on the inside of his wrist to make it less conspicuous. On one side of the face was the dial by which he could adjust the time, which he did frequently, but on the other side was a small button.

Leonard closed his eyes and pressed the button with his thumb.

The hairs on the back of his neck stood prickled as if anticipating being struck by lightning. The muscles in his abdomen clenched, involuntarily, as they always did. Even with his eyes closed he sensed the brilliant, purple flash. It had no heat, but his body still felt the energy crackle—

—and then it was gone, and Leonard opened his eyes.

Perfect dark.

Elizabethan Southwark, Globe Theater and all, was gone. Everything, in fact, seemed gone; he couldn't make out the brushed metal walls he knew surrounded him.

Blazing blue light above him. It swept down his body, pausing briefly at his eyes and fingertips.

Then: a crack in the darkness. A seam slid away, a section of wall whisped aside, and Leonard stepped into the brilliant whiteness it had revealed.

3

Chance awoke to bumps and shudders, a wailing, backward-rushing cacophony and the furtive rustle of crinkling plastic. Something clung over his nose and mouth, and pain throbbed in his head. His first thought was of his father and the gunman. His first emotion was panic. His first action was to sit up as he reached toward his face, where his fingertips brushed a mask.

Quick movement. A man to his left crouched over him. He wore a crisp, white shirt with a gold-and-black patch and put a latex-gloved hand on Chance's chest. "Take it easy."

"My dad." Chance's breath fogged the mask. His voice didn't make it past the plastic.

"We're taking you to County."

Chance tried to rise, but the man pressed back against his chest, whispered something about sedation if necessary, and then, when Chance wouldn't calm down, when Chance couldn't calm down, made good on the warning. Chance felt a pinch near his elbow, looked down to see a clear plastic syringe with numbers on its side jammed to its hilt into his arm. He didn't see the man depress the plunger, only felt calm, warm indifference spread like infection through his body before he sank slowly again into the darkness.

*

Chance woke on a thin sheet on an uncomfortable mattress: did it feel familiar because hospitals are all the same? Electronic beeps, metal clinking, the sharp scent of disinfectant over something biological. He tried to swallow but his tongue was too dry, and a dull ache throbbed through his tightening shoulder. He tried to move it to work out the kink, but pain sliced through his deltoid and made him groan. His blue eyes had always been sensitive to light, and he squeezed them shut to clear his vision.

Trish Lackesis appeared at his side. Her hair was swept back in a tight ponytail, and concern had drawn her lips thin, crinkled the corners of her green eyes.

"Aunt Trish," Chance said. Trish wasn't actually a relative, but her family—which included her husband Nick and their children, Cassie and Dan—had lived across the street from Chance all through his childhood.

"You're awake," Trish said.

Chance attempted to nod, but he felt like his brain had become a giant storm cloud; a few thoughts flashed across like lightning, but mostly there was just a lot of rumbling. He licked his lips. "My dad."

"I haven't heard. How do you feel?"

"Groggy."

"They sedated you."

Chance remembered the white-shirted man, the syringe, the panic. Chance hated hospitals. The last time he'd been in one, a few years before, his father had undergone an emergency bypass. The time before that he'd lost his mother to terminal cancer.

"They said you'll be okay," she told him.

Chance considered his shoulder, which throbbed like it didn't plan to let him forget about it anytime soon, but said nothing.

A perfunctory knock on the curtain surrounding Chance's bed, and a man in a suit stepped around it. He identified himself as Officer Burdick from the local police force and apologized for having to ask Chance a few questions. "If that's okay."

Chance nodded.

"First, there were shots fired but no one else seems to have heard anything—."

"I think he had a silencer."

Burdick took a note in a small notepad. "You get a look at him?"

"He had a ski mask on. But I did hear him tell my father to give him something. Sorry it's not much to go on."

"Any little bit can help," Burdick said, then produced a plastic bag that clinked and jingled as he gave it to Chance. "Paramedics took these off you when you came in."

Chance took the bag and opened it, letting its contents fall to the sheetfolds over his stomach: his wallet, his cell phone, his keys, and then a ring. When he picked it up, memory rushed back so hard he thought he heard his father call his name, heard himself whisper to his father not to talk.

"What?" Trish said.

Chance hadn't realized he had spoken aloud, his attention caught by the ten glittering diamonds, the elaborate crucifix etched with a large sapphire set behind it. The rosary ring his mother had given Chance on the occasion of his confirmation into Catholicism, and the ring his father had pressed into his hand earlier. Each diamond marked a decade to designate ten "Hail Mary"s and an "Our Father," prayers Chance had learned in a private elementary school and had continued to recite with some frequency until his mother had gotten sick—

The diagnoses and the white rooms. The doctors with hushed voices. The oxygen tank that had put his mother in perpetual danger of tipping over.

He had prayed until he could no longer find the words, until he had felt empty. He had turned his attention away from Heaven and to his mother, and he had given her his ring. He had told her he hoped she found comfort with it.

She had worn it around her neck until the end. His father had offered the ring back when she passed away, but Chance had told him to keep it. He wondered whether he had hoped his father would find comfort with it or he just hadn't thought it could do any good any more.—

"Chance?" Burdick asked.

"It's just an old ring my mom gave me once. My father gave it to me just before—," Chance said, but his voice caught on him. He clenched his fist around the ring.

Burdick nodded. "I'm going to call this in. Excuse me," he withdrew.

Even as he did so, two other people entered: the first a man in green scrubs, a surgical mask loose around his neck. His glasses had no rims, but the lines in his face made up for it.

An older black woman followed him. She wore a lavender suit over a white blouse with a collar so high it nearly reached her chin, and a pair of gold-rimmed glasses hung on a pearl necklace down to her bosom. She held a metal clipboard in the crook of her arm.

"Chance Sowin?" the man asked.

Chance nodded, but he was only barely listening. His attention was caught by the clipboard, which looked like bad news.

"Are you Mrs. Sowin?" he asked Trish.

"No. A friend of the family."

"I need to speak to Chance alone."

Chance shook his head. "She stays. She was the only one here when I woke up, and she'll be the only one here after you tell me whatever you have to say."

The man nodded. "I'm Doctor Beldowicz," he said, hesitated, and in that hesitation Chance lost the world. It slowed, and when the doctor spoke again, Chance found he couldn't quite grasp the words.

"Multiple gunshot wounds."

—*another shot, and searing pain*—

"Best attempts to resuscitate him."

—*an antiseptic emergency room where a heart monitor tweeped like a metronome, and a cluster of men and women stared somberly down*—

"Failed."

—*the beat became a steady tone that went on and on and on*—

"Sorry."

Those other words had felt dense, but that last one was a black hole, so strong and explosive it pulled everything Chance knew into it before bursting it out the other side. Up until then, time had played tricks on him, two-step shimmying helter-skelter forward when he'd first gotten home until sedation and shock had slowed it to an ooooozing near-stop, but finally it snapped.

Trish gasped, but suddenly she seemed a long way away. The world seemed bigger than it had a moment before, and more empty; his body didn't feel heavy so much as suddenly and excruciatingly hollowed: this is what it feels like to become an orphan.

This is what it feels like to know you're alone in the world. This is what it feels like to realize that the people you always counted on to be there for you, to help you and keep you safe, no longer can because they are gone.

Chance hadn't expected that. After his mother had succumbed to cancer, he realized, he had expected his father to always pull through, because surely if you lose one parent, the other one has to stay. Surely the only parent you've got left can't abandon you.

No tears came. It might have surprised him, but he remembered running from the crumbling-down World Trade Center just weeks before; he hadn't cried then, either. Some pain is just too big right away. Sometimes there are too many emotions, and sometimes the sadness is just too dense, like the dust that clouds the streets and avenues you were only just learning by heart. Sometimes you just want the world to be normal again, secure again. Sometimes you just want to go home.

But what if going home doesn't bring the comfort, the safety, the normalcy you thought it might? What if you go home and find busted doors and bullets? What then?

The woman who had come in with the doctor spoke. Chance attempted to follow her words as best he could: "Talk to someone." Something about funeral homes and considerations, and then she inquired after his father's organs. His father had not made arrangements, and so Chance signed a form the doctor hurried away with, and the woman asked in a slow, soothing voice if Chance wanted to see his father, or if Chance needed anything.

He sensed he did, though not what, and he wasn't ready to see his father, not when some part of him still hoped it wasn't true. He shook his head.

The woman nodded and stepped from the room as another doctor entered. This one—bald like he chose it, built like he worked at it—introduced himself though Chance missed his name, checked Chance's chart and the dressing on Chance's shoulder. "It's a nice graze," he said, with a vaguely British accent, "But I don't think you need a sling. Just some rest. You were sedated, so I think I'd like to keep you overnight—."

"No. I don't want to stay here. I just want to go home," Chance said. He didn't want to be there anymore. He wanted a shower, and a real mattress on a real bed.

"The police were still there when I left," Trish said. "But you can stay with us. And we'll keep a good close eye on him," she told the doctor.

*

Down the highway home, past familiar houses on familiar corners, mom-and-pop convenience stores and banks with brick facades. The sun was setting, but a storm cloud like a bruise approached from the east, its dark body blazed brilliant orange on its edge.

Trish followed a winding road through their development to park in her driveway. Across the street, two boxy, white Crown Victorias clogged Chance's driveway. He assumed they were unmarked police cruisers by the antennae both had behind their rear windows.

He wondered if the police had any leads. He worried he hadn't been helpful enough.

Chance had already shouldered his door open with his good arm by the time Trish got around the hood to offer her hand. She led him up the walk to the large, white, Tudor house whose siding gleamed like eggshells in the fading daylight. Up the steps, and she opened the big, wooden front door with its etched glass windows to let Chance into her house, where he paused in the foyer. His body didn't ache so much as it felt slow, like he was hungover.

"Why don't you have a seat in the living room? I'll bring you a cup of my special coffee," Trish offered.

Chance had drunk her spiked, spiced coffee during many evenings when their families had dined together. "That'd be great."

*

The first thing Chance noticed when he stepped into the living room was the collage of pictures and family portraits hanging above the hearth opposite the entryway: Dan in a singlet pinning another boy to the mat; Trish in a one-piece black swimsuit, her hair dark and sleek-back from a swim, a book open on her abdomen and her sunglasses hiding her smile; Nick in a fisherman's hat, holding up a trophy-sized, green and grey trout and staring at it like he couldn't decide whether to eat it or hang it above the mantle.

Chance found Cassie's small senior college portrait, and he swallowed. Of course she had changed. Everyone does, and she was no exception, but instead of the usual swelling of curves or loss of hair . . . her glasses were gone, which meant they no longer hid her blue eyes, and her smile was free of her braces. Her porcelain skin and wavy black hair rendered him unable to think except in clichés.

Longing: noticing her, first, when he'd begun to notice girls in the ways that young men do. He had asked her if he could go out with her, once upon a time when he'd been a sophomore in high school, she a freshman, but she had only chuckled and said, of course you can, Chance, we always go out together. The tone of her voice, the way she had said it, had prevented him from correcting her, from telling her he meant it in a completely different way—

He had kissed her once. Just once, at the lake. He'd been twelve and she had been eleven, and they had found themselves beneath a maple tree behind the snack shack where they'd bought watermelon ropes and cherry Cokes. The memory of that day was so strong Chance felt again the sun on his back, tasted her cola lips and smelled the coconut oil-sheen on her skin. He remembered, all over again, the ignorant lust her lips had stirred in him when they'd met his own, the absolute knowledge that he wanted more of her and the complete absence of any idea what it might have been.—

Some things change so hard they shock you, but other things never do. Chance took a deep breath, and by the time he'd let it out, his lips had curled into a faint smile. Which surprised him, because he hadn't thought he had a smile in him. Not then.

A knock behind him, and a voice: "Chance?"

He turned to see Nick in the doorway. Tall, with Kennedy-thick dark hair. He wore a green polo shirt and khakis, but looked like he should have been all in white and on a tennis court.

"Hey, Uncle Nick," Chance said.

"How are you, Chance?"

He didn't know what to say. He wasn't sure yet.

Nick moved to put a hand on Chance's shoulder, but Chance dodged sideways.

"Bad shoulder," he explained. "Doctor said the bullet grazed me."

Nick looked at his shoulder, nodded. "Sorry. And sorry about your dad."

"Thanks."

Nick stuck his hands in his pockets. "Jerry Nazor's in the dining room," he said. Nazor was a detective in the local police department; as a teenager, Chance had worked with Nazor's son, Bram, at the local hardware store. "He'd like to talk to you, if you feel up to it."

"Again? I just talked to one in the hospital."

Nick shrugged. "Seems like Jerry's in charge."

Chance nodded. "Do they have any leads?" he asked even as he started to leave.

Pain jittered through his arm when his uncle grabbed his hand. "Wait."

Chance yanked his hand away, gasping. He flexed his fingers, but the pain already felt distant, like it was in somebody else's body. He wondered which was having greater effect, the painkillers or the sedatives.

"Sorry. It's just—they might have a lead."

"A suspect?" Chance asked.

"More like a motive. Few weeks ago, your father came over and asked if we could talk. I invited him in, but he said it wasn't safe. So we went down to Main Street Bar, and he told me he'd built a hidden room in the basement after you left for school—."

"What? Why wouldn't he tell me?"

"He said he hadn't wanted anyone to know. He seemed nervous."

"So why'd he tell you?"

"He thought someone had found out about it, and he wanted me to destroy it if anything happened to him."

"Destroy it?"

"He told me he built some security mechanisms into it—."

"Did you tell the cops?"

"They found it themselves. But I didn't tell them he wanted me to destroy it. I—I wanted you to hear it from me. Before I did."

"What? You can't. It's evidence," Chance said, trying to keep his voice low.

"Your father—."

Chance cut him off. "My father's dead, and I want to know why, and I'm not going to let you destroy the only clue we've got so far."

"That's not fair."

Chance shrugged his good shoulder. "Sorry. I've seen a whole lot of not fair in the last few weeks. Now if you'll excuse me, I'd like to talk to Jerry, so we can figure out who killed my father, and why."

4

Geneva, Switzerland. October 31, 2001.
Conseil Internationale pour la Recherche Temporel et Nucleaire
(CIRTN, pronounced 'certain').
The Safe.

H undreds of meters below the Operations Center, Leonard strode across the Schrodinger Chamber at the core of the Large Hadron Collider. Behind him, the Safe looked like a gunmetal cigar resting on its unlit tip, rising twenty feet before its tapered top intersected with the bottom of a down-pointing, porcelain white cone. Because the entire room was brilliant white as a laser-treated smile, its exact dimensions were elusive; its only visible feature besides the semi-cylindrical chamber was a small, dark-glassed screen next to a large door.

Leonard placed his palm on the screen, and a bright blue laser scanned his palm. It sped his fingerprints through CIRTN's electronic databases before the door next to it whirred open. Leonard stepped through, into a long, white corridor where a man wearing the CIRTN uniform, khaki fatigues and dark shoes, waited.

The man half-raised his arm to salute, but paused at Leonard's outfit. "Lieutenant Kensington," he said, with an accent Leonard couldn't identify.

"At ease," Leonard said as he strode past.

The man fell into step behind him. "Grand Marshall Atropos asked me to brief you," he said. "I'm Private Madison—."

Leonard nodded. "There's a problem."

"We upgraded our hardware this morning. We updated the quantum supercore to match the new hadron accelerator. It's a better processor, and the new design allows for more memory to extrapolate and triangulate—."

"How about we pretend I already know about the fancy gadgets and you just tell me what the problem is?"

"Right," Madison said. "There's an anomaly."

"Yes, Race said. He also said that you weren't sure what it is."

"It's got a different signature pattern than anything we've ever seen."

"But we might be able to prevent it."

"If we can determine when and where it will occur and stop it before it does."

"Which is precisely what the word 'prevent' means. So what do we know? Time? Place?"

"Neither," Madison said.

"What are the computers telling us?"

"They can't trace it."

"What about these new processors? What are the screens showing?" Leonard asked. One entire wall of CIRTN's Operations Center was an 18-foot-by-32-foot bank of high-definition monitors, each of which could display its own image or contribute to a larger mosaic. Quantum supercomputers chugged and crunched Greek-character variables to determine which uncertainties would occur. The *Conseil*, then, used the information to monitor the continuum.

"Nothing. They're blank."

Leonard stopped so suddenly Madison bumped into him. "Blank?"

"The computers can't get a lock on it. They can detect it, but so far, that's been it. They don't know what it is. Or where."

"Or when."

The corridor ended at an elevator. The two men stepped in, and the elevator began to rise through the concentric circles of the different levels of the particle accelerators. Leonard always imagined he could feel, at a purely physical level, the million-billion revolutions of mesons and bosons and gluons speeding so fast through those tunnels that they arrived at each sensor almost before they had left the source in the first place. Of course he couldn't see them, just the walls of the elevator, so shiny it showed their reflections.

The elevator stopped, its doors opening to reveal the operations center. In four, stadium-style rows of computer terminals, men and women wearing crisp, white shirts typed frantically on keyboards and stared intently at screens. At the front of the room, all those screens blazed uniform electric purple as characters blurred so fast Leonard couldn't tell how, exactly, they were moving. He cursed under his breath.

"That's what we've been saying," Race said, as he approached the two men. Horatio Atropos, the Chief Operations Officer of CIRTN and the Heisenberg Project, was a tall, lean man with a trim beard and short, brown hair. If the Schrodinger Chamber and its Safe were the heart of CIRTN, the Heisenberg Project and its Operations Center were both its brain and its reason for being. In that room, CIRTN had used those screens and computers to monitor the space-time continuum since science had first rendered it useless.

In seven years, Leonard had seen those monitors display presidents and dignitaries, battles and bombs, but never those blurring characters. He looked at Madison. "I thought you said they were blank."

"They were when it was potential," Race said.

"It's not anymore?"

"We were hoping to prevent it, but it's definitely going to happen."

"So what do you need me for?" Leonard asked. Leonard was a researcher for CIRTN, skilled in reconnaissance. The *Conseil* used facilitators for missions that required more action, not men like him. Leonard had traveled back to 1593 to investigate the death of Christopher Marlowe; had the *Conseil* wanted to intercede, they would have then sent someone else.

"Because it's not just years and space. Remember how Einstein once said that all his research and work suggested that there might be alternate realities, higher dimensions with infinite probabilities?"

Leonard nodded, knowing what Race was about to say.

"It's not our timeline. That, up there, is the closest we've been able to get to an alternate universe."

5

The Lackesis dining room was large, with an enormous, deep mahogany table and matching, cushion-seated wooden chairs. Jeryn "Jerry" Nazor, his dark hair flecked with grey, his brown eyes sharp and focused, rose to offer his hand when Chance walked in. "I'm sorry to hear about your father, Chance," he said, his voice low, dry and soft as desert wind over a dying accent. Bram had told Chance his father had come to America from Bosnia nearly two decades before.

"Nick said you wanted to talk to me?"

"If that's okay. I know it's not the best time——."

"I don't know what more I'm going to be able to tell you besides what I told the guy at the hospital," Chance said. Trish motioned him to a place where she had set a mug of steaming coffee and a bowl of stew. Chance thanked her, picked up the coffee to sip it—hot, the scent of dark beans and scotch, tangy, burning down his throat as it chased the gloomy fog from his head—then tried the thick, hearty soup.

Jerry pulled out a pen and a notebook. "At this point, we're mostly concerned with the room your father hid in the basement. Did you know about it?"

"Not until Nick told me."

When Jerry looked sideways at Nick, the latter raised supplicating hands. "I wanted him to hear it from me."

Jerry scribbled in his notebook. "I remember Dennis talked to some magazines last year, about his work. Were you familiar with it?"

Chance shook his head. His father had taught physics at Princeton's Institute for Advanced Study, but Chance had studied history and philosophy at Fordham, and his father's research had always been beyond him. "He talked about it sometimes, and I know he got boxes of books to read and review, but other than that?" he shrugged his good shoulder.

"So you don't know what he might have been working on in that room?"

Chance shook his head. "But whatever's in there, the guy who killed him wanted it."

Jerry nodded. He flipped a notebook page. "You told Officer Burdick the gunman demanded something."

"He asked where it was."

"Can you be more specific?"

"Not really," Chance shrugged again without thinking. Pain tightened across his upper back and just up his neck. He took another sip from the coffee, hoping that the alcohol might help relax him more even as the caffeine made things more clear.

"Did your father respond?"

Chance thought back again. Back to the basement, back until his father said: "I've worked too hard on it."

"But you don't know what he was working on."

"My daughter might," Nick said.

"Cassie?" Chance asked.

Nick nodded. "Princeton just hired her as your father's research assistant. She was supposed to start next semester."

"I thought she was in Germany," Chance said. Last he'd heard, Cassie had just been accepted into the Max Planck Institute for Physics near Munich.

"She was, but she finished her master's and moved back home over the summer. Princeton offered her a job working with your dad, but it couldn't start until spring, so they asked her to work in the library until then. She should be home soon."

Jerry sighed, scanned his notebook. "Okay, let's go back to the beginning."

"I've already told you everything."

"Your neighbors mentioned seeing some strange cars coming and going recently. Do you know anything about them?"

"Strange cars?"

Jerry consulted his notebook. "Several over the past few months. A few Lincolns, a late-model Nissan, an exotic sports car with a logo like a pitchfork."

"Mazerati," Chance said. Nazor cocked an eyebrow. "I worked in the financial district with guys who made three million a quarter. They couldn't spend it all on drugs."

"Did they ever talk to your father?"

"Dad and finances? God no."

"Did he have financial trouble? Maybe he borrowed money?"

"Like a loan shark? Dad was never into gambling."

"People borrow money for lots of things," Nazor said. "Like research."

"I think that's reaching."

"Maybe, but motive is just about our only lead. And this room we can't get into."

"You haven't gone in yet?"

Nazor shook his head. "The entrance is behind the bookcase, but we can't move it. We found a lock in a dummy thermostat, but it's got a complicated key. Our guy said whatever it is has an odd shape, like a letter, or a crucifix. I'm not entirely sure, myself. I . . ."

Chance had stopped listening by then. He was thinking of a crucifix. "I think I know how to get into that room."

*

The sun was gone, but the dark cloud had stuck around, and Chance followed Jerry through a cool drizzle, across the street to his house. Up the slightly overgrown lawn, up the brick steps of the stoop. The yellow tape. "POLICE LINE DO NOT CROSS."

Chance's strides slowed the closer he got to the door. He clomped up the front steps, but by the time he reached that door, he found he could not move his feet. Jerry ducked under the yellow tape, disappearing without looking back, but Chance just stood there a moment, staring at the torn jamb. He touched the yellow tape, watched it crinkle in his fist.

You've been here before.

Again the hairs on his neck prickled with something more intense than memory. Again the sensation of infinite busted doors on endless broken days—

"Chance?"

Chance looked up. Jerry had reappeared and was eyeing him as if concerned. "Sorry. Just—bad memories, I guess."

The detective nodded. "Come on. Just don't touch anything."

Chance wiped rain from his forehead as he followed Jerry into the house. The detritus of everyday life cluttered the living room like a small but powerful domestic bomb had gone off. Jerry led him past the kitchen entrance, through the basement door, down the simple, creaking wooden steps into the cellar. They crossed to the office, where a man in dark jeans and a turtleneck stood concentrating on something on the wall. Signs of the earlier struggle: the overturned desk chair, the scent of ozone from the broken monitor, finger-sized holes punched through the wall to reveal nothing but hollow blackness.

Jerry nodded toward the holes. "That's how we found the room."

The man in the turtleneck turned. He had dark hair and a brown beard with hints of red in it. "Still working on it, Jer."

Jerry nodded. "This is officer Mackenzie. Our lock expert."

"Was until I saw this bad boy. Bugger. Strangest key I've ever—."

"Mind if I take a look?" Chance cut him off.

"What? I mean, I guess," Mackenzie said as he gave Jerry a questioning look.

Mackenzie had flipped the thermostat open to reveal a metal plate with a vertical slit, and Chance was impressed by the façade; he never would have guessed it wasn't actually a thermostat. He wondered if he'd ever questioned it before, if he'd ever even noticed it, but he couldn't remember; his father's office had always been his sanctuary, and Chance had rarely intruded.

"It's this weird shape. Hitting both tumblers . . ."

If Mackenzie kept talking, Chance didn't hear it. He reached into his pocket, closing his fingers around the hard, metal points of the rosary ring, and pulled it out. Jerry spoke behind him, but he didn't pay attention, just turned the crucifix sideways to stick it into the slit. He felt the tumblers slip as the cross slid home, and he twisted. Something mechanical in the wall clicked, while something else began to spin with *whrrr*—

The bookcase first lifted and then began to revolve on its left side, opening like a door, and leaving in the wall behind it only a hole into a dim room Chance couldn't make out.

Chance didn't know what to expect. Part of him, the irrational parts, thought of the Batcave. The Shakespearean bust with the hidden switch, strange markings like hieroglyphics. He'd always been fascinated by secret passages—as all young boys are—and he wondered where this one led, and what he'd find beyond it. He started toward it.

"No, wait," Jerry said.

Chance looked at him.

"Everything in that room will be evidence—."

"I might recognize something if I see it. Something you wouldn't."

Jerry hesitated. "All right, but I go first."

Jerry passed him, past the edge of the bookcase and through the door, where he paused and sought a switch, which he must have found, because suddenly Chance could see into the room his father had hidden behind the office wall . . .

Which was really just a physics lab. In a basement. Just a room a lot like the physics laboratories his father had lectured in at Princeton. Overhead fluorescent fixtures ran the length of the room, about twenty feet end to end and ten feet deep. A marbleized bench sat in the center, on top of which were several instruments Chance had long ago forgotten the names of. Squiggly marks decorated the white dry-erase board on one wall; Chance was sure they probably meant something, but he couldn't guess what. It smelled like what he remembered his father's lab and office at Princeton smelled like:

singed circuitry, cloying transformer oil, and pipe tobacco.

To Chance's right, along the wall, was a long workbench strewn with a couple of screwdrivers and a soldering iron, a circuit board, but there were several other instruments Chance had never seen and wouldn't try guessing the function of. One was about the size of a small paperback, with a matte metal casing, an LCD screen, and several buttons and dials—

you've seen this—

even though he hadn't, even though he'd never been in that room before, and he reached for it as reality superimposed over his memory, but withdrew his hand when Jerry spoke. "I'd rather you didn't touch anything for right now."

Chance nodded. Looked around the room, the board, the lab bench.

"If we can figure out what he was working on," Jerry began, but stopped when Mackenzie poked his head through the doorway.

"Hey, Jer? Couple guys just arrived. Sayin' they're government."

"Feds?" Jerry's brow furrowed. He started out of the room, glanced at Chance. "I'll be right back. Don't touch anything."

But what was there to touch? Chance had been more impressed at the Princeton physics department, even just in the lobby, where a deep trophy case displayed things like plastic scintillators and spark chambers across from a large portrait of Richard Feynman.

He had expected more. Especially if this room was the reason his father was dead, especially if someone, somewhere, wanted something in it. What was there? A board, a bench, a couple of instruments anyone could pick up at a specialty supply vendor, if not simply a comprehensive electronics store. A couple of notebooks. Nothing that looked dangerous, or valuable. Nothing impressive. Just a bunch of stuff Chance couldn't find a reason to care about in a room he couldn't imagine a reason to hide.

He heard Jerry raise his voice outside the office, and he poked his head around the doorway. Jerry was talking to two men, one a tall blond with eyes like a bird of prey and a nose crooked like it had been broken and improperly set many years before, the other a shorter, dark-haired man with an icy blue gaze. Both wore immaculate white shirts under charcoal suits whose cuffs were damp with rain, and both looked like all the federal agents Chance had ever seen in movies and television, striking just the right balance between authoritative, mysterious, sinister, and clichéd. The dark-haired man carried a large, empty cardboard box.

"But I haven't even reported it to anyone higher up," Jerry was saying.

"We've been monitoring Dennis Sowin——."

"What?" Chance asked.

The dark-haired one's jaw clenched. "Who're you?"

"I'm Dennis Sowin's son. I'd've thought you'd know that if you were monitoring him."

"You're Chance," Blondie's tone was less confrontational than Brunette's, but salesman-slick.

Chance didn't nod. "You are?"

"I'm sorry, where are my manners? I'm Agent Hanley," Hanley said, flashing a leather wallet open-closed so fast Chance didn't see anything in it. "And this is my partner, Agent Geisel. We're here about your father."

"My father died several hours ago."

"We're very sorry for your loss. But we have reason to believe that the man who took his life would also have taken his research had he had the opportunity, and we're here to prevent that from happening."

"So you know what he was working on?"

"We haven't actually seen—."

"Then what makes you so certain you can prevent anything? Because I'll be honest with you, from where I stand, the most important thing to prevent would have been his death in the first place, and you guys obviously dropped the ball on that one."

Hanley looked at Geisel, who merely shrugged. Chance guessed he didn't know what to say. Hanley spoke instead. "Yes, the loss of your father was unfortunate—."

"Yeah, tell me about it," Chance struggled to keep control of himself.

"As I said, we're very sorry for your loss. But we have reason to believe your father was conducting research that could be very dangerous were it to fall into the wrong hands. Rest assured we will have our most qualified and knowledgeable experts working around the clock to figure it out. We will, in addition, be collecting full statements from all parties involved, and will assume full responsibility of the investigation."

"Which is all just the long way of saying you're taking control," Chance said. "And you said you're agents? FBI, or something?"

"We're with the Joint Terrorism Task Force. We work in conjunction with the FBI and local law enforcement personnel. As you can imagine, we've been very busy since the attacks last month. Our job is to investigate those, as well as prevent any new ones from occurring, and we have been monitoring your father because we have reason to believe that he was in some way connected to al Qaeda."

It was a verbal suitcase nuke, a spoken dirty bomb that left in its aftermath devastating silence like radiation.

Chance's body broke into goosebumps identical to the ones that had formed as he'd run from the encroaching dustcloud of the World Trade Center's collapse.

Jerry's voice, when it came, was soft but reasoned. Calm, but forceful. "You have some evidence of this?"

"Unfortunately, that information is classified. Suffice to say, with the provisions newly allotted us, and under the jurisdiction provided by the PATRIOT act, we have reason to believe last month's attacks were just the beginning," Hanley said, then looked from Chance to Jerry and back again. "But we're getting ahead of ourselves, gentlemen. Why don't the three of us walk back across the street, where we can discuss the matter both reasonably and at length? Peter, go through the office and collect anything you think might be relevant."

6

"Leonard?" Race said, like it wasn't the first time.

"What?"

"I asked what you thought of it."

The first time Leonard had stepped into the Safe's giant cylinder, which used an electromagnetic field to create a pocket in the space-time continuum in which the laws of physics and concepts like yesterday and forward no longer existed, icy panic had seized him. The thick-walled cylinder had sealed shut around him, and then bending nausea had waved through him as the field had engaged. He had put his hand out to steel himself against those brushed metal walls, only to discover—

They had disappeared.

In less time than it had taken for him to blink, so quickly he had missed seeing it occur, all evidence of

CIRTN had vanished, giving way instead to panoramic desert as far as he could see. By the time he had returned to the complex, Leonard had become fascinated enough by quantum mechanics to enroll in advanced study, which had led to his promotion through the organization. Many physical concepts had remained elusive, but Leonard had understood that the possibility of higher dimensions suggested the existence of alternate universes, and now those blazing purple characters on those vibrant screens proved it.

"I have no idea. I don't know if I ever expected to actually see it. Or what it might look like if I did," he said, finally, then, "What now?"

"As soon as we realized it's an alternate universe, we sent all the data to Kaku and Greene. We're hoping they'll be able to make some sense out of it."

"And then?"

"And then we need to figure out how to get there. You should probably change into something less conspicuous. Something simple, maybe? What is that, anyway, a doublet and hose, or something? Elizabethan England?"

Leonard nodded, and then Race's meaning finally sank in. "You're sending me?"

"I don't trust anyone else."

"What about Leudeker?" Johannes Leudeker was CIRTN's most qualified operative and the one used for the most important missions. When a young German named Himmler had attempted to keep Gavrilo Princip from assassinating Franz Ferdinand to catalyze the Great War, Leudeker had prevented the temporal interference.

"I don't want anything done. I just need to know what's happening, where, and when so we can figure out what to do."

Leonard clenched his jaw, nodded. "Okay."

"Where do you want to go?"

Leonard considered. "Manhattan," he said. Because if he was going to find any facts about any universe, he was going to find them in Manhattan.

"Manhattan?"

"I went to school there," Leonard said. He'd left his parents' English countryside cottage to attend Columbia University in New Holland, and he remembered the streets and byways well, because you never really forget them. Manhattan had always stood, in his mind, proudly perched on the bleeding edge of now. It was the most dense city Leonard had ever known and changed the most quickly, time-lapse evolution like a millennial second; Manhattan's breakfast could change the entire world by lunch. Given alternate universes, Leonard had the feeling that Manhattan would be each one's soul, an urban fingerprint that both reflected and summarized its world.

Race nodded. "In the meantime, why don't you change?"

"Plainclothes?"

Race nodded.

"When do I leave?"

"Yesterday."

Leonard nodded, turned. The elevator doors opened the moment Leonard pushed the button, and he hit the button for an upper floor. He'd request new clothing, shower, change out of the Elizabethan garments, then leave. Yesterday.

It was a figure of speech, but only just.

7

Chance, Trish, Nick, and Jerry sat around the Lackesis dining table. Hanley had set a brown leather briefcase, the lid of which he'd propped open, on the table, but he did not sit.

Trish had made Chance a second mug of coffee when she'd seen him walk in from the cold, driving rain just behind Jerry and Hanley. Raindrops had plastered his hair to his head and dripped down his face, and his shirt was moist and damp. Even inside, Chance could hear the rain had picked up, pludding against the roof, liquid-tapping down the windows.

"I know you've all had a lot to process and not a whole lot of time to do so, but my colleagues and I are with the joint terrorism task force and hope to resolve this situation quickly," Hanley told them. He'd already twice flashed his identification wallet, once to Nick and then again to Trisha.

"I think I've missed something here. I thought it was a burglary," Trish said.

"They think Dad was connected with *al Qaeda*," Chance said. He wasn't sure he believed the allegation, but he had learned the month before to be careful trusting his instincts; had anyone told him on September 10th that terrorist attacks would level the World Trade Center the following day, he wouldn't have believed that, either, but that wouldn't have kept it from becoming true. "They haven't said if they have any evidence of it, though."

"Our information is classified—."

"You said," Jerry cut in. "And that you're here to confiscate Dennis Sowin's work."

"We're concerned it might fall into the wrong hands."

"But don't they need a warrant for that?" Trish said.

"Not after the PATRIOT act," Jerry said. "Just passed last week, and it basically means they can do and take whatever they want."

"It's a matter of national security," Hanley said, withdrawing from his briefcase a manila folder he opened. From within he pulled a thick stack of photographs, passed one to Nick. "Tell me, have you or your wife seen this car recently? Say, over the summer, perhaps?"

Nick looked at the picture. His eyes widened as he nodded, and he showed the picture to Jerry. "This is the car I mentioned. The one I didn't recognize the logo of. The—what'd you say it was?" he asked Chance.

"Mazerati," Chance replied. Pain pinched through his neck when he tried for a better look.

"I'm sure Mr. and Mrs. Lackesis can corroborate having seen the car several times," Hanley said, as he withdrew another photograph from the envelope. "Tell me," he said, looking from Nick to Trisha and back again, "If you can remember ever having seen this man before."

A grainy, black-and-white shot, obviously taken at a distance but with telephoto. A small, outdoor café, and the main subject was a young-ish, professional-looking man, dark-skinned and with a wiry, unkempt beard, who appeared to be of some vaguely Middle-Eastern ethnicity: Saudi, perhaps, or Afghani, Chance wasn't certain. For several years, Chance had lived in Jersey City, which had one of the most dense populations of Middle Eastern immigrants in the United States, but that only made Chance more aware that identifying ethnicity or origin by sight alone was difficult at best.

The man in the photograph was as likely Egyptian as Iraqi. He was dressed in an immaculate, light-colored linen suit, and on his head wore a white covering from which thick curls of black hair sprung at the bottom. He sat alone.

"That's the guy who was always driving the car."

Hanley set another picture on top of it: the same man, in the same attire, stepping into that brilliant, beautiful car. "Until just a few weeks ago, Fajid al Zawqiri was just another Islamic fundamentalist with too much money and too much access to too many automatic weapons. He was trying to insinuate himself into the lower levels of *al Qaeda*. Given that he is a rich man with vast resources to both fund and implement just about any operations his associates could think of, they took full advantage of him."

Another photograph. Chance's breath caught: the same man, the same clothing, the same car, in front of the house Chance had grown up in. The picture might have been black and white, but it was crisp and clear and showed more details than he wanted to see.

Something wasn't right. Chance knew photographs could be easily doctored, but that wasn't it. He drained the remainder of the coffee in one long pull, sighed as warm coffee and hot liquor burned down his throat.

"More?" Trish asked him, reaching for the mug.

Chance put his hand up to stay hers. He felt better, but he feared that any more alcohol would have an adverse reaction with the sedative the paramedics had administered earlier. "So he was at my house," he said.

Another photograph: Zawqiri walking up the lawn of Chance's house, and Dennis Sowin standing in the door, watching him. Another: Dennis Sowin standing aside to allow Zawqiri entrance. "All the evidence we have suggests your father was in contact with him, and we believe he had an unhealthy interest in your father's research. We want to know why," Hanley said. As he said it, the sound of the front door opening carried into the dining room, and footsteps approached the dining room.

Those footsteps echoed through Chance's brain, supercolliding and meeting themselves coming, going, and sideways. The world became hyperintense: the rain outside sounded like applause, the light seemed brighter, the contrast between Hanley's white shirt and his dark suit greater.

"You think he killed my father," Chance said. His own voice sounded distant, the question scripted.

"One of his associates, certainly," Hanley told him as Geisel, appeared in the doorway, carrying the same box as he had been earlier. "Ah, Peter. Wonderful. Is that everything?"

Geisel nodded, might have said something, but Chance couldn't follow; just that quickly, the echoes left his brain, leaving him wondering only what they had meant.

He looked at his empty coffee mug, trying to collect his thoughts, wondering if it had been aftereffects of whatever they'd given him, or if perhaps he'd drunk more alcohol-spiked coffee than he'd realized.

"That's all you're taking?" Nick asked.

"All we need are the notebooks and any significant hardware."

"Significant hardware?" Jerry asked.

"Most of his equipment could be purchased fairly easily," Hanley reached into the box and pulled out the small, boxy device with the LCD screen Chance had seen earlier. "But the devices Dennis Sowin was working on," he said, set it on the table, then reached again into the box and withdrew something that looked like a telescope crossed with a stun baton, "These are what we're interested in."

"But what about the writing on the dry-erase boards?" Jerry asked.

Geisel reached into the box to withdraw a digital camera.

Chance eyed it. Was he being paranoid that nothing seemed to add up? "So what you're telling us is that my father was talking to some low-level *al Qaeda* flunky, who then hired somebody to kill him, just to get his hands on a box of homemade electronics?"

"That's a fairly accurate, if oversimplified, summary of what we know so far."

Jerry spoke up, then. "If that's all you know so far, I think we're in deep trouble."

Hanley seemed about to respond, but then the front door opened again, and Chance stopped paying attention. Approaching footsteps triggered again that strange, hyperreal intensity—

you've been here before—

returned the moment he saw Cassie, who paused in the doorway, her eyes darting from Hanley and Geisel, to Jerry and her mother and father, and finally to Chance.

The portrait hadn't done her justice. It might have caught the deep, blue-green color of her eyes, but it had missed entirely their liveliness and spark. Rainwater had damped down the chestnut waves of her hair, which dripped dark marks on her shoulders. She wore a black turtleneck that clung tight to her body under a tweed jacket complete with brown leather patches at its elbows, plus a pair of tight-fitting jeans she wore easily over her long, lithe legs.

"Chance?" she whispered. "What's going on?"

"Someone broke into Chance's house, Cass. They shot Uncle Dennis," Nick told her.

"Is he—," she stopped like she didn't know what to ask.

"They couldn't save him."

Chance watched her reaction, which hovered somewhere between confused and incredulous.

"This is Agent Hanley, and his partner, Agent Geisel. They're all trying to get to figure out who did it, and why."

Cassie looked at Hanley and Geisel. "Agent?"

Hanley nodded. "FBI, joint terrorism task force. And you were Dennis Sowin's assistant."

"I—yes, but—," Cassie twice began, but stopped each time as if whatever thought had crossed her mind had blinked away. Her gaze continued to dart, from the agents to Jerry to Chance to the cardboard box still on table to the small metal-cased device Hanley had set next to it.

"We need you to answer a few questions his research," Hanley said.

She looked at him a moment, then stared directly at Chance. "I need to speak to Chance."

Hanley paused, as if what she had said had been the last answer he'd expected. "Okay," he nodded. The chair groaned as Chance rose. Everyone was looking at him expectantly, but he ignored them. He followed Cassie out.

*

Cassie sat on the couch, nearly folding into herself, her elbows on her knees, and she ran her hands back through her hair. Her expression looked as though she were trying to puzzle out a complex physics problem.

"You okay?" Chance asked her.

She looked at him. "Yeah," she started, then, "God, I'm so sorry," she rose, her arms opening to embrace him.

He barely had time to recoil from her embrace, even as much as he wanted to be in it. He indicated his shoulder, pulled up his sleeve. "Dad wasn't the only one who got shot."

Cassie's hand found his tricep. "Is it bad?"

"Just a graze."

"Does it hurt?"

"Feels like I worked out too hard and strained something."

She nodded, and then her gaze wandered. He followed it to look through the window, at his house. The police cars had left, and the only sign that anything out of the ordinary had occurred was the yellow tape still slashed across the door. The dark Lincoln sedan the agents had drive was parked out front.

"They found the hidden room in your basement, didn't they?" Cassie said.

"You knew about it too?" He thought of his father's telling Nick about it, the darkened bar and too many beers. He moved toward the window, stopped, half turned. He wondered how his father had told Cassie, and when. "Jesus Christ, am I the only fucking one he didn't—"

"Chance."

"Tell? I mean, when did he tell you? How long after you signed on—?"

"Chance," she said, louder. Shorter. More abruptly.

Her tone stopped him. He looked at her. "What?"

"He didn't tell me, Chance," she told him. "You did."

8

Another CIRTN elevator stop, two floors above the Operations Center, where Leonard found a reception area with grey carpet, a black-leather-and-chrome sofa and a so-modern-it's-from-tomorrow desk, behind which sat a young woman in a dark green business suit. Her auburn hair was swept back from her smooth, lean neck, and she didn't look up from the computer's monitor when Leonard stepped out. Her slender fingers danced on the keyboard.

Leonard cleared his throat.

Jennifer looked up. "My favorite lieutenant," she exclaimed as she rose from behind the desk and stepped around it. She opened her arms as if to pull him close, but then stopped. "Oh."

"Is that an 'Oh, I want you so bad I can't contain myself' oh, or an 'Oh, I must restrain myself while on the job, for people may well be watching and to act on my visceral instincts would be a breach of etiquette' oh?"

"That would be an 'Oh, how I would love to give my wonderful man a kiss I would feel against my thigh, but what on Earth does he smell like?' oh. Because seriously."

He realized, then, he couldn't actually recall the last time he had bathed, because when in Elizabethan Southwark etc. "That bad?"

"On the positive side, I'm sure you fit right in. So how was it?"

"Fine as you'd expect."

"Burbage?"

"Voice like aged Scotch. So thick you could pour it. But Shakespeare was better."

She doubletook. "You saw the Bard?"

"I had no idea how talented he was. Couldn't take your eyes off him."

"And the plays?"

"Totally his. He played that audience like a bloody piano."

"Wow," she said. "Swordfights?"

"Unfortunately not. Bloody interrupted right before."

"I was going to say. It's only been a few days."

Leonard had wondered how long he'd been gone. CIRTN coordinated Safejumps to end precisely one week after they began, because, due to temporal fluctuations, time passed differently on either end of the jump. Depending on mission objectives, some jumps lasted a few hours or days, whereas others, such as the one Leonard had just returned from, lasted months; he'd been in Southwark nearly two with another on schedule. "Got called back. Priority."

"Here to see Darren?"

Darren Manningly was the equipment coordinator at CIRTN, who in addition oversaw the research and production department. "Not yet. For now, I just want to change."

"Though the medieval attire certainly does become you so. So what can we get for you? Kevlex?" she asked him as she returned to the other side of the desk, took out a form and ticked a box on it. Kevlex was a light, impenetrable body armor.

"Perfect," he leaned gently against the desk. "Black?"

She looked at him over her glasses. "You look better in slate, honey."

"Single-breasted? Three buttons?"

"Check and check. Shall I bring it down to you?"

He pushed away from her desk. "Nothing would please me more," he told her as he turned and tapped the elevator button.

"Oh, I don't know. We could certainly try a few things."

The elevator doors opened. "I'm going to go down and change out of these clothes."

"And shower."

"And shower," he agreed.

*

The dormitories in the temporary quarters were small because no one ever stayed there very long anyway. They universally contained: a tan-sheeted, full-sized bed, the room just a few feet bigger on every side; a dresser; a mirror; and a cloth curtain hiding a small closet. A bathroom only slightly larger, just a shower and a basin and a commode and not enough room to turn around in without bumping his knee.

As he unbuttoned his doublet and began to unwrap the leather and rough cotton, Leonard wondered if, somewhere else somewhen else, another Leonard Kensington was standing in a dormitory and hating it every bit as much as he did. When he didn't have to stay at the complex, he shared a small Geneva apartment with Jennifer, and lately the idea of leaving CIRTN behind forever, to settle down with Jennifer in Switzerland or even to move on completely, had become more attractive. To bring her back to the English countryside where he'd grown up, or return to her family in Lesser Jersey on the Atlantic side of the North American Union.

He drew aside the thin closet curtain to toss his doublet into the hamper, wondering as he did so if there might be a—what would they call it? An alterniverse? An alternity?—different reality in which something very much like that had already occurred. If somewhen else Leonard had already married her, and they were together raising two and a half children and had a white picket fence. He wondered if there wasn't a son whom he'd taught to throw a mean slider, if somewhere else he wasn't a rockstar and somewhere else he wasn't a doctor and somewhere else again he wasn't already dead.

He pulled the hose from his legs, sighing in relief as he released himself from their constriction, and strode into the small bathroom. He ran the hot water and stepped under it, sighing with relief as he washed off a layer of grime that was at the same time both just several hours and more than three hundred years old. When he heard a knock, he wrapped a towel around his waist and padded back into the main room to whisper open the door, revealing—

A great, growling werewolf with latex fangs and plastic hair above a body like men can't think around. A rubber-gloved paw held up his suit, while the other tucked up the mask to reveal Jennifer's smile. "Brought your suit," she told him, then growled at him.

"I see that. Come in, come in," he took the suit and hung it in the closet. "What's with the mask."

"Halloween, silly."

"Oh, is it?" he said, then turned and kissed her, hard, hungrily. He had missed her. He didn't get to see her nearly as often as he would have liked, and due to the nature of his travel, the time he spent with her was often sporadic and always too brief.

Which was why he treasured her. Her firm lips on his, her soft breasts pressed to his chest even through her blouse, which he had already begun to unbutton, revealing a white lace bra. At the same time, she unknotted the towel from his waist, then kissed down his chest and abdomen, went to her knees before him as if in prayer, and he struggled to keep his knees from buckling.

"You started the shower without me," she told him just before she took him into her mouth.

He pulled her up to him, against him, removed that smart grey skirt and slid down her white lace panties and carried her into the shower with him. There he kissed her and held her and moved with her; the water sluiced down their bodies. As he held her there, as they moved in that water, as it danced and bounced and cascaded on their bodies, Leonard forgot to wonder if, some other where, some other when, he was doing exactly the same thing in exactly the same way.

There and then it didn't matter. There and then, he held her. There and then was enough.

9

Chance plunked himself down on the couch but never looked away from Cassie. "Me?"

He wasn't sure anything else Cassie could have said would have surprised him more. Not that she had always had feelings for him. Not that she and his father had begun a clandestine romantic relationship. Not even that she had gone to Munich not to study physics but rather to enter rehabilitation for an addiction to black tar heroin.

His brain was misfiring. Thoughts vanished before they could fully form. "But—but how?" he asked, even though there were a thousand other incoherent questions suddenly bursting in his head. He thought of the pervasive *déjà vu* he'd been experiencing since the moment he'd pulled in front of his house.

"You. You told me. Last night—"

"But I was in my apartment in Jersey City last night. Packing. And I just found out about it myself. Your dad said he was the only one who'd known."

Cassie shrugged, looked out the window, toward Chance's house. Quicksilver raindrops coursed down the pane, obscuring the street beyond. As he watched, lightning blazed the window, followed a few seconds later by a sound of thunder.

"You know how sometimes you get late-night phone calls you barely remember the next morning? The ones you only sort of remember they even happened in the first place? Nevermind what you said. And you think you remember them but you're never really sure they happened?"

"So you don't actually remember what happened?"

She turned. "My dad knew about the room."

Chance nodded.

"And the two agents. They're saying your father worked with al Qaeda."

"They have pictures."

"I just remember I woke up and you were in my bedroom. You told me about that room, except you told me it was a lab. You said your father had built it in your basement, but he'd told my father to destroy, and that the government was after whatever was in it."

"I think I'd remember being in your bedroom."

"It's too much to be a coincidence."

"So do you know what he was working on?"

"They don't know?"

"They're trying to figure it out."

"They think I'll know?"

"Weren't you helping him?"

"Not until next semester."

"But you'd probably understand it, wouldn't you?" he asked her.

*

By the time Chance and Cassie walked back into the dining room, Hanley and Geisel had both taken seats. Hanley was in the one Chance had left and had set the photographs out in front of him, while Geisel had pulled one of the extra chairs from against the wall, spun it, and sat on it backward, his hands steepled over the back. Two devices had been removed from the box and were on the table: the odd-looking electronics gadget and the one that resembled the telescope.

Hanley rose when Chance and Cassie reappeared. "Glad you're back. Please," he indicated the chair he'd risen from.

Chance looked at Cassie. "Go ahead."

Hanley looked at Geisel, twitched his head sideways. Geisel rose, too.

"You too, Chance. We'd like to continue where we left off. We're especially eager to speak with you, Ms. Lackesis."

"Chance told me. But I wasn't scheduled to start working with Uncle Dennis until next semester."

"We know," Hanley withdrew a notebook from the copy-paper box and offered it to her. "But I'd wager you might figure out what he was working on."

Cassie eyed the notebook, hesitated, but took it.

"I'm sure Chance has told you what we know so far," Hanley said.

"I'm not sure I believe it, but I'm more interested in seeing if I can figure out what Uncle Dennis was working on than in arguing with you." She opened the notebook. Her eyes scanned down the page. "What do *you* think he was working on?"

"We're not certain."

"If you've been watching Uncle Dennis for as long as Chance said you have, I have a feeling you have at least a bit of an idea."

"We think Dennis Sowin's research included several different areas. Alternative energy sources. Quantum mechanics. Lasers and optics."

"And you think *al Qaeda* was after those things?"

"Any one of those things might well have attracted their attention. *Al Qaeda* generally draws its resources from either oil or opium. If your father had made some significant advancement in the field of alternative energy sources, that might spell trouble for oil conglomerates."

"But aren't there a lot here, too?" Chance asked. "What's Cheney's company? That give him that big kickback the other year?"

"Halliburton," Jerry said.

"And there are a bunch of refineries right down the highway."

"Which is why we don't think it was just the energy research," Hanley nodded. "Have you ever heard of a quantum bomb?"

"What?" Cassie asked.

Hanley hesitated. "We don't know much about it. Our best sources have told us that, if it is possible and Dennis Sowin managed to build one, it would make an atomic bomb look like a Roman candle."

"And you think he was doing it to help al Qaeda?" Chance said. It didn't make any sense.

"We have no real definitive proof about what your father's connection to *al Qaeda* was, only that he met with Zawqiri multiple times. It's entirely possible Zawqiri was simply being persistent, or even actually coercing your father into sharing his research. In light of today's occurrences, however, the best working theory we have is that your father resisted and Zawqiri got tired of trying."

"So he had my father killed and just planned to steal it."

"He probably would have been successful if you hadn't interrupted. You may well have single-handedly prevented the next terrorist attack on the United States. At the very least, you postponed it."

"Yeah, well, I—," he was about to say he just wished he'd been able to single-handedly save his father, but even as he did so, he realized why it didn't make sense, and it gave him chills. "That's not how they'd attack," he said, looking at the pictures on the table. Grainy, black and white images. Zawqiri and the Mazerati. Then back up at Hanley, who was watching him, then at Nick and Trish, Jerry and Cassie. "Think about it. Just about the single worst terrorist attack in the history of the world, and the most sophisticated thing they used was a boxcutter."

"It was all they had access to. Which is why they were after your father's research."

"But why would they waste time on undeveloped technology? This quantum bomb thing? Nobody's ever heard of it, much less used anything like it, and that's not what you use if you want to attack someone. You don't use a gun that may or may not work. You use the simplest thing you can find that'll do the most possible damage. Like an airplane."

"They already used airplanes," Hanley said. "They wouldn't again."

"They've been using Anthrax," Trish said. "Those letters. Not far from here."

The letter scare had centered around the office of Tom Daschle, who had done business with the law firm where Chance had temped, so he remembered the news very well. "You use something you know would be effective. You don't try to use something some random physics professor built by modifying something he bought at Best Buy."

"We're not certain it's a weapon. All we know is that your father's research had attracted the attention of people like Zawqiri."

"And you," Nick said.

Hanley looked at him. "Pardon?"

Nick indicated the photographs on the table. "You'd obviously been watching Dennis for quite a while——."

"We had every reason to believe——."

"Right, you said. And my wife and I both saw that man, in that car, coming and going several times."

"He was interested in the research."

"But why wait?" Cassie said. "You've been watching him, you know that people with ties to this terrorist organization are contacting him, so you must have known he was getting into trouble. Why didn't you do anything before now?" She closed the notebook with a decisive thwap and set it on the table in front of her. "Why didn't you do something several hours ago? You're saying you want to prevent his research from falling into the wrong hands, but why didn't you prevent those wrong hands from killing him in the first place?"

Hanley hesitated, looked around the room at five sets of expectant eyes. Glanced over his shoulder at Geisel, whose jaw clenched. Geisel shrugged, and Hanley turned again, taking a deep breath. "I know this is a difficult time for everyone. I know you've lost someone" he said, eyeing Cassie, Nick, and Trish. "And I know, Detective Nazor, that you were just beginning your investigation when my partner and I arrived. I know that these are difficult circumstances, what with a connection to al Qaeda on top of betrayal and infidelity, but——."

"Infidelity?" Chance asked, cutting Hanley off.

Hanley looked at him, then at Trish and Nick, then at Cassie. "I didn't imagine we would be the ones to break the news," he said. He pulled another envelope from the briefcase, this one smaller in both width and length, and from it he withdrew several snapshot-sized photographs. "One of the things we discovered during the course of our investigation of Dennis Sowin, Mr. Lackesis," Hanley began, and as he did so offered Nick the photographs, "Was that he and your wife were having an affair."

"What?" Trish asked. "That's ludicrous."

Chance had never seen the color drain from anyone's face until he watched Nick's face fall. The muscles in his jaw slackened and his mouth dropped open, and he seemed to stop breathing, too. He seemed surprised to watch his hands take the photographs from Hanley, and then he flipped through them as if on auto-pilot.

"It's a lie, honey," Trish said. "They're making it up just like they made up everything else. They couldn't get us scared, so they're trying to turn us against each other."

"They didn't make it up," Nick whispered. "We both saw that car. We both saw Zawqiri," he told her. He set the pictures down on the table as he rose from the chair, and he strode deliberately out of the room.

"Honey," Trish called after him. "Nick."

But Nick didn't turn, didn't respond, didn't do anything except keep walking, and Trish hurried after him. The front door opened just long enough to allow two people to pass through, then slammed so hard it rattled.

Cassie rose. The device with the metal casing was still on the table, and she reached as if she were gathering her things to leave.

Hanley grabbed her wrist.

"If you don't take your goddamned hands off me this instant, I swear to Christ I'll straighten your nose back out."

"I can't let you go anywhere with those."

"If you want me to figure out what this research concerns, I need to take these notes and these instruments into the other room, where I can give them my full attention. Because frankly, this *al Qaeda*-FBI-infidelity circus is too much of a distraction."

Hanley held her eyes, released her wrist. She brushed her forearm against her blazer, rotated her hand as if to work out a kink, then picked up the device and stormed out.

Chance got up to follow her. Hanley and Geisel both eyed him, but neither said a word.

*

It was only after he'd stepped into the hallway between the foyer and the dining that Chance realized he had no idea what to say. Or do.

So much had changed. He realized he couldn't remember the last time he'd seen Cassie before that evening. He thought back to the weekends he'd returned home, the special occasions he'd made specific excursions for. He'd returned for his five-year reunion, and he'd gone out with his friends, but he couldn't recall having seen her. Surely his college graduation party, three years before, couldn't have been the last time.

He crossed the hall to the living room entrance. Cassie hunched forward on the sofa. The notebook she'd taken lay open on the table before her, and she held the device Chance thought looked familiar even though he was certain he'd never seen it before.

"Hey," he said, and immediately hated himself for it. Everything that had happened, everything Hanley had told them, and all he could muster for her was "Hey?"

She didn't look up from the notebook.

Chance stepped forward. "You okay?" A little better at least.

"Just trying to figure this out."

"What he said back there——."

When she looked up at him, her eyes seemed distracted, calculating. "I think I know what your father was doing."

"What?"

"I'm not—it doesn't seem possible. It shouldn't be possible."

"Is it really a bomb?"

Outside, lightning slashed open the world, and thunder blasted out of the rift it had left behind.

Cassie shook her head, her brilliant blue eyes sparkling. "No. I don't think they knew what they were talking about. He wasn't using a different source so much as using energy differently."

"What do you mean, 'differently'?"

"It looks—it's complicated, but it looks like he figured out how to amplify energy."

Chance wasn't sure he understood. You don't grow up the son of a physicist without picking some things up along the way, but then again, you don't learn physics by studying history and philosophy in college and then working as a temp in a law firm, either.

Cassie pressed a button on the device, and its LCD display lit up brilliant white like Times Square on New Year's Eve before it settled to become bright, purple-pink neon. She pressed two other buttons, then turned one of the dials.

A chill prickled over Chance—

you've been here before—

like tiny, hyperactive pins and needles over his whole body.

He exhaled. "What're you doing? What is that?"

Her eyes glittered. Flashed and shimmered like twinkling stars. "It's the Higgs field."

He remembered his father's having mentioned the Higgs field, but they were interrupted before Cassie could explain anything: the front door burst open, and

Trish stormed into the house with a wake of wind and rain, and the door slammed behind her like thunder. She crossed the foyer toward the dining room.

Cassie never put down the device as she rose and joined Chance around the corner.

Trish seethed at Hanley, her face so close she sprayed his with spittle through clenched teeth. "How dare you make those accusations."

Hanley shrank back, and Jerry moved around the table to grasp Trish's wrist.

She twisted her wrist in his grip. "They're lying to us. They doctored those pictures—."

"Getting angry isn't going to solve anything."

"I love my husband," Trish said. Quiet. Simple.

"Where is dad, anyway?" Cassie asked.

"He went to Chance's house," Trish said.

Hanley stiffened. "What?" he didn't bother trying to keep either the anger or the fear from entering his voice. He looked at Geisel, ticked his head sideways, and they hustled out of the dining room, crossed the hall and the foyer, yanked the door open. Outside, the storm was loud and furious.

Chance, Cassie, Jerry, and Trish hurried after the two agents, out of the house and into the thunder and lightning and torrential rain falling in sheets and gusts. Wind howled down the street.

Hanley and Geisel tore across the Lackesis lawn. Chance and Cassie only a few steps behind. On the stoop, Jerry put his arm out, stayed Trish, then followed down the lawn himself.

Lightning flashed so bright it turned night back into day, and thunder pealed across the sky on its heel.

Chance swept a hand across his forehead. The rain came down so hard it was like a cold shower. His skin prickled, and below the cold, below the frigid raindrops, he could still feel the tingling that had begun when

Cassie had turned the dial on the device she still held; was it his imagination that everything felt so intense? That the rain splashing against his skin seemed to sizzle? That Cassie shimmered like a vapor trail in the storm?

Jerry, sprinting full-out, passed Chance on the left.

Hanley and Geisel reached the curb and started across the street.

All three were yelling, but their voices didn't carry over the tremendous sound of rain.

On the far side of the street, the yellow police tape trailed loose down the right side of the jamb, and Nick appeared in the door.

"Stop right there Nick," Hanley shouted to make himself heard over the rain

Nick started across Chance's lawn. Chance wondered if Nick hadn't heard Hanley.

Lightning flashed so hard it hurt Chance's eyes. Its afterimage glowed in his head.

Hanley stopped in the middle of the street, planted both feet. He reached for his waist. He shouted, but thunder shattered like the universe had cracked open, and Chance never heard it.

Nick didn't stop. He was halfway across Chance's lawn.

Blood slammed through Chance's head. His pulse icky-thumped like an electric bass, and his breath whooshed like he expected to blow his own house down when he got there.

Hanley drew his pistol. "I'm warning you, Nick, stop right there and put your hands in the air." His voice was high, each word like a perfectly enunciated bullet.

Dominoes:

Jerry pulled his own sidearm from his holster. "No need for a gun, agent Hanley."

Geisel: "Drop your gun, Nazor."

You've seen this.

Nick's feet stuttered. Stopped. He looked at the three guns, as if confused.

Everything seemed to slow.

Chance found himself struck paralytic. His body couldn't find a coherent movement.

The four men's eyes ticked back and forth among each other, but no one moved. The rain rushed and the wind howled and thunder grumbled like an angry dog, but nobody moved.

Next to him, Cassie shielded the device within her blazer, but she twisted the dial as she ran.

Before Chance could ask what she was doing, before he could get even a single syllable out, his house exploded. A spectacular fireball shroomed into the night.

A gun fired.

Every hair on his body stiffened so hard he thought they meant to jump off. He shielded his face from the hot, percussive blast he expected,

but the world wrenched around him

as something whirled inside his head and then

nothing.

Silence.

Chance had been on the Hoboken ferry, in the middle of the Hudson river, when the third building of the World Trade Center had fallen. He remembered counting as he watched, wondering if a nuclear blast lasts long enough to feel. If someone shoots you in the head, do you hear it, or does everything just go black? Does a quantum bomb annihilate everything in its wake to leave behind neither death nor destruction but absolutely nothing?

He lowered his arm.

The world had

stopped.

The rain didn't fall.

The wind didn't howl.

The thunder didn't rumble.

Nothing moved.

Not the raindrops in the air,

not the great explosive cloud paused

mid-bloom over his house.

Even the lightning flash: frozen.

He realized he was holding his breath. Like the whole world seemed to be.

He let it out.

The world did not.

10

Leonard lay comfortably on the bed. Jennifer curled against him, her auburn hair wet against his neck and cheek, and he played his fingers through it.

She sighed against his chest. "You missed me."

"Always do."

She curlicued lazy circles in his chest hair. "I wouldn't miss me. I mean, you just went to a Shakespeare play, and not just Brannagh and Denzel doing *Othello* on Broadway. An actual play in actual Elizabethan England. Was Elizabeth there?"

"It was the public performance. She'd already gotten a private performance at her court."

"I'd say you just gave a fine private performance yourself," she told him. She propped herself up on her elbow. Her hair hung in damp, curling waves; her breasts rested against his chest; her green eyes sparkled. "Speak of, how 'bout anutha, Guv'nuh?" she asked in her best British accent, which actually wasn't so far off from Leonard's, as she grasped him.

Leonard gasped, but then the implant in his jaw began to vibrate. He hated to move from her, but he sat up. "Race," Leonard explained when she looked at him, confused.

She pulled the sheet to her chest. One look at her made him want to ignore the buzzing in his head, but he sighed, rose from the bed as he tugged on his earlobe.

"I'm here," he opened the top drawer of the pine dresser, pulled out a pair of boxer-briefs.

"We need you here. Now." Race's voice was quick. Urgent.

Leonard frowned. "Everything okay?" he asked. He rolled his eyes to let Jennifer know he wasn't talking to her.

"We got the trace. You need to get here now. Five minutes ago. Get here before I buzzed you," and then, deep inside Leonard's skull, a disconnective click.

"Everything okay?" Jennifer asked him.

"Didn't sound that way."

"How did it sound?"

"Worried," Leonard said as he pulled aside the closet curtain, took out the white shirt Jennifer had included with the suit, slid into it. He stepped into the slacks, too: charcoal grey like a London sky. Jennifer always picked the best colors for him.

"You're going again."

"That's why they called me back," he said.

"Any idea where?"

"I requested Manhattan."

"Requested?"

"Long story."

"Any idea for how long?"

"On your end, or on mine?"

"Either," she said.

He shook his head. "Not yet." He wished he had a better answer.

He stood, went to the closet and slid into the grey blazer, then back to the bed, sat next to her. He twirled one of her curls between his fingers. "Can I ask you something?"

"Of course."

He hesitated, then: "How long have we been dating?"

He saw her hate the question. Hurt flashed across her face, but flickered away to sympathy, even if he wasn't sure it was understanding. He wondered if she could understand. "On your end, or on mine?" she asked, and he realized she did.

"Yours."

"Well, let's see. Started working here myself a few years ago. And we flirted … I guess we started dating when you invited me to Manhattan with you for that week. Well. That month, really," she corrected, because one of the unique aspects of being involved with CIRTN was that time was fluid, there. Days lasted months lasted seconds, which sounded like it should have wrought havoc on the system, but in fact the temporal decompression that accompanied time travel was like mainlining jetlag: intensely fatiguing, but brief. "That was my vacation, the middle of last year. And it's the end of this year. So I guess almost two years, give or take. Has it been more on your end?"

He tried to smile. "I lose track sometimes."

"Some days I'm surprised you even remember your own birthday."

"November second," he said.

She stroked his cheek. "And how many times have you seen it?"

He looked around, then, taking in the dormitory. The sad, sparse room. He wondered, again, if another Leonard Kensington in another time and place was lying in bed with another Jennifer. He wondered if that Leonard was looking around another room, and contemplating leaving another CIRTN. He wondered if that Leonard already had and, if so, if he was happier.

He didn't know. All he really knew, in fact, was that the simple idea of infinite Leonards in infinite rooms chilled him.

He felt Jennifer's hand on his. "Honey? You were a million miles away for a minute there."

"Just, I've been thinking. What if I said, after this trip, we retire? We find something else. We could stay here and travel around Europe, or we can go back to the AU. Be closer to your family," he told her, but her lip was quivering, and he couldn't read the look on her face. "I mean, it could be anywhere. Wherever you want to go. I just thought—."

She sprang forward, and he found himself suddenly in her arms.

"I don't care wherever or whenever we go, so long as I can go with you," she laughed into his ear.

"So that's a yes, then?"

"Of course it's a yes, you dear, sweet, silly man," she kissed him. "Yes." Kiss. "Yes." Kiss. "Yes." Kiss.

He couldn't stop smiling. "Okay, okay," he rose. "All right. I need to go talk to Race. I need to do this thing for them, go to Manhattan. But I'll tell him. And when I get back, we can talk more about it. We can figure out where to go."

*

When the elevator doors opened to the Operations Center and Leonard saw the bank of monitors directly opposite, he had several visceral reactions: shock, fear, disbelief. Their combination stunned him. His bowels tightened, and he swallowed.

Across the room, the monitors were a mosaic of Manattan midnight. Office lights glittered like the stars had fallen to the City, and the Brooklyn Bridge jutted out to the left. The view was of the island itself from the west, so downtown Manhattan loomed before him, and in the center of the mosaic, precisely where the twin towers of the World Trade Center should have been anchoring the City's southern tip, two beams of light blazed into the darkness.

"You said you wanted to go to Manhattan," Race said. "We set the computers to lock the trace there. We just nailed the signal a minute ago, and that's what appeared on the screen."

Leonard felt as though he'd woken up to find his bedroom rearranged and his bathroom backwards. His brain seemed to be holding on to the memory of what he should have been seeing while his eyes supplied different information, and somewhere between the two a circuit shorted like an overloaded breaker.

"We're still trying to figure out what happened. We rewound it back to when the World Trade Center was built, and it was approximately the same there as it was here. So we've got it extrapolating forward, and we're hoping—."

"Sir." Midway down one of the four rows of computer terminals, a man in a white shirt had raised his hand. "I think I've got it."

"On screen."

A beautiful day. A brilliant sun just rising. If it hadn't been on the monitor, Leonard would have thought it should have been a commercial. It was exactly the Manhattan he'd fallen in love with at first sight, in a way he'd never fall for any woman: home. Adventurous, sophisticated, elegant home. Home in a slinky black dress and pearls, home with sleek blonde hair, home with long, black gloves and functional heels that could go for miles.

Seeing Manhattan at a long distance reminded Leonard of quantum physics. From the Operations Center, the city appeared almost still unless you knew where to look: the congested, crawling streets that slowed within the nucleus, but the outer highways, the expressway and the bridges and the tunnels where the particles had more room, because there were fewer about, where they got some elbow room and could blur. Move closer and get sucked into the energy, the thriving, buzzing cacophony of cars and people and life.

"I want a tighter shot of the buildings," Race said.

The image on the screen swooped toward those two silver towers, gleaming in the morning light. The Operations Center did not have a camera trained on the alternate reality; rather, its computers crunched through quantum mechanical and electrodynamic information to extrapolate visual imagery and the auditory information that went along with it.

"Closer. Lower," Race said.

The perspective tightened on those two buildings, perhaps from Fulton or Canal. Leonard couldn't quite place any landmarks to tell: the buildings looked different there. Some of the names of the stores—Century 21, Strawberry's—were familiar, some not.

"Sound," Race said.

Besides the quantum imaging, the computers could extrapolate sonic information to the sidewalls, turning them into giant speakers that made the image suddenly more real, because suddenly there were horns and engines, construction and sirens. If Manhattan was the heart of the world, its sounds were the lifeblood pulsed through Leonard's ears; and the complex seemed to disappear. In the Operations Center, thousands of miles from the Manhattan he knew and impossibly distant from the one he was looking at, Leonard Kensington smiled because he'd fallen in love all over again.

But then: a foreign sound. The tiny hairs on his neck cringed; it wasn't a Manhattan sound. Engines and jackhammers and people with megaphones and homeless men screaming at the sky are Manhattan sounds. This— it grew louder, a distant, rumbling hiss that whined into a deafening shriek, and then Leonard's stomach froze as he watched a jet plunge into one of the towers as if it had been aiming for it. A percussive blast jarred his bones, and his breath left him as he watched debris burst from the side of the building.

Several people in the Operations Center cursed. Leonard couldn't tell who, nor if he'd done so himself.

"A plane?" Race asked. "It was a plane?"

No one answered. They all watched the screen, the tower, the wreckage. That proud building with its huge, red, gaping wound. Smoke oozed out from the building as if the plane had stuck a vein, inking into the sky as blood through water.

Sirens. Noise, but muffled, muted. A hush falling.

"Is it a movie? It must be a movie. You must've—."

"No sir," the man who'd raised his hand said. "The computers indicate it fell a few hours later."

Race's brow furrowed. "Tighten on the impact."

"Sir?" the man said.

"The impact. The crash. Close in on it," he said, looked back at the screen.

The image swooped again, until the monitors were full of fire and dark smoke and jagged metal like unraveled mesh.

"Stop."

The image locked, flame frozen, smoke halted, detritus paused in the air.

"Back it up."

Though the image started backward, the only difference was that the smoke oozed back in: the dance of backward fire looked the same. The smoke rushed back in as if to fill the wound, then coalesced and brightened into an orange fireball, out of which appeared the tail of a plane—

"Slow it."

The plane emerged from the building as if gently pulled.

"I want all the information on that plane," Race said. "I want to know who's flying it right this very second. I want the company, I want the flight number, I want to know what those people were eating for breakfast. I want everything you can—."

"Sir," a woman called. "There's another plane. Approximately eighteen minutes later. From the opposite direction. The other tower."

Race looked at her, then: "Show me."

The image on the screen changed. The second Tower, the unblemished one. Behind it, the smoke from the first tower plumed out to the side.

And then: that foreign sound again, except it wasn't so foreign anymore. Leonard felt his muscles tighten: not again. Please, not again, even as the plane screamed overhead to collide headlong into the building: a brief flash of orange and then the whole world stopped dead. He didn't gasp that time.

"So, what, they collapsed? Is that even possible? Speed it up."

It only took a minute. The pluming smoke, the gathering dust, and then first one tower collapsed before the other followed it.

Leonard saw that Race had looked away, staring at the ground, before he sucked in a breath and looked back at the screen. Then at Leonard. "You still want to go there? That's..." he didn't say what it was.

He didn't need to. Leonard knew. He'd seen it for himself. "Where else would I go?"

"I'm sure you could find information just about anywhere."

"Not like there."

"If you're sure."

Leonard thought of something. "But send me to the day before."

Race raised an eyebrow.

"Think how it's going to be if you send me over there right now," Leonard said. "Tighter security, for one. Especially if that was an attack."

"I think we can rule out that 'if.' One plane might have been an accident, but two? That hit as precisely as those two just did?" Race said, then seemed to think of something. "Run a global search. See if there were any—."

"Ahead of you, sir," the woman who'd noted the second plane said. "There were two other plane crashes at approximately the same time. One of them crashed into the Pentagon. The other went down in Pennsylvania."

"Pennsylvania?" Race asked.

"Further extrapolation indicates that national airspace was shut completely down except for military aircraft for a week afterward."

Race looked at Leonard. "You're probably right about the security then. We'll set the machine for the day before—what day was that?"

"September the eleventh, sir. Last month," the woman said.

"So you're going to September tenth," Race told Leonard. "Get all the information you can, and then we'll send you to the point of digression. Which will actually be the point of intersection, now that I think about it," Race said rubbed his forehead. "This stuff makes my brain hurt."

"Try going," Leonard told him.

Race looked at him, nodded. "I've never envied you."

Leonard nodded, then: "Speak of . . . I was thinking of maybe making this my last run."

"You mean retire?" Race asked.

Leonard nodded.

"I think it could be a possibility."

"No, that's a possibility," Leonard nodded toward the monitors.

"That's a reality, and you've got to figure out where it stopped being ours. When you get back, I'll recommend your honorable discharge to Claudius," Race told him. John Claudius was the head of CIRTN's review board.

"Okay," Leonard nodded. He turned and strode to the elevator, knuckled the button. His movements were precise and used no more motion than was required, because he was being careful to control them; otherwise, he worried, he would tremble. He controlled, too, his thoughts, because he kept thinking of how it would feel to leave CIRTN after his mission, of Jennifer in his arms, and those thoughts made it difficult for him to consider how he might prepare for the alternate reality of those planes. When the elevator arrived and he stepped on, he turned toward the buttons, tapped the one for requisitions, and he looked up only after those doors had safely closed and the elevator had begun its descent.

He exhaled, then. He hadn't realized he'd been holding his breath, but it didn't surprise him.

PART II
ALL OUR YESTERDAYS

"IT IS UTTERLY BEYOND OUR POWER TO MEASURE THE CHANGES OF THINGS BY TIME. QUITE THE CONTRARY, TIME IS AN ABSTRACTION AT WHICH WE ARRIVE BY MEANS OF THE CHANGES OF THINGS."
        -ERNST MACH

"LORD, GRANT ME THE SERENITY TO ACCEPT THE THINGS I CANNOT CHANGE, THE COURAGE TO CHANGE THOSE I CAN, AND THE WISDOM TO KNOW THE DIFFERENCE."
        -TRADITIONAL GAELIC PRAYER

"THE SOLE PURPOSE OF HISTORY IS TO BE REWRITTEN."
        -OSCAR WILDE, "THE DECAY OF LYING"

"I BELIEVE THAT EVERY RIGHT IMPLIES A RESPONSIBILITY; EVERY OPPORTUNITY AN OBLIGATION; EVERY POSSESSION, A DUTY."
        -JOHN D. ROCKEFELLER

11

Every hair on Chance's body had tensed as if it planned to jump from its follicle, and goosebumps singed up his back and around his arms and legs. Even his lips tingled.

The lightning blazed the sky around it electrostatic blue-white, which faded first to purple, then indigo, and then finally into darkness. Raindrops like crystal pebbles filled the air, and a giant smoke cloud, highlighted by orange flame, smudged the night where Chance's house had been.

Hanley, Geisel, and Nazor all stood paused in the street like mannequins, pointing their guns at each like characters in comic-book panels, their faces stunned, angry. A tiny burst of white clung to the muzzle of Hanley's gun, and a thin curlicue of smoke like a prehensile tail trailed upwards from it without ever moving at all.

Chance took everything in without ever moving his head. His gut had clenched, his hands bunched into frightened fists, and his whole body had locked up tight, not like it couldn't move but rather like he was too petrified.

"What'd you do?" he whispered. He barely moved his lips when he did so, and he didn't turn his head to look at her.

When she spoke, her voice shook between awed, desperate, defensive, and apologetic. "I had to. Everything you said would happen was—I needed to think."

"So what, you paused time?" His attention focused on the millions of frozen raindrops, each like a glass bead. "Can we move? Is it safe?"

"Should be."

Without coordinating the movement, both raised their hands before them, their fingertips tracing through the rain. Drops burst on tiny impact with their skin, vaporizing into lingering mist in which Chance could discern each smaller droplet. "What is this? What happened?"

"Remember I mentioned the Higgs field?"

Chance nodded, turned to look at her. Each small movement added to his confidence that he could make the next one, too.

Cassie's blonde-streaked hair and bright blue eyes stood out against the static grey of that motionless world, vibrant against the utter stillness of suspended time, and Chance thought she looked as if she'd been superimposed over the background. "Do you know what the Higgs field is?"

"I remember my dad mentioning it was how subatomic particles get their mass. But isn't it theoretical?"

"Your father made a breakthrough. He proved it can be manipulated," she looked down at the device she was still holding. Its LCD blazed blue. "That tingling earlier . . . it basically taps into that field, and then it can alter it. Right now, we're excited at a subatomic level, and after that it's just light-speed theory."

"Einstein?"

She nodded. "As an object's velocity approaches the speed of light, time slows down. If you accelerate all of the subatomic particles in an object, time around them will slow."

"Or stop," he had begun to speak at normal volume. "So can it—." The question froze on his lips as possibilities flooded his brain. He thought of *Back to the Future* and Michael Crichton, science fiction and *Quantum Leap*. He thought of other things, too, things that were less imaginary: John F. Kennedy in his Dallas motorcade and Martin Luther King at that motel. "Can it go backward, too?"

She nodded, slowly. "I think it can."

His jaw clenched. In his mind he saw the World Trade Center collapse as if it had grown tired of standing all those years, story upon story upon story crumbling into themselves and piledriving down down down into the ground.

In his mind he saw his house. The busted-in front door, the dim hallway. Creeping along the hallway and down the stairs and across his basement. In his mind he saw his father on the floor.

"We could save him," he felt that sentence so hard he wanted to gasp. They could save him. They could save him.

"You told me you were going to say that," she said.

"What?"

"Last night. When you told me about the room and the agents and what this was," she indicated the device. "Otherwise, I wouldn't have been able to figure it out. Not that quickly. But I recognized it the moment I saw it."

He looked at the jagged scar of lightning. "But what does that even mean?"

"I don't know," her voice betrayed her: high and desperate and just on the verge of breaking.

"But if it's really a time machine, if everything I said really happened, and if I was actually in Jersey City last night—."

She closed her eyes, nodding. "I know what you're thinking, and yes. It's possible."

Chance looked out at the unmoving raindrops in the middle of the shocking-white lightning. The small flash at the end of Hanley's bright muzzle, and the giant fireball that should have been billowing into the darkness and the night sky but wasn't.

You've been here before.

Had he? Had he stood there next to her, terrified to move, contemplating reversing time to save his father? How do you think about the future when there's a possibility it's already occurred? "But if it's possible, and all this is possible, isn't—," he meant to suggest there was a chance that it might be different this time.

"Yeah," she cut him off. "It is."

Staring out at the frozen world in front of him, he believed it. "So shouldn't we at least try?" he asked. His mind felt hot and dense, but he thought it was with purpose moreso than fear. "Is there really so much harm in trying?"

"I don't know."

Chance considered that, then considered the rain and the lightning, the wind that had died in its tracks, extinguished. He looked up, at the angry storm cloud that should have been roiling, its billows and fruts rumbling and stumbling over themselves; it didn't move at all. "When I was a kid, I went to summer camp, for Scouts. We learned CPR, but before we did, our instructor warned us that if we ever found ourselves in a situation where we should use it, we had to. That all the information he was about to give us could save someone's life, so we should try to use it as best we could."

"But that's CPR. Not a time machine. Just because we can doesn't mean we should. What if—"

"What if what? What if we can do it? What if it works? What if we save him?"

"What if everything you told me last night comes true?"

"What else did I tell you?"

She hesitated.

"You don't remember."

"I was half asleep. And you—," she stopped.

"I what?"

"You weren't all that coherent, Chance. You seemed halfway between drunk and exhausted. You were talking about time machines and FBI agents and your dead father, and you didn't make much sense. So I'm sorry I don't remember everything you told me. I'm sorry I can't stand here now and tell you why it's not a good idea to save your father, but I don't think it is." The words poured out, and her shoulders heaved.

Chance touched her arm, moved closer, tentatively, slid his palm down her arm until he could feel her close to him.

"I didn't mean—It's just—it's a time machine, Chance," she told him. "He did it. Not only did your father prove it was possible, he managed to make it possible." She looked out at the paused world. The frozen lightning reflected in her eyes. "And somebody killed him for it."

"So you think we shouldn't use it."

She looked at him but said nothing.

"You know more about it than I do, and you had the crazy dream. So if you think we shouldn't do it," he paused. He was about to say, "We won't," but realized he didn't want to.

"We don't even know that it will work."

"But you—," he gestured. "Look at the rain. Look at the fire—"

"I'm not denying the special effects, but it's not like we've tried going backward yet. Who's to say it wouldn't just futz out like a bottle rocket? Or what if it works, but we can't actually intervene because of some bylaws of physics no one's discovered?"

"That's a lot of what ifs," Chance said.

"Which is the whole point, isn't it? Who knows? Maybe we'd try to save my dad, but we find out we can't actually change the past because of some divine intervention."

"Right, because there's been so much divine intervention in the past few thousand years. Look, we won't know until we try. We can argue about it until time starts back up, anyway, whether we want it to or not, or we can try to use it and see if it works."

"You realize if we save your father, we'd never find the time machine and we'd never have to use it to save him. Which would create a paradox based on causality; if we never had to save him, we'd never find the time machine, which would mean we'd never have to use it to save him, but if we didn't, we'd—."

"And then what?"

She paused. "What do you mean?"

"What happens then? Do you and I cease to exist because we didn't have to save him and continued living our lives and never went back to the past?"

Cassie shrugged. "I don't know. It's not like there's any data to go by."

"So we won't know until we try."

"But what if we can't go back to our regular lives because we're already living in them? What if nothing happens, and we don't cease to exist, but your father doesn't die? Then there's us, living in a whole new world we can't really be part of because two other versions of us already live in it."

Chance considered that, then: "I'm not sure I care. I know you've got something to lose. You've got a nice job at Princeton lined up for January. I was just a temp. I was waking up every day and putting on a stupid tie, and I'd already decided I had to give it up even if I didn't know what else to do. And after last month—," the thought of the World Trade Center stopped that sentence before he could continue.

Cassie, for her part, said nothing, just waited.

"I figured I'd come home and figure things out. Find myself, or some damned thing. Find something that didn't feel like I was doing exactly the same thing over and over every day for the next forty years. But now there's nothing here, either. Somebody killed my dad, and my house just exploded, so now I've got no place to go and nothing to do, except this. My dad came up with a way to make a difference. I want to use it. I want to save him. I want to do something right. Because last month made me feel so useless," he nearly spat that last word. Still it made him feel indignant. Tears had come to his eyes, and he wiped them away like he was irritated with them.

She put her arms around him, gently, careful of his injured shoulder. Still she said nothing, just held him, just held him.

"Last month, I felt like I couldn't do anything. And I wanted to. So badly. I just want to do something," he said, quietly, but it was like a mantra. Just the idea had power. "Will you help me?"

The moment in that paused world stretched longer, so long it might have gone on to the end of time before it crossed dimensions and looped back around. Chance didn't know what he would do if she—

"I'll help you," she told him, and it felt for all the world like a sudden new universe had flashed into existence with an entirely different set of rules and laws and physics, in which time and space were not just entangled together but malleable and flexible and words like "yesterday" and "tomorrow" had no real meaning at all.

12

Leonard rode the elevator to requisitions, where Jennifer was already seated behind her desk. Her hair had waved into loose crinkles, and her cheeks still held a blush. "That was quick."

"They got the trace. Just wanted to make sure I still wanted to go to Manhattan."

"Dangerous?"

Leonard considered those shrieking planes, the towers bleeding into the sky before they crumbled down into a cloud of dust and ash. "Nothing I can't handle," he told her; the way he'd handled war-torn Afghanistan in the early nineties was why CIRTN had recruited him. In less than a decade, Leonard had executed reconnaissance missions over at least six millennia. He had watched the tidal wave inundate Crete, giving rise to the myth of Atlantis; he'd watched the druids map the stars to assemble their great Henge. To Egypt and the pharaohs, to the ten plagues of the Torah; to a time when the only recorded history had been drawn on the walls of caves to finally corroborate, once and for all, evolutionary law.

"I don't doubt that. I was just wondering if I should worry about you."

"Don't you always worry about me?"

Jennifer shook her head as she chuckled to herself. "Are you just here to say hello again, or do you need to see Darren?"

"How about a little of both?"

She pressed a button on her desk, and the brushed-metal door off to the right of her desk slid open.

*

Beyond the doorway, the cavernous room resembled nothing so much as an enormous manufacturing factory. A six-foot wide walkway cut a swath Leonard followed; to his right, a man with a dark beard honed what appeared, under a shower of blazing-orange sparks, to be an obsidian spearhead. Further on, a man wearing glasses as wide as his head under a green visor counted out rainbow-colored currency whose spectacular holographic strips blurred iridescent under his fingers. Further on again, a man watched a bank of monitors, all of which showed different temporal eras; he scribbled in his notebook as the images shuddered by, while, opposite him, a man wearing a jeweler's loupe hunched over a table on which were spread passports, drivers' licenses, and employee identification cards.

Leonard strode past to approach a circular desk, behind which stood Darren Manningly, a young man with long black hair and bushy eyebrows that nearly met behind the thick frames of his tortoise-shell glasses. He pressed a soldering iron to a circuit board, and a thin wisp of smoke curled up around his head. Leonard cleared his throat.

"Just one second, Len. Be riiiigght with you, yes, that's it, that's—it," Darren said, the latter part to himself, almost whispered. He set aside the soldering iron, and then, with careful fingers, held the green circuit board up to the light. "Indeed," he said, then set it aside, and looked at Leonard. "So, what can I do for you, Lenny baby?" Darren was the only person in the complex, besides Jennifer, who might get away with calling Leonard "Lenny baby," and Jennifer would never try.

"A smartcard," he said. Disguised as credit cards, smartcards contained what CIRTN called 'intelligent' magnet strips, which could adapt instantly to all situations. Their versatility wasn't limited to monetary transactions, however; they could, in addition, open any lock that required a keycard or trick any reader that required magnetic strip identification.

"Wouldn't leave CIRTN without it. Anything else?"

Leonard thought of those purple-blurring screens. "I'm not entirely sure."

"Where are you going?"

"Manhattan."

"So let's see, then. A passport, probably European? Maybe Welsh. Some currency—"

"No currency."

"You're just going to rely on the smartcard? Okay. Well. Smart phone, then—"

"No phone," he said, because who knew what frequency cell phones would operate on there?

"Going back before then?"

"I'm not actually sure yet."

"You don't know when you're going?"

"I don't know where I'm going."

"But you just said you were going to Manhattan."

"It's not that Manhattan."

"What other Manhattan is ther—?" Darren cut himself off as his eyes widened in surprise bordering on shock. "It's not our Manhattan."

Leonard nodded.

"Wow," Darren said, looked away as if he were absorbing the information, then looked back at Leonard. "So it's true, then? Alternate realities really do exist?"

"This one does."

"You've seen it?"

Leonard thought of those planes. "Yeah."

Darren low-whistled. "That's amazing. Wow. I mean, all those theories—if even just the one exists, that must mean that all of them must, too, right? The philosophical implications alone—."

"Could probably support several philosophers' careers, but we're not philosophers, and I've got things to do."

"It's all research?"

Leonard nodded, rubbed his forehead. "So far. I just know they did some sort of major upgrade this morning, something about better hardware—."

"Right, yes. I was the lead on it," Darren moved around the desk, gestured for Leonard to follow him. "Old hardware was outdated. Couldn't've detected a quark even had you told it that's what it was looking at."

"A what?"

"A quark. Subatomic particle. Inside protons and neutrons. Standard-model fermions and—well. Doesn't matter. Tricky little buggers, and I'd tell you more but you'd need an advanced physics degree to understand it and I'd have to draw you some, like, Feynman diagrams—."

"Feynman? Like, Richard? Guy who helped found us?" Feynman had been one of the several American and European physicists who had first proposed the *Conseil*

European pour la Recherche Nucleaire. During the 1990s, when CERN had finally detected the Higgs field, it had subsequently unlocked the mysteries of quantum mechanics, relativity, and space-time. The new physical advancements had inspired a new, global perspective; the inclusion of all nations on the *Conseil*, and a name change.

"So you're not just another pretty face," Darren winked. "Point is, with all the recent research from guys like Greene and Kaku, we had to make the upgrade to be able to handle new levels of quantum uncertainty."

"Well, your upgrade detected an anomaly. So we ran a trace on it, and it turns out it's not from our continuum—."

"Which we knew was possible in theory, but never proved in practice."

"Which means we have to approach it differently, and I'm the guy they're sending to do it. We need to figure out what happened, and we can't do it from here. So they're sending me, and that puts me in a bind, because who knows what's going to work over there? They might have different money, different wireless protocols, different—."

"Those sorts of things shouldn't be much of a problem." They arrived at the ID bench. "Martin, do we still have the passport Leonard used when he was in Britain?"

A few months before, Leonard had investigated Prime Minister Lennon's involvement in an international scandal. His exoneration of the former Beatle had prevented a war the likes of which hadn't been seen since before Marx and Emmanuel had helped initiate the European Union.

Martin zipped a key from his belt to unlock a steel cabinet behind him. He pulled open an interior drawer, thumbed through a stack of passports, and then tossed a maroon-colored booklet with gold-leafing on the cover onto the bench.

Leonard opened it. His face, his name, his signature, too, stamped Switzerland, Germany, and Austria. "Perfect," he tucked it into the breast pocket of his suit.

"And a smartcard," Darren walked up to the banker, and picked up a small leather billfold, which he handed to Leonard. "I think you should take a serious gun," he said. Serious guns were small, stun-gun like devices that produced quantum electrodynamic pulses to disrupt the body's bioelectrical energy and induce spontaneous tachycardia. Leonard had always thought the name was just a bad pun: they were serious as heart attacks.

"I've never needed a weapon," Leonard thought of the automatic rifle he'd once carried in Lebanon, the feel of squeezing the trigger. Just the idea made him skittish.

"You've never gone to a different reality, either."

He followed Darren to the bearded man, who'd set aside the spearhead to sharpen a quick, wicked knife against a stone. He withdrew from a drawer beside him a small, silver, ceramic pistol, then handed Darren both the gun and a shoulder holster.

"And now we might not know the wireless protocols, but we do have a new device I've been wanting to test, and this might be the perfect opportunity."

"Like I'm a guinea pig?" Leonard said as he followed.

"You're much too tall for that. It's not like it's dangerous."

"What is it?"

"Oh, once you see this, you're not going to want to turn it down, Lenny baby," he said, then turned to the man at the monitors. "John, have you got the Oracle handy?"

John reached into a drawer next to him and withdrew a small white device and a pair of athletic sunglasses. Darren took the device when John handed it over his shoulder and offered it to Leonard. It was about the size of a deck of cards but heavier, and one side was mirrored chrome while the other was immaculate white with a large circle.

"Put the glasses on," Darren told him.

Leonard looked at him uncertainly.

"Oh, just do it. It's not going to fry your eyeballs. I wouldn't do that to you. You have such nice eyeballs."

Leonard slipped the sunglasses on. The tint of the lenses was light enough that he could still see clearly through them.

"The lenses themselves are a special polymer that react to ambient light and increase visual acuity, all of which just means you can see better when you wear them. John here was working on some optical applications when he was designing them. Which also led to our breakthrough. Here, let me show you," Darren told him. He plucked the device from Leonard's hand, and suddenly Leonard saw a giant, translucent image before him as if there were a large menu hovering in midair. The options read, simply, "pause," "rewind," "forward," and "settings."

Darren chose "pause."

Nothing happened.

Leonard waited.

Nothing continued to happen.

He turned his head to tell Darren the device wasn't working, and the world seemed to move with his head. Everything seemed to superimpose over everything else. He turned the other way, and the image followed there, too. He fumbled with the glasses, pulled them from his face.

The world returned to normal.

Leonard held up the glasses to peer at the image on its lenses, which didn't change. "What the hell?"

Darren laughed. "We're calling it the Oracle. It's a portable version of SecondSight. Isn't it great?"

SecondSight, which allowed for stationary observation of the past but not participation in it, was the commercial application of the breakthrough that had come with the discovery of the Higgs particle and the globalization of CIRTN. The *Conseil* regulated cross-temporal travel, but it licensed SecondSight to certain institutions to allow the public to observe the kinds of events Leonard had been able to experience firsthand. Visitors of Gettysburg could watch Lincoln deliver his famous address; in Philadelphia, visitors at the Constitution Center could observe details of the Convention that had birthed the United States. In Vienna, *Karntnertortheater* displayed a deaf Beethoven mock-conducting his Ninth Symphony, which had debuted in the theater more than a hundred years before.

The *Conseil* had initiated the Shakespeare Project and Leonard's trip to Southwark after the Globe theater had applied for just such an installation. CIRTN hoped to reveal conclusive evidence of the plays' authorship to the public before approving the installation, as was its custom. Some applications, such as the Jerusalem Project, still awaited approval; intratemporal devices failed during a time window crucial to the origins of Christianity. The Catholic Church called the failing one of science before the mystery of faith, while the *Conseil* cited an inexplicable temporal anomaly. In an address to the NAU, Prime Minister Clinton had said: "We have made great technological advances and major scientific breakthroughs, but that does not mean we will not, now and in the future, encounter areas where our technologies are only as advanced as our knowledge and imagination."

Leonard put the glasses back on. The image Darren had paused superimposed over the lenses. "So it freezes an image?"

Darren chuckled. "Oh, no. You can also increase the opacity of whatever you're looking at." The superimposed image seemed to gain density and clarity. "Then you move around whatever you're looking at." The image revolved around a center access so that Leonard received an around-the-world view of the room and himself in it, as if he were watching a movie. "You can focus in on a particular aspect." The perspective zoomed in until Leonard seemed to be standing right in front of himself, "And you can lock it, and then," Darren said, with emphasis, "You can start it backward and really watch the fun."

Everything Leonard had just done, accepting the gun, taking the leather billfold with the smartcard inside, pocketing the passport, approaching Darren's desk, walking into the room, talking to Jennifer... it all unhappened.

"You can start it forward again," Darren told him, and the image paused, then seemed to continue at a normal pace. "And it can broadcast sound via your cellular implant."

That was quick.

They got the trace. Just wanted to make sure I still wanted to go to Manhattan.

Dangerous?

Nothing I can't handle.

Leonard realized, then, he hadn't told Jennifer about the alternate reality and the danger it might pose. The sight of those falling towers had been too fresh in his mind.

I don't doubt that. I was just wondering if I should worry about you.

Don't you always worry about me?

Leonard watched her blush then. He hadn't noticed that the first time he'd spoken to her.

Are you just here to say hello again, or do you need to see Darren?

How about a little of both?

"You can change the focus, too," the image switched from Leonard to Jennifer, started backward again; she looked down at the desk, then, in sped-backward time-lapse, walked back around the desk backward into the elevator, and the doors closed in front of her. The image stopped and faded. "And if you go into settings, you can set both the temporal and spatial coordinates."

"So I can watch pretty much anything anywhere?" Leonard asked. "I think I'm obsolete."

"Just because we'll be able to see it doesn't mean we'll understand. Which is where you come in," Darren said. From beside him, he picked up a nylon bag. "And here. Laptop and cellphone, both with protocol detectors. I can't imagine it would be that different over there."

Leonard took the bag, unzipped the front pocket, and slipped the Oracle into it. He slid the glasses into his breast pocket.

"Anything else you need?" Darren asked him.

"I think I'm good."

*

"Wow. You're packing light," Jennifer said when he walked back into the elevatored vestibule. "Where's your usual duffel bag of tricks?"

Leonard smiled. "Not this time. Not that sort of assignment."

"So what sort of assignment is it, exactly? You said it was Manhattan…"

"Early last month."

"Really? I don't remember reading that anything major happened there."

"It's not… it's not our Manhattan. That's why Race called me down to make sure I still wanted to go. It's… the first time we've seen an alternate universe. So I need to figure out where it diverges from ours."

"Wow," she said, paused. Absorbing. "So how different? Have you seen it?"

"So far, all we know is that there were four attacks using airplanes last month. Two of them hit the World Trade Center there."

"The Trade Center? My brother works there. Do you think—."

Leonard cut her off. "It's a different reality. There's really no telling."

"So what's your plan?"

"The library. The cyberweb, if they even have it over there."

Jennifer bit her lip. "So when are you going?"

"On my way now."

"No, I mean, there. When will you arrive?"

"September tenth. Day before those planes."

"Will you do me a favor, then? Will you check on my brother? He works at Cantor Fitzgerald. Will you go there and see if he's there, and warn him if he is? For me?"

"I can't—I mean, I'm not—."

"I know you're not," Jennifer didn't let him finish his sentence. For that he was grateful, though only until she leaned farther forward and, lowering her voice, said: "But what little difference would it make if you go to the World Trade Center, and just see if Gabe is working there, and maybe just tel—"

"Think about the chain reaction. If he believes me, he'll tell his friends, who will tell theirs, and on, and on—."

"And you'll have saved all those lives——."

"But that's not my job," Leonard struggled to keep his voice from rising and almost succeeded. "You know that."

Jennifer backed off the desk, crossed her arms, but said nothing.

"It's not that I don't want to. I just can't go and start trying to save people I've no business saving. It's just not how it works."

"It's fine. If you can't do it, you can't do it. I understand."

Leonard's implant vibrated. He tugged his lobe, to answer it, but said, "Hang on, Race." He looked at her. "I've got to go."

"I know," Jennifer told him.

He moved closer, to hug her, to kiss her, but she withdrew. "Just go," she told him. "I'll be here when you get back, but for now, just go."

He bit back anger, instead took her hand, kissed her fingers. "I'll see you soon."

"I know."

"I love you."

"I know."

He didn't want that to be it, but he knew it was. He knew that Jennifer meant it when she said she would be there when he returned, but for right then, that was all the goodbye they were going to give each other.

He got into the elevator, tugged his earlobe to retrieve the call. "I'm on my way."

"The machine is programmed. You'll arrive on the southeast corner of 40th and 8th at oh-eight-hundred on September 10th, 2001. That'll give you one full day at the library. We think that will give you enough time."

Leonard pressed the button for the Safe's floor, rode the elevator down.

The same white hallway. Another door similar to all the others, and it opened to allow him entrance to the inner vestibule. At the next door, a laser scanned his retina while another scanned his palm, and then that door, too, swished open, onto the brilliant white Schrodinger Chamber. He crossed to the silver cylinder, and when the chamber door closed behind him, he put his hand on the cylinder screen. Another laser scan, and then the final door slid open to let him enter the Safe. The door slid closed behind him.

Total darkness save for a purple ring around a small button in front of him.

He tugged his earlobe. "Okay, Race, I'm in."

"Just give us one second. It's warming up."

Leonard nodded. At his sides, his hands bunched into tight firsts. He knew the matte-silver inner walls of the cylinder were at least three feet away in any direction. He hated the moments within the Safe just before the jump, those long, uncertain moments that stretched beyond time and space into uncertain nether-dimensions without feature. He knew those walls could never close in on him, but that didn't stop him from believing it was possible anyway.

"Okay," Race said. "Go time."

Leonard pressed the button.

A sudden feeling of compression, like the air within the cylinder compressed or gained density. The hairs on Leonard's neck tensed and his entire body
>clenched<
and then the inner-walls of the cylinder shimmered with fantastic purple-pink that spiraled around Leonard, leaving in its wake daylight-clear Manhattan, New York vitality, buildings and people and bustle, the raw, exuberant vigor of life at the very bleeding edge of now, life in this present moment without thought to any other. Leonard took a deep breath of urban air that tasted of

streetcart candied almonds and the sort of eye-burningly strong coffee that makes people forget about the night before in favor of the day in front of them and, without pause, began walking in midtown Manhattan, aiming directly at the sun.

13

Chance didn't want to let go of Cassie. It wasn't just that her hair smelled so clean, or even that the mere feeling of her body close against his was comforting; it was that until the moment she agreed to help him, he hadn't realized how alone he had felt. Until that handful of words, it just hadn't fully sunken in. He'd gone through anger and fear, but he understood finally that most of all, he'd felt lost, which released him from it. His body felt lighter, his head more clear.

The emotion that came next surprised him, and he had difficulty identifying it because it had two facets. Part of it was full-on, heart-heavy grief that his father was gone, that besides some extended family, he had no one else.

The rest, however, was hope. His body flooded with the kind of elated relief he imagined might have come if he'd gone skydiving wearing a jammed parachute, and at the last panic-rushing moment remembered the back-up.

She rubbed his back. Still said nothing. Just let him be.

He thumbed his eyes dry. "Sorry. I just—."

"I know," she told him.

"No, you don't," he said, reluctantly withdrawing. A moment before he might have said it with anger, but he said it then with acceptance, and just as quickly moved on: "So how do we do it? Just go?"

"I need to do something first," she started to take the first step either had taken since the world had stopped, but stopped when he gripped her wrist. "What?"

"Is it safe? To move around?"

"We should be fine. We'll stay in an excited state until we shut it off."

"Oh," he said. He realized how tightly he'd gripped her wrist and released it, and she opened and closed her hand, flexing out the kink. "So what're you doing?"

She gestured towards Hanley. "He fired his gun."

Which was why, Chance realized, the muzzle looked like a flashlight; the bright burst at the end was the explosion-wake of a gunshot. "But how come we can see it?"

"What do you mean?"

"You said light-speed theory. Which has that other clause that nothing can travel at the speed of light, because it would get too dense. So we can't be traveling at the speed of light. So how come the light doesn't seem to be moving?"

"You know, you put up a good charade sometimes, Chance Sowin, but I knew you weren't just another pretty face. Einstein never took into account the Higgs field, which is what we're seeing right now. All this interaction is taking place at the Higgs level."

"Isn't that subatomic?"

"We're seeing its effects."

They had reached the spot where Hanley stood, his legs spread and locked, arms thrust out and gun ablaze. The gunshot reflection shone in his eyes, lips pulled back almost in a snarl. Cassie bent close to Hanley's arm, turned her head sideways to sight along his gun. "He shot at my dad," she said, and with that she kicked him in the crotch so hard that, though Hanley's body didn't move, didn't flex, didn't twitch, his feet rose a solid inch from the ground, where they remained. Chance pointed that out.

"Still the Higgs. Your dad had thought it would affect gravity and air pressure, and he must have been right," she told him, and she moved from the muzzleflash in a straight line. He followed her until she paused.

At first, he mistook the bullet for a raindrop. The only difference between the small slug and all the droplets of water around it was that the bullet was darker. When Chance looked closer, he also noticed that it looked hazy, as if it was affecting the air around it. He reached out to touch it, but she caught his hand before he could. "What?"

"See how the air's hazy around it? That's the Higgs interaction. It caught the heat."

"So we can't move the bullet? What do we do, then?"

"We move my dad."

Nick had raised his arm to shield his face from the explosion. Orange light from the fireball illuminated his body, and the way he stood, the bullet would have pierced his right side just below his armpit. Chance pressed his good shoulder into Nick's waist and wrapped his arms around him, pushed, and was surprised that Nick's body gave way so easily. He stumbled, tripping as he tried to regain his footing, twirled and stopped. He'd moved Nick several feet to the left.

"You okay?" she asked him.

"He moved way more easily than I'd expected."

"Same as Hanley's feet. Gravity and air pressure."

Chance didn't fully understand, but neither did he really think he had to. "Well, he's out of harm's way. So let's get on with it."

*

She showed him how to use the time machine first, what buttons activated which functions, when and why and how to turn the dials, how to input spatial coordinates. Chance tried to keep up, and thought he understood how to use it, even if he didn't think he actually understood how it worked. At first, he worried, but then he realized how many things he used daily without really knowing how they worked. Cars, computers, credit cards: he didn't understand internal combustion, processors and memory and electricity; plumbing and magnetic strips. The only thought he ever gave when plunking down his card to pay for dinner was whether he had enough money in his checking account to cover the food.

Cassie led him into her house, where she composed a letter to her mother. "If it works, they'll never know, because this set of events won't ever have existed. But if it doesn't—."

"Right," Chance nodded, because that was the part he didn't need her to explain to him. He understood what would happen: he and Cassie would vanish without a trace. Someone might suspect that something had happened to them at the moment of the explosion and leave that as the official explanation, but leaving Trish a letter would let her family know she was still alive, somewhere, somewhen. Cassie folded the paper loosely and slipped it into her mother's pocket.

*

They weren't going far. Spatially, they weren't moving at all.

Chance remembered the display on his cell phone when he'd called 911. It had been 1:57 in the afternoon, and so Cassie set the time machine for 1:40.

"When I press the button," she told him, "The field is going to increase our excitement level. Substantially. Until all the particles that make us up are simultaneously moving faster than light. Once that happens, time is going to start going backward."

"So we're going into the past."

"More like we're bringing the past to us. But my point is that this might hurt."

"Might?"

"Your dad's notes weren't clear."

Chance looked at the time machine, then nodded. "All right."

She nodded back. Offered her hand. "Ready?"

The truth was he wasn't ready, not really, but he took her hand anyway.

Just as he did so, Cassie pressed the button to activate the field, to reverse the continuum or spiral back the present or whatever they were doing. Chance didn't know.

The feeling that bloomed through him when he took Cassie's hand was like exploding through déjà vu and coming out the other side. He felt rooted to the spot, constancy in the world like he'd never felt before, like right at that very instant, that place in time and space was the only one he was supposed to occupy.

He had a sudden memory of an amusement park he'd visited often as a child, and its Gravitron; years later, in a freshman chemistry course, he'd understood that the ride had merely been a big-enough centrifuge that people could walk into it. Chance and his friends had done so, going to the nearest padded section of wall to wait with tense stomachs for the door to close and for the ride to begin, which it soon did, spinning

spinning

round and round

until centrifugal force increased and rooted him to the padded wall, which had then risen mechanically until his feet hung a foot from the floor. Chance's limbs had felt as if they'd been bound to the wall.

He felt that way then standing there with Cassie, rooted in that instant like it had become stronger and more intense. As if time were compressing around him, bearing down on him from all directions, all dimensions. As if the universe were distilling into him.

As it did so, as that feeling intensified, the brightness of the paused lightning began to fade. Color bleached out of the world. Chance seemed able to feel the darkness prickling around him, in him, through him. The darkness

squeezed

singing his body electric

tenser

tighter

until the universe

s   t   r   e   t   c   h   e   d

blurrrrred

became unstable

and reversed

—SNAP—

reversed and

the colors in the world inverted like a photographic negative. Darkness blinked away, leaving behind a world shocked robin's egg blue. Street and houses shifted grey-white that hurt his eyes. Lawns blasted iridescent lavender

unstable became

blurrrrred

s   t   r   e   t   c   h   e   d

into clear borders that ran together in a suddenly Cezanne world.

His brain argued with his eyes because all the colors had gone negative, inverting on themselves, and the idea of light as darkness and shadows as highlights was just too foreign. The smoke cloud where his house had been bleached out blue, highlit by dark streaks like backward sunspots. The fire seemed to have gone black—living, breathing darkness that seemed to be trying to escape consumption as it collapsed in on itself.

He felt not only as if he could not move, but also as if he were already in motion. Time like mercury, quicksilver retro like watercolors under rain speeding skyward into clouds blazing salmon-orange. Motion pulled at his body, and he felt like a modern-day Gatsby standing against a current bearing him ceaselessly back into the past.

His stomach squeezed, and his gorge rose, but he kept from gagging because he worried he would retch so hard he might turn himself inside-out. Anything seemed possible under that iridescent sky in a going-backward universe that seemed to be collapsing into his sudden density, and he realized that was about what was happening, body fixed with inertia like concrete. He wondered if he would ever move again. He felt bigger than his body, and like it might just burst trying to contain him.

He groaned softly, more in his chest than in his throat. The reverse colors intensified, lost their contrast until livid neon burned into his soul;

slowed to calm.

Back to them again the once-errant prodigal hour returned, and as it did so, that insane darkness ruptured and the universal pressure that had made his whole body feel like lead let go. His knees buckled and he crumpled to the ground, his hand slipping from Cassie's to break his fall, and on his hands and knees he gagged so hard his lower back convulsed. The taste of sour alcohol and bitter-laced honey and heavy beef broth rose to his mouth, but only enough to make him spit throat-burning bile to the ground. He felt Cassie's hand on his shoulder and knew it was there for support, but he couldn't decide whether she was offering it or needed it herself.

He shut his tearing eyes, and shook his head to clear it. He feared that he would shake his brain lose, or perhaps that he wouldn't be able to synchronize with it again, that somehow his consciousness and his body might separate and continue on in diverging directions, one borne inevitably into the future while the other continued backward through a photo-negative past. He felt like he might blur across dimensions he'd never understand.

You've been here before.

14

Close-up: a giant fireball, orange with golden highlights shocking against the darkened sky of a stormy night. Track along the blast radius to Nicolo Constantin Lackesis, who begins to twist his body, his attention drawn by the explosion, as he raises his arms to shield his face from the blast.

Less than twenty feet away, Agent Richard Hanley fires his pistol. The sound of the report is sounds like it's clearing its throat against the domestic percussion of the explosion, the loud wind and howling rain, the suddenly roaring flames and the still-grumbling thunder.

Nick Lackesis shifts: sideways. From one instant to sudden next, he stands several feet from where he had just a moment before. He shakes his head.

Besides the ringing in his ears, he hears nothing. Not the flames, not the wind or the rain. Certainly not the gunshots.

There are several.

*

Richard Hanley might have sighted Nick down the barrel of his gun after, but he does not when pain explodes through his lower abdomen and he realizes his feet are no longer touching the ground. His fingers slacken, and his gun falls from his hand, clattering to the street.

Even as his gun falls, he fills a percussive crack like an internal snare drum. He staggers, the side of his chest numbed as though punched by concrete. At first, he believes a stray chuck of debris from the exploding Sowin house struck him, but then he touches his side. He withdraws his hand to see slick blood on his fingers; by the time his knees hit the ground, he is finding breathing difficult.

He exhales.

He does not inhale again. He tries, but he feels as though he is attempting to draw a breath underwater. His lungs stop trying before he does. Blackness.

*

Jeryn Nazor raises his gun as he spins, quick, but he is not fast enough; the shot comes from his left side, and the sound of its report makes his ear ring such that he clamps a hand over it. His throat feels like his tie has tightened around it, but when he drops his gun as he fingers the knot, the fabric yields to his hand. He looks at it as he pulls it from his neck before he understands. He falls to his ass, his neck shuddering as breath whistles like wind in his throat, and then he falls backward. The hole in his neck fills with raindrops and blood he drowns on.

*

Peter Geisel wipes the sweat from his brow but removes only rain. He pivots, fires two shots: one catches Nick Lackesis in the chest, the other in the head.

He hears a scream behind him and turns toward it.

His next shot pierces Trish Lackesis through the frontal lobe, just above her left eye. Her scream dies in her throat as her body crumples to her lawn.

Geisel turns just slightly more, finger tight on the trigger, but stops.

Chance Sowin and Cassie Lackesis are gone.

Geisel continues to spin. He scans the street. He walks a few steps in several directions before he stops.

When satisfied they are truly gone, he stalks back into the Lackesis house. His shoes leave grimy footprints on the hardwood floor of the foyer as he crosses to the dining room, where he picks up the cardboard box full of Dennis Sowin's inventions. He curses when he realizes Cassie has disappeared with the one she had taken.

He is relieved when he finds the notebooks she had taken into the living room. He picks them up, adds them to the box, and takes it out to his car. He slams the door after tucking it onto the passenger seat.

He collects each body and drags each one into the Sowin house, over which fire is spreading with vigor. Flames are reaching into the foyer when he drops Trish's body onto the hardwood floor, and he pulls his cell phone from his pocket as he crosses the lawn to return to his call. He dials 911 to report the fire, and the dispatcher informs him that several units are already on their way. He clicks his phone shut.

He gets into his car and pulls into the street just as the first fire engine screams around the corner, among the wind and lights the great figure five signifying the town's fire shield. Sirens howl and gongs clang, and then Peter Geisel turns in the opposite direction the firetruck came, leaving behind him four dead bodies burning in the house.

*

Among the property destroyed in the fire will be a note in Trish Lackesis' pocket that no one will ever read.

*

In the weeks that follow, Peter Geisel will be interrogated by no fewer than a dozen times by FBI agents and counter-terrorism officers. He will tell them the same story every time.

Some will believe him. Others will not.

Eventually, they will grow bored of Geisel. After confiscating the research he recovered, the FBI will add the names of Chancellor Terrence Sowin and Cassandra Moira Lackesis to its most-wanted list. Soon after that, they will forget both; they will be too excited by the reports their physicists make, based on the research of Dennis Joseph Sowin. They will discover that the two electronic devices are a high-powered laser and an engine that proves the existence of the Higgs field, yielding unlimited energy from finite resources. The engine will revolutionize the energy industry, and they will mass produce it to install in cars, heat and cool homes cheaply, and then even power cities.

The alleviation of dependence on fossil fuel will create great turmoil in the Middle East, which the world will eye warily in the years to follow. When the United States government formally declares war on Iraq in 2003, it will train the sight of the Sowin laser on the palace of Saddam Hussein, and a conflict that might have dragged on for years will end in a matter of hours, with the complete vaporization of that single palace in Baghdad and everyone within it.

In North Korea, Kim Jong Il will regard the use of the Sowin laser as a crime against humanity, and he will retaliate. Pearl Harbor will gain new notoriety as the third place in history upon which an atomic bomb was dropped.

Due to an error in triangulation and changes in air pressure and wind speed, a second missile intended for Los Angeles will instead strike Whitney Peak in California, causing a landslide that will destroy General Sherman in Sequoia National Park. Scientists will eye the San Andreas Fault for weeks before finally the expected quake will shift all of California west of the faultline northwest by 35 miles to form what will become known as the Pacific Archipelago. Aftershocks of the quake will loosen enormous ice shelves in Antarctica, and tumbling chunks will plunge millions of innocent penguins to their deaths.

Sea level will rise by several inches, causing the inundations of New York City, Boston, Philadelphia, and Miami. Heavy storms will flood New Orleans and London.

*

Peter Geisel will be the only person who will trace those events back to a single, fateful evening. When the Sowin laser destroys Saddam's palace, Geisel will become quiet for days, and his coworkers will question his mental stability. His superiors will recall that Geisel was the agent who recovered the laser. They will in addition remember that evening's body count, and that two people, as well as some key research and a third device, remain missing.

Geisel will know they remember this. He will begin to take precautions.

They will not matter.

One day, while Geisel drives south on I-95 to keep an appointment in D.C., an eighteen-wheel truck hauling flammable chemicals will slow suddenly before him. Geisel will slam on his brakes.

They will fail.

His tires will squeal; his bumper will crumple; his windshield will explode. His seatbelt will rip due to a small tear he never would have noticed, and his body will pitch forward. The steering wheel will disintegrate, and its column will crack his sternum before shattering through his ribs, ripping his lungs apart and pulverizing his heart.

When the paramedics finally pull him from the hulk of wreckage, they will need to use his dental records to identify his body; his teeth will be just about all that will remain of him.

15

Leonard passed an HMV and two movie theaters across the street from each other. The sidewalk in front of him sparkled in the early morning light. He saw a bank of telephones, too, which marked the first such kiosk he'd seen in many years.

The first thing he needed was money, and he found a convenience store on the next corner. In his experience, just about anywhere that had refrigerated drink cases would have a money machine. He scanned the brands as he passed the case: Coca-Cola, of course. Pepsi as well, and Dr Pepper. But he didn't see Lymon or Sparkle.

Past the case he found the small machine he'd been hoping for. He wondered, briefly, what "ATM" stood for and who Star was, but disregarded both as he swiped his smartcard down the strip. The machine took a moment to recognize his card at all, then asked for his preferred language. He chose English, punched four random numbers when the machine asked for his PIN, approved a 3-dollar transaction fee, selected a 200-dollar withdrawal, and then waited as the machine processed his request. A small motor hummed ten crisp 20-dollar bills into the tray below the screen.

Greenbacks? Leonard hadn't seen greenbacks in years. He thumbed through them. He had to squint to confirm the large portrait was still Jackson, but the bills, overall, were quaint, with no holographic strips or iridescent ink; CIRTN's banker could have counterfeited them easily. Wondering what smaller denominations looked like, he took a Diet Pepsi from the drink case to the cashier, offered one of the twenties, and pocketed the change to check later. He twisted the cap off the soda and took a swig; Pepsi tastes the same no matter where you go.

He crossed 7th Avenue, and the next street was Broadway. Times Square. Enormous monitors showed a newscaster, and just to the north, the red Virgin logo blazed while, slightly further on, a giant Samsung monitor displayed another newscast. Enormous models looked out at the world from billboards several stories up; by the waistband of his underwear, Leonard guessed the lean young man's name was Calvin Klein. Opposite him, a buxom woman wore only barely more clothing, and Leonard wondered if her name was Victoria and what her secret was. He crossed the street, past a Warner Brothers store and approaching a giant neon sign that blurred numbers straight across, each accompanied by letters Leonard sensed meant something he could not discern.

He couldn't really tell if anything was different, because everything was. Different billboards with different beautiful people, different faces on giant screens, different acronyms gaining or losing different percentages . . . the details were different, perhaps, but the things those details signified were not. Somehow, the reality to which he had traveled might have been completely different, but Manhattan was exactly the same as he remembered.

16

The past wasn't what Chance had expected.

He didn't know what he had imagined. Time-lapse backward, and when it all stopped the world would glow iridescent, shimmering like magic. But the past was nothing like that, because, he realized, it no longer existed. The moment he looked out over the street on which he had grown up, expecting it to be different when it was the same as it always had been and might always be; he realized that the past was suddenly now.

A favorite anecdote of one of his history professors at Fordham concerned cartographers and the way they had marked territories no explorers had yet charted. Wizened monks loomed over sturdy parchment, biting their tongues as their careful fingers traced thin lines to demarcate the world for intrepid men who refused to stop to ask for directions both because they wished instead to make their own and because the only direction that had existed was forward. When those cartographers depicted as-yet-unexplored land, forests and mountains and scapes that hadn't yet been mapped nor even described in any detail, they would mark those sections of maps with a simple warning to future travelers: "Here be dragons."

Ptolemy and Al-Idrisi, Amerigo Vespucci and Christopher Saxon. Lewis and Clark, Simeon De Whitt and James Wilson. To that list Chance would have added both his own name and Cassie's.

Cassie still had her hand on his good shoulder. Her eyes were closed. She wobbled.

"You okay?" he asked her.

She exhaled, nodded as she opened her eyes. "Yeah. I'll be—I'm fine. I should have prepared us better for that."

Chance laughed. "It's okay. I think the alcohol on top of the sedatives they gave me earlier messed up my system, but I feel totally sobered now. And besides, I'm not sure you could've, Cass." He thought of all those traveling men with their quills and parchments, with their boats and their spears, and if he had possessed a compass, he would have taken it up to rechart the world before him, dragons be damned. This place was his. He claimed it. The present we share, but the past and the future belong to Chance.

*

The deadbolt, again: busted. Cassie eased the time machine's dial back, restoring motion to the world as Chance eased the door open, wincing as it creaked. Golden daylight behind him spindled his shadow across the hardwood floor. Chance crept forward, wondering where the gunm—

"Stop right there."

A curt voice. Its tone didn't expect argument, and its owner rounded the corner of the living room, silencered pistol already raised: the deep, black muzzle. "Don't move," the man said. His aim shifted: Chance to Cassie.

Instinct: Chance lunged. The gunman had already killed Chance's father. He wouldn't get Cassie, too.

Cassie turned the dial on the time machine to pause time just as Chance slammed into the man's midsection. The gun chuffled twice, shots soft and embarrassed as coughs during a eulogy. Behind him, Cassie flattened herself to the floor, even as Chance piledrove the man to the wood. Pain flared in Chance's shoulder, but it seemed distant and filtered through adrenaline and rage. The man dropped his gun as he struggled, but it hung in mid-air and never dropped to the floor.

Chance grappled with the man, whose limbs were long and muscular. He tried to crook his elbow around the man's neck, but the man was too fast, too wiry. He didn't notice Cassie had grabbed the gun until she smashed it across the man's face, the impact of which left him stunned long enough for Chance to get him into a tight headlock.

Chance squeezed, hard, flexing his bicep even as he pulled his hands together. The man made a sound in his throat like a growl, his hands scrambling at Chance's forearm, at first ineffective until his fingers found the nerve in Chance's wrist; icy pain seized through Chance's forearm so hard he could no longer keep a fist. The man wriggled free, kicking Chance in the gut as he did so, stumbling backward and around the corner, into the kitchen, even as Cassie blurred past him.

Seeing her moving so quickly pushed Chance forward, around the corner just as both Cassie and the gunman, a writhing, struggling mass of slapping hands and elbows, crossed the jamb together. The man pushed Cassie into the wall, so hard the magnets on the fridge rattled, and she groaned when her head struck solid.

Chance twisted around the man and hooked his arms under the man's armpits in a full-nelson, yanking backward so hard the man stutter-stepped until he let his legs relax, which made him seem to gain fifty pounds and pulled Chance off balance. Chance's heels skidded on the linoleum-tile floor, but he twisted even as he fell with the man. He felt as though his brain were several steps ahead of his body, analyzing, planning, through a rush of adrenaline and some other body's pain. Taking in details: the wide-open basement door. The center island's corners—

Chance pulled the man's body sideways, slammed the man's head against the closest corner of the kitchen's island. The man's clear blue eyes off-focused as his head struck, just above the ear, hard enough to jar Chance's hands. If the man bled, his mask absorbed it, but Chance used the rebound to slam the man sideways, toward the dark basement door. The man's body passed the threshold, and then his weight pulled Chance down several stairs before Chance could find balance to stop, but the man, even in his daze, pulled, and Chance nearly toppled right over him. Pain seared across Chance's neck, and tiny stars danced behind his eyes as his head banged the railing.

Muscles have their own memories, and Chance's then recalled their dojo training, punches and kicks, grapples and throws. Chance stuck out his knee to fulcrum the man sideways, over it, down the steps. The man's sudden downward motion pulled Chance forward, away from the banister. His hands slipped from the man's arms, seeking purchase as he snaked an arm across the man's chest while the other slid around the man's neck, and then—

bony resistance, vertebral popping like hard-cracking knuckles. Chance felt the man's neck twist and the bones within it give way.

Fingers so tense they trembled, muscles in his arms bunched, a sound midway between a grunt and a scream escaped Chance's throat. He gasped, again, again. He couldn't get enough air, and when those inhalations came out, they did so as sobs.

He heard a footstep behind him, and he turned to see Cassie in the doorway. She moved with urgency until she looked past Chance, saw the man's body on the stairs down below. Fear crossed her face. "Is he—?"she didn't finish the sentence, the silence of the missing adjective defeaning. She put her hand on his good shoulder. "Are you okay?"

"I'll live." He kept seeing the gunman aim at Cassie, and the anger overwhelmed anything else. "I think—I think I broke his neck."

Cassie looked at him like she didn't believe it. He leaned sideways as she eased past him, down one step, and two.

The adrenaline rushing through his system began to seep out of it, and the distant pain of his shoulder approached as if at a gallop, throbbing to pulse through his neck and bag. Chance sagged sideways, against the banister.

At first Chance thought she intended to check for a pulse, but she did not. Her fingers sought a seam around his neck, and when they found it, she twisted upward and pulled the gunman's mask from his head.

Chance groaned when he saw the man's face. "Oh, Jesus Christ, you've got to be fucking kidding me."

Because the man whose neck Chance had just snapped like so much wicker, the man from whose head Cassie had yanked that black mask, the man who, in another few minutes, would have shot and killed Chance's father, was Federal Agent Peter Geisel.

17

Leonard continued east along 40th, crossed Broadway to arrive at 6th, where Bryant Park surprised him. In the still brightening, September morning light, the emerald leaves of the park's trees rustled in a breeze Leonard couldn't feel at street level, shielded as he was by concrete monoliths and their multi-colored awnings. In the Manhattan Leonard knew, junkies referred to Bryant as Needle Park, and anyone not looking for a fix avoided its thriving heroin trade and the auxiliary prostitution micro-industry that supported it.

Leonard followed a slate-grey stone walkway past business people sitting in skeletal chairs next to small, metal tables. Dew evaporated off grass so green it shimmered. Leonard approached the library from its backside, where brilliant white walls and arched windows shone beyond a few white-and-green-awninged kiosks hawking tourist maps and magazines. He continued to the side of the library, rounded the corner at 5th Avenue and jogged up the giant, concrete steps, on either side of which presided prideful lions, to approach the three entrances dwarfed by their enormous archways.

The one closest to him shuddered in its frame when he pulled its handle, and he paused before he noticed the library's hours posted on the center door. He checked his watch, but cursed before he even saw the time. Mondays were the only day of the week the library was closed, which September 10th, 2001 happened to be. He retreated down the steps, paused at street level and noticed a coffee shop across the street, its storefront obscured by a construction scaffold. His stomach grumbled when he saw the bagel illustration on the window, and he wagered, too, that they would have newspapers for sale. Some food and some news would help him consider his options.

At the shop, he found a copy of the New York Times in a small display stand. He scanned the front page as he pulled it from the rack. Something about a recession, Democrats and Republicans. In Manhattan itself, a debate between Badillo and Bloomberg, two mayoral candidates.

If the newspaper's dimensions hadn't made it difficult to unfold and read on the spot, Leonard might have been unable to resist the urge. Instead, he tucked it under his arm, approached the counter and ordered a cranberry muffin and a tall coffee at the counter. He procured a spot at one of the small tables nearby, then spread open the newspaper. As he began to read, a small, dense pit formed in his stomach. The paper detailed only the previous few days, but still he began to sense the greater enormity of the differences between the alternity and the world he knew.

The United States was still the United States, and still had a president. The North American Union had not been formed, no Prime Minister was in place, and no Union-States seemed to exist. Leonard had to concentrate to remember when the Union had formed. He knew FDR had set its formation in motion, but also recalled the first Prime Minister hadn't come for some years afterward. It had been another several years after that before the formation of the Union-States, but he was sure that had occurred before Kennedy had become PM, because he was certain Nixon—the then president of Atlantica—had been the one who'd alerted JFK about the Indo-Russo Korean Union's installation of a missile base in Cuba.

The business section was the first to include stories and details familiar to Leonard. Disney and Pepsi, of course, though he wondered who AOL was, how they related to Time Warner, and why they were pursuing a purchase of AT&T. Which also meant AT&T had survived the large anti-trust settlement in the 80s . . .

Leonard closed the newspaper. He stared out the window, watching the library, before he slugged down the last of his coffee, chomped the final morsel of his muffin, and rose to leave the shop. Whatever coincidence this alternity shared with his reality, wherever and whenever that common event had occurred, it had done so long before, though the city still resembled the Manhattan he knew. Some of the brand names were different, and he had never heard of Starbucks, the name of the shop he had just left, but Times Square had seemed familiar. And, he realized, standing there and looking at the library, that too appeared exactly as he had remembered it. He crossed 5th Avenue again, began to skirt the concrete foundation of the library, stopped when he spotted the big, rectangular stone slightly darker than the rest of the wall, with a white number etched into its face: 1911.

If the library was the same, if so much of Manhattan was similar, but there was no NAU, the divergence must have occurred sometime between 1911 and the mid-1960s. In fact, the formation of the NAU could well have been the difference, or something to do with Kennedy. If the attempted assassination had been successful, it would have prevented the man's work with the UN—

Leonard looked down 5th Avenue. In the distance, the towering buildings on either side of the street appeared to move closer to meet. In the Manhattan he knew, 5th Avenue continued until it hit Washington Square Park, in the Village. After that was downtown, the financial district, Wall Street and its Journal. The World Trade Center. He thought of its concourse: the upscale clothing shops, chocolates and coffees, high-end accessories and high-tech electronics. He would've bet one of those boring old greenbacks the ATM had given him that there would be a bookstore there.

He'd seen a subway stop back toward 6th Avenue, near the north end of Bryant Park, and he doubled back.

While he was in transit, he also realized, he could coordinate with Race. He tugged on his earlobe. Waited.

He turned the corner, found a chair and sat near the topiary. The fragrant scent of newly trimmed flowers brightened the air.

No response came.

Leonard pulled on his earlobe again. The implant in his temporal lobe had never malfunctioned, and its quantum design ensured that it would work across millennia. At first he worried about speaking aloud, but he noticed that several people held what he assumed were small phones to their ears. He mimicked their stance by pulling the Oracle device to his ear even as he tugged its lobe a third time. "Race? You there?"

City sounds around him, but silence in his head.

He tugged his lobe, again, again, never even let it go, until pain shot through the cartilage above it and he worried it would come right off if he kept pulling. "You've got to be bloody kidding me."

He pulled his sleeve back, squeezed the buttons on his watch, expecting the ab clench. The gooseprickles sizzling on the back of his neck. A sudden lurch as Bryant Park and Manhattan around him vanished to give way to—

darkness, of course, like always. The familiar darkness of those familiar, brushed-steel walls—

All around Leonard, people continued to talk on their small phones. Pigeons continued to peck at the humble remains of portable breakfasts. Tree limbs continued to sway in the breeze, leaves to rustle.

Bryant Park continued to exist, and Leonard continued to remain in it.

He squeezed the buttons again, hard. He clenched his own abdomen as he did so, trying to will it to work, trying to make it happen, take me back, take me back, but the universe ignored him. When his skin prickled, it was from chilly fear rather than temporal displacement.

"Come on, you've got to be bloody kidding me," Leonard Kensington said aloud, again, as he looked around at the pigeons and people, the buildings and the trees, and realized that he was stranded in an alternate reality.

18

Nothing surprised Chance Sowin anymore. He understood this as he sat on the hard pine stairs, staring down at the federal agent he had just killed.

Not long before, the discovery that his father's murderer had worked for the government might have iced Chance's insides, but sitting there, Chance understood something he had begun to realize when the doctor had told him his father had died: surprise no longer existed. Since that day a month before when he'd felt the bone-jarring crash as he'd ridden an escalator up the World Trade Center concourse on his way to his office, whatever receptors felt surprise had vanished. Chance's life had begun to defy expectations immediately: the World Trade Center landing above him should have been reduced to chaos, but policemen in dark uniforms had turned employees away from the elevators even as firefighters had dashed around with deliberate expressions on their faces.

Workers had funneled straight from the subway out to the street beyond. Beautiful sunlight on a bright September morning, but the smell was of burning. Chance had tried to place the smell as he had followed directions until there weren't any more directions to follow, until rescue workers believed that they had passed to relative haven, which was the moment Chance had paused to look back and realize that the burning smell was the scent of jet fuel and the martyrdom of madmen and heroes alike. Later, when those towers had fallen, whatever tiny mechanism in his brain had held the ability to register awe had tripped like a fuse in a haunted house, exploded like a mason jar attempting to hold lightning.

Which was why, sitting there and looking down at the body of the federal agent whose neck he had just snapped, Chance wasn't surprised. He wasn't surprised to discover the man who would have killed his father had worked for the government, nor that his neck had snapped so easily. He wondered if *al Qaeda* was just a convenient scapegoat Hanley had used so that he could steal Dennis Sowin's work.

Cassie moved up the stairs again, to his side, placed a hand in his thick hair. "Are you okay?"

Chance considered that but no longer knew how to answer, or where one might begin. Instead, he said, "He didn't stop."

Cassie hesitated as if unsure what he meant.

"I saw you twist the dial. And when we were wrestling and he dropped his gun, it didn't fall. Just hung there. So why didn't—."

"You tackled him right when I turned the dial. You brought him into the pause with us," she said. "And now we need to warn your father. Because otherwise, I'm betting Hanley's going to show up to finish the job."

He looked up at her. He found he didn't know how to respond.

She held a hand out to him.

"I just can't—I can't believe it was Geisel. I don't get it," he said, taking her hand and letting her pull him up, then: "I thought he was going to shoot you," like he was defending his actions.

"You saved me," she said. "Thank you."

He half-shrugged. Pain seethed like dying embers in his shoulder. "Couldn't let anything happen to you."

"Always the hero."

"Nah. Just always trying."

*

Cassie turned the dial to let time move forward again. Rapid-fire double-banged in the foyer as two bullets from Geisel's dropped gun punched into the wall of the foyer. A second or so later, Chance heard a mechanical sound come from his father's office, and then his father's long shadow appeared across the floor of the basement.

Dennis Sowin had thinning grey hair and bright blue eyes under a well-lined forehead, and doctors had, several years before, used vessels in his left leg to complete a quadruple bypass; his gait had never returned to normal. Even still he used a dark, wooden cane as he limped across the basement, pausing at the foot of the stairs. "Chance? Cassie?" he said, then, at the sight of the body. "What's going on? Who's he?"

Chance would have responded but couldn't figure out how. His jaw clenched.

His father looked between him and Cassie, and then he recognized the time machine. "Oh, bloody hell," he said. He'd been born in Scotland and educated at Oxford, and though he'd come to the States many years before, still spoke with a prominent accent halfway to a burr. "You were in my lab. You found my research. You—it worked."

"You never used it?"

"He couldn't," Cassie said. To Dennis: "The field would have shorted out your pacemaker."

"I could start it, and see some of the effects, but I couldn't increase the field intensity enough to actually use it."

"Why didn't you tell me what you were doing?" Chance struggled to keep his voice even and almost succeeded. "Didn't you trust me?"

"I was trying to protect you."

"I'm not a child."

"You're my child!" Dennis rubbed his forehead. "So it works. And you—."

"We gave up our lives to come backward in time to save you, yes," Chance said. "If that's what you were going to say."

"Not in so many words," Dennis said. "What do you want me to say?"

"You're sorry would be a start. And then maybe you could explain why a government agent killed you."

"The government?" Dennis asked.

Chance nodded toward Geisel. "Oh, bloody hell. You're sure he's government?"

"That's what he said—," Chance said.

But Cassie cut in. "Except we're not. He said so, but did you ever get a good look at his badge? And what about all the other accusations?"

"What accusations?" Dennis asked.

"That you were talking to *al Qaeda*, for one. But they're lying, right?"

Dennis started to respond but hesitated.

"Tell me they were lying, dad. Tell me you weren't working with *al Qaeda*."

"It's more complicated than that."

"What's complicated? Either you were or you weren't."

"Oh, don't be so bloody naïve. Look, this isn't—there's a bloody corpse on the stairs, and let's face it, you can't stay long, because so far as I know, I'm expecting you to walk through that door in ten or so minutes. So look, right now, come down to the lab, and I'll explain. At least as far as I can figure, and there are some things about the time machine I should tell you," he glanced toward Geisel. "And then I'll figure out what to do with him."

*

Chance watched his father pull the chain from the collar of his shirt, flip the thermostat and stick the ring into the lock. The bookcase swung aside, and he and Cassie followed Dennis into the lab, where Dennis caned a floor-button Chance hadn't noticed before; the back of the bookcase slid shut, closing them into the lab.

Chance leaned against a metal chair he pulled from near the workbench, crossed his arms. "So did you ever plan to tell me about this room?"

"Actually, yes, I had," Dennis said. "Today, in fact. When you moved back in. I figured you should know."

"Mighty big of you."

"This conversation might be easier if you stopped acting like a pompous little brat."

"I'm just trying to make sense of things. Like losing my father. And then having the FBI show up to tell me he was working with *al Qaeda*."

"Which is bollocks."

"So you weren't, then?"

"Working, no. Talking—that's complicated."

"Then make it simple. Explain to me why you built this lab, and why you never told me about it, and why the government killed you for whatever you were doing in it."

"I was trying to keep them from attacking us again. There was one particular man—."

"Zawqiri," Cassie said.

Dennis nodded. "Zawqiri tried to buy my research. I told him it wasn't for sale, but then after last month—I knew he had connections to *al Qaeda*, and I tried to capitalize on his interest in my work. I told him I might be interested in selling it, but I wasn't ready yet."

"You were stringing them along?" Cassie said.

"I was just trying to keep them occupied."

"So they found out you'd invented a time machine—," Chance said.

"The Sowin device. But my work wasn't really about time travel."

"You named it after us?"

"Spelled the old way," Dennis said, which was 'Samhain,' and which was how Chance's family had spelled it until one of Chance's ancestors, Terrence Samhain, had become a chancellor in a church and altered the spelling to distance his name from the ancient Pagan feast of harvest. "Because it fit. Wizened old blokes with pointy hats and noses, and nubile young lasses shedding their clothes to dance round the fire. Samhain is when magic works, and that's what this is, isn't it?"

"It's certainly close," Cassie said.

"But you said your work wasn't about the time machine?" Chance said.

Dennis shook his head. "The time machine was an accident—."

"How do you invent a time machine by accident?"

"It was the energy, wasn't it?" Cassie said. "You figured out how to enhance energy."

"Something close to. Consider relativity and its implications. The potential energy of any system is equal to—take yourself as an example. What do you weigh now, Chance? Twelve stone or so? Say a hundred and fifty pounds? Times nearly three hundred meters per second," Dennis said, then added: "Squared. Which is simply astronomical. Unfathomable. I mean, in mathematical terms, a number like that is completely the opposite of realistic. When you talk about numbers, there are irrational numbers like *pi*, and then there are imaginary numbers, like the square root of negative one, and then you get a number like the one we're speaking about, which I believe falls under the 'ludicrous' category. Except with one major caveat."

"It's a real number. It's possible," Cassie said.

"Or should be. So I started rethinking energy. And that was about when I built this room. Because that was when I got a campus visit from some prigs from Halliburton. Bunch of buttoned-up poncers. They wanted to buy me out of my research. Princeton, to their immense credit, backed me up when I refused, but they told me not long afterward that I might want to scale it down a bit. Thing was, I was getting close, and I couldn't very well just give it up, could I?"

"No, you couldn't," Cassie said.

"Of course I couldn't do. So I built the wall in last summer and started doing the work on my own. I didn't need much," he went to the workbench, where he picked up the time machine, held it up, and indicated the one Cassie was still holding. "Some electronics components. There's a processor, a small harddrive to store the spatial and temporal coordinates, and of course the Higgs engine is the real heart of it. That was where the breakthrough came, and how I ended up with a time machine. See, I got to thinking, what if I could access just a little of that relative energy, which made me realize that the energy was already there, and I thought—."

"Instead of trying to get it out, put more energy in," Cassie said.

"Exactly. Which created a sort of feedback loop, and I was getting more energy than I'd started with, which was when I realized I was onto something. Unfortunately, that was also right around the time I was approached by a bloke named—."

"Zawqiri," Chance said.

Dennis shook his head. "Zawqiri came later. First was a bloke named Hanley."

Chance looked at Cassie, who shrugged.

"What'd I miss?" Dennis said.

"The guy on the stairs," Cassie said. "Geisel. He showed up with someone called Hanley. They said they were partners. They also said you'd been having an affair with my mother."

"What? Heavens no. Your mother is a beautiful woman, Cassie, and she's been the best kind of friend to me when I've needed it. After Miry—," he started, but he choked on the name of his wife, and suddenly Chance understood. Not the research, not the work and the time machine and the physics; a ten-minute crash course wasn't going to help him understand the Higgs field.

Chance had followed his father into that room wanting answers and ready to demand them—who were the agents? Who was after him?—but, he realized, the room was his father's answer to the single greatest lingering question in life: what now? When your wife dies, what now? When your son decides not to come home, what now? When the only thing you have left in your life is your work, what now?

You build a room. You hide your pain and your grief and your love away, because you worry that the world is too big and scary for them. You hide away the parts of your life that matter because you worry about losing them; you want to protect them from the elements and perhaps from a world you don't believe deserves them. You come home to a big, empty house that once upon a time contained the laughter of your wife and your child but now reverberates with silence, and you build a small, secret room within it, a place that's yours, a place where you can try to work through the pain and where you can hope the pain won't find you. You conceal a part of yourself from the world, and you attempt to preserve it the best way you know how.

And when people try to find it, when people try to help you, you only withdraw farther, because they can't understand. How could they?

Chance only half-listened to his father tell Cassie that Trish had helped him through several tough moments of his life, first when he had lost Miryam and then again after Chance had moved away to Fordham and then remained in Manhattan even after he'd graduated.

"I was surprised when you didn't move back home," his father told him. "And more than a little disappointed."

"Better late than never, though, right?" Chance said. "If there's even such a thing anymore."

"Right, and if you've used the time machine, you need to be careful and watch how it affects you. There's no guarantee it's safe. Even besides the electromagnetic field you've just exposed yourselves to," Dennis said, even as they heard furtive movements above them, from upstairs. Dennis looked up toward the ceiling.

"That's either Chance or Hanley," Cassie said.

"Then, crash course: the other thing to worry about is more important than field exposure. Because now that you've used it, time's gone a bit—wibbly-wobbly for you, hasn't it? There's really no past or future anymore, and you've changed what you knew as the past but what will be my future. Which means there might be consequences in terms of causality and what most people would call paradoxes—."

"Might be?" Chance asked.

"Well, nobody knows, do they?"

"You're not going to tell me we're going to unmake the universe or something, are you?" Chance said.

"Highly unlikely. It's been here long enough nothing you can do is going to affect the Big Bang. At least, I don't think so. What I was going to say was more concerning you two than the universe, and that's that the Sowin device is going to keep your particles—all your particles—in a constant state of excitement. Even when you're not actually manipulating time around you, it's still locked on those particles so long as the field is activated, but it's locked on them at the frequency of spin and rotation—."

"You're losing me," Chance said.

Just then, though, they heard Chance's voice call "Dad!" from above them.

"At least we know it's me," Chance said.

"He's not losing me," Cassie said. "Electrons spin. And they were doing so at a specific frequency when we started the time machine's field. But if we just created a new timeline, where we're going to exist now, the time machine is going to keep our particles at their original frequency from the timeline we just diverged from. Until we shut the field off."

"Is that bad?"

"Doubt it's ever happened. If it will happen. But if it does, you might experience some uncertainty—."

"I feel like uncertainty's been the story of my life for the past month," Chance said.

"I meant quantum uncertainty."

"That doesn't sound comfortable."

"If it happens, comfort is about the least thing you're going to need to worry about," Dennis said just as Chance's voice called for him again, this time higher in tone and more urgent. He'd probably just seen the body on the stairs.

"We've got to get going," Cassie said, taking Chance's hand.

Chance resisted, though, and moved to hug his father, who returned the embrace but then patted his back and inched him away. "Go, go," he said, waving his arms as if to shoo them both away, just as Cassie took his hand again and turned the dial on the Samhain. The world stopped, freezing his father and all the rest of the world and time around them.

*

They crossed the dim basement, toward the wooden stairs. Chance reached for the railing—

—but his fingers closed on nothing, and no step met his foot, which fell further than his brain and leg had anticipated, causing him to stumble forward before he reached out to catch himself using the small side table in the foyer—foyer?—where a small sliver of autumn light came through the crack between the busted jamb and the slightly open door.

Before he could react or surprise could set in, Cassie's voice called his name from behind him.

He turned, started back toward the kitchen. "Yeah, I'm her—," he—

—found himself instead staring directly at the front door, a yard or so closer to it than he had been a moment before.

Cassie's voice again: "Chance?"

Chance didn't move. "I'm by the front door, Cass," he called. He waited until she came into the foyer behind him.

"You okay?"

"I was about to start up the stairs and then I was suddenly in the foyer."

"I think it's because you were in the kitchen."

"I never made it to the kitchen."

"No, not you. You, from before. You were standing at the top of the stairs."

"I—what?" Chance said, then realized what she was saying: his former self, his past self.

"There must be some kind of quantum safeguard to prevent you from interacting directly with your past self. Makes sense," she said. "Like we were just talking about electron spin. The universe might actively prevent identical atoms from existing in the same space."

"So I couldn't get close to myself."

"The electrons would be identical. So rather than let that happen . . . there must be some form of repulsion at work. Get too close, and you get displaced to a safer distance. We were heading out of the house. You must have skipped ahead."

"If I didn't know better, I'd say the universe was trying to kick me out of my house."

"It might. Walk back toward the kitchen," Cassie told him.

Trusting her, Chance moved again toward the kitchen—

—late afternoon autumn sunlight blazed down on his front lawn dotted here and there with stray leaves and tufts of weeds.

Chance turned to watch Cassie walk out the front door of his house. "You just vanished. There was this pop and then you were gone."

"I'd really be happier not being your guinea pig."

"If you didn't want to be an experiment, we never should have used the time machine to save your father," she said as she descended Chance's front stoop and brushed past him to stride across the lawn.

Chance turned to follow her away. The world was more still than ever he would have imagined it. It wasn't just the still of an autumn day without a breeze, nor a mid-week afternoon during when no one was home because everyone was at work or running errands; this was stillness without even the potential for motion. Stillness they had caused, and stillness they had reversed to suit their needs.

"We did it," Chance said, following Cassie across the lawn, toward the curb and the street. "We did it," he repeated like he was still testing the reality of the phrase. Like he was examining how it felt, and what it meant. The sudden high of newfound possibility rushing through his body flooded images his brain—

the roiling dustcloud that had been, for so many agonizing days, all that had remained of the brilliant silver towers that had reached above the Manhattan sky.

The peaceful civil rights advocate with his baby face and his small mustache: "The ultimate measure of a man is not where he stands in moments of comfort and convenience, but where he stands at times of challenge and controversy."

The light-colored convertible and the thick head of hair on the most charismatic president in history: "Ask not what your country can do for you—ask what you can do for your country. My fellow citizens of the world: ask not what America will do for you, but what together we can do for the freedom of man."

The tall, spindly man with the large nose and the mole, the beard beneath the stovepipe hat and the stentorian voice of confident oration: "You cannot escape the responsibility of tomorrow by evading it today"—

"You realize what this means," he said. "We could go anywhere. Do anything. Change—."

"No," she shook her head as they crossed the sidewalk.

"I thought—."

She turned. "No, Chance. You didn't. We didn't. I turned on the time machine because everything was happening too fast, and—it's not that easy. I mean, it's—the repercussions are—I can't even imagine what might happen."

"But we don't have to."

"Are you not listening? It's great that it worked and that we managed to save your father, but we've fundamentally changed the universe."

"And it's fine," Chance told her. "Look around. Same trees. Same sun. Same sky. We didn't fucking unmake the universe or anything."

"But on some fundamental level—."

"On some fundamental level nobody'll ever know the damned difference anyway. Who does? When was the last time you saw a boson, Cass?"

"April," she said.

He hadn't expected her to answer, and it stopped him cold.

She began again to walk, toward the corner. "Look, Chance, I remember when you used to wear your Scout uniform to help with the fundraising stuff at school. You were always volunteering for some damned thing, and I know exactly what's going through your head right now—."

"I seriously doubt—."

"I'll bet you were thinking of people we could save. I'll bet you were thinking of JFK and his brother—."

"I never thought of Bobby."

"But you don't deny thinking of John."

"We could save some people who didn't deserve to die when they did."

They had reached the corner. Chance followed her when she started west. "But you're leaving out the part about traveling through time to do it. And you heard your dad——."

"I heard him say that it might be a danger for us, but not that it would hurt the universe in general. I mean, think about it, Cassie. We could try to stop those planes."

"Are you joking? We still barely know what happened, and they're still saying more attacks are coming. Nobody really knows what's going on and there's no information available because it's all classified, so unless you want to try to teleport us onto each plane——"

"So what now, then? Where are we going?"

"We're going to the library to figure out where we're going to start over."

Her voice and tone left little room for argument, and Chance huffed as he walked along with her, as he thrust his hands into his pocket, where his fingers found the ring. He thought of his mother and her rosary. He thought of the church where he'd been confirmed, of classes about transubstantiation and mysteries of faith. He wondered: "What if we didn't change anything?"

"What do you mean?"

"You're saying you don't want to change anything in the past——."

"I'm saying we shouldn't change anything because we don't know what might happen."

"But what if it's more about research than anything else?" Chance asked, fingering the sacred contours of the holy ring in his pocket as he said it.

"I think you're stretching the limits of academic freedom to call going back in time 'research.' Especially since, if we're talking about a legitimate historical event, there'd be a ton of books on it."

"But only a few primary texts."

"Primary texts? What're you—?" she started to say, but then she stopped. Her eyes widened.

Chance nodded. "Jesus."

19

Leonard did not panic.

He had studied political science and philosophy at Columbia in New Amsterdam, then joined Work for Peace to build hovels in Johannesburg before he'd served in Afghanistan. When he had joined CIRTN, he had studied not only rudimentary physics and quantum mechanics but also global history. Between his education and service, Leonard Kensington was well trained to do many different things, but panicking was not one of them.

He got up from the spindly chair, adjusted his sport coat. He yanked the cuffs of his shirt as he strode through the park, his gait deliberate.

Improvise.

He'd already been planning to go to the World Trade Center. Its concourse would almost certainly have a bookstore.

He thought, then, of Jennifer, and Jennifer's brother. Gabe, she had said. Leonard remembered the worry that had crossed her face when she had said that Gabe worked in the building.

Which would be attacked—he looked at his watch—in slightly less than 24 hours. Which meant he had to either figure out what was different here and when it had become different in the first place, or find a way out before sunrise.

Hopefully, both.

*

A green-railinged F-M-V-train stop adorned the northwest corner of Bryant Park. Leonard descended the stairs through the familiar, invisible subway smog of humid urine and body odor that might have dated back to the train's first run. Four yellow and blue computer terminals with MetroCard signs lined the wall to his right. He assumed they were the equivalent of the WayPass cards used in the Manhattan he knew, and he bypassed them, swiping his smartcard through the slot. Electric blue letters informed him he had three exclamation points and a hashtag worth of rides left, and he pressed through the turnstile to wait for the train.

The subway cars were hideous orange, with tan tile floors and alternately tan, orange, and brown seats; Leonard crooked his elbow around a pole. The large map near the stand-clear-of-the-closing doors showed alpha-numeric routes, a Crayola circulatory system in kindergarten colors, orange F to brilliant red 1. Down to Cortlandt, where platforms connected upward upward upward, and Leonard found himself in a labyrinth of interconnecting walkways, signs: Vesey, PATH, WTC. Leonard followed those latter signs to the giant, gorgeously clean concourse that gleamed like the future. The marbleized white floors and the black-and-glass store facades that displayed designer clothing, coffee and croissants, sportswear, and gourmet chocolate.

Directly ahead of him, he saw exactly what he had hoped for: the entrance to an enormous, three-story Borders Books & Music.

*

The first words Leonard noticed in the history section: World War II. The sections broke down into easy subsets. World history. American history. Egyptian and Middle Eastern history. World War I. Vietnam.

None surprised him. Regional histories, of course: everywhere had a past, and everywhere liked to celebrate it.

But the wars . . .

Intimidating tomes full of bricks of words, too many dates and names, too much plot and not enough character development. They might have helped Leonard had he possessed world enough and time to study them, but he did not. He could skim major details, which proved enough to confirm what he already knew. Most wars begin the same way, with men fighting over parcels of land and escalating each minor conflict using the fine art of throwing things.

He chose three books that seemed to recount facts without overwhelming detail, then left the aisle, headed for the small café. Along the way, he noticed the bargain section, where he found a selection of coffee table books that looked more like what he needed, and he tucked away the three books he'd already chosen to pick up a new stack. He bought an iced tea at the café, along with a pen and a leather-bound notebook.

Perhaps because he had traveled so far in so many ways, Leonard Kensington had an innate feel for history. It was in his bones. Which is why, when what he learned began to frighten him, as he realized that this unfamiliar history was far darker and more bleak than the one he knew, he could feel it chill through his marrow.

He began with the first World War. To Leonard, the "Great War," which had occurred during the early part of the century. It appeared that its superficial cause was still the assassination of Ferdinand, and its deeper conflicts and tensions seemed familiar, as well.

The second had broken out around the end of the thirties. During that decade, a man named Hitler had been appointed German Chancellor, instead of Jarres, and pursued his own imperialism, invading much of Europe and even Russia. Roosevelt had helped bolster English and French troops against Hitler's Germany, and Italy, too, before Japan had bombed a naval port in Hawaii . . .

The war had culminated with Hitler's death, and Truman beginning the nuclear age by dropping atomic bombs on Hiroshima and Nagasaki. Tensions between Russia and the USA had heightened and begun what the text referred to as a "cold" war; a lot of tension, some not-so-veiled threats, but little in the way of actual violence between superpowers. When Kennedy became president, the same tensions that had existed in Leonard's reality had caused a confrontation—the Cuban Missile Crisis—but it had failed to escalate into the October Crisis.

Kennedy had never sent Cuba back to the Stone Age. Castro had survived. The United States had never annexed Puerto Rico or Cuba; the United Nations had never proposed a formation of a North American Union to balance power in the north-western hemisphere; no Union-States had been formed. Which meant the coincidence occurred sometime before the second World War, but a lot during that time was different. Especially in Germany. Hitler. It was certainly a solid lead.

He looked sideways, out the large, floor-to-ceiling windows at the financial-district buildings, as he considered it, and then he remembered the Oracle. He pulled it from his pocket. Darren had said it should work no matter where he went.

He slipped the glasses on, pressing the button to activate the device, and waited as the menu appeared before him. The same four options: pause, rewind, forward, and settings.

He selected the latter. A menu of options by which he could enter latitude and longitude coordinates, as well as a time and date, appeared. He took off the glasses and returned to the books. Several mentioned the 1934 Nuremberg rally, and so he rose, returned to the history and then the geography sections, setting the Oracle coordinates to correspond.

He returned to the café, to his table, sat, and pressed the button; the bookstore disappeared, replaced by—

A giant, outdoor gathering. Groups of attendees had blocked together in formation, and the sound of it all made the muscles in Leonard's groin tighten. Thousands of cascading voices in colliding frequencies, all filling his head via the implant in his temporal lobe.

Drums.

A cadence like a militaristic march.

Using the Oracle, Leonard could swoop down among the attendees,

boys no older than fifteen or sixteen, with many substantially younger. Their young, lithe bodies seemed coiled with tension building to a crescendo, and they all wore khaki uniforms with red epaulets, twisted neckerchiefs, and proud swastika armbands . . .

The books Leonard had been reading mentioned that this man, Hitler, had employed it as a national symbol.

Suddenly, the driving beat of the drums gave way to added intensity, a battle-cry of teenagers. Hormones and rage and uncertainty, all unbottled and given cracking voice, and every head turned to concentrate on a single entrance. All the youth in attendance raised their right arms in salute to the several men who emerged, one of whom was the man Leonard had just been reading about.

He was short. With beady little eyes and hangdog cheeks, a soft face and a razor-sharp part, from which his hair plastered left across his scalp. He wore similar khakis with a similar swastika armband, and as he emerged, the crowd began to chant:

Heil.

Heil.

Heil,

And the man surveyed the crowd as if to absorb their applause and their approval. He made his way to a podium toward the front, pausing as he did so to raise his own hand in response to their salute. Each time, he drove the crowd into greater frenzy, and there is nothing quite like the frenzy of sixteen-year-old boys.

Trumpets sounded and more young men screamed, until finally one man broke from the officers to address the crowd.

One of the requirements CIRTN had made Leonard fulfill was a vast knowledge of foreign languages, and so he could understand the German spoken:

"A youth that knows no class distinction—the youth of our nation is shaped in your distinction. Because you are the epitome of altruism, the youth wants to be altruistic. Because you are the epitome of loyalty, the youth want to be loyal."

Adolf Hitler stepped forward, to even more applause. He waited a moment, allowing it to build into a frenzy before he began to speak. The moment he did so, the crowd hushed.

"My German youths, after a year, I again greet you. You here today are merely one part of what is spread all over Germany. We want you, my German boys and girls, to absorb all that we expect of Germany. We want to be our own people, and you, my youth, are to be that people. In the future there must be no races or classes and you must not let them grow in you. We want to be one nation, and you must educate yourselves for it."—

He seemed the sort of hyperbolic villain who would have twirled his moustache had it not been limited to a tiny swath above his lip. If he'd read of Hitler in a story, Leonard would have thought him some a kind of caricature, a short, insecure man with a Napoleon complex some lazy novelist had invented as an easy foil for a hero who embodied the ideals of democracy.

"You must learn to accept privations and collapse. No matter what we create today or what we do today, we will pass away, but in you Germany will live. And when nothing remains of us, then you must hold in your fists the flag we tore from nothing. I know this cannot be otherwise, because you are flesh from our flesh and blood from our blood. The same spirit that dominates us burns in your young minds."

Leonard felt in his pulse the cheer that rose from the crowd. Hitler was bolstering all those young men and their flagging esteem. Hitler knew their insecurities because they had been his own, and he helped them believe that, by force and power, they might overcome their every inadequacy.

"And we know around us is Germany. In us Germany marches, and behind us, Germany follows."

Leonard removed the glasses as Hitler retreated to the back of the stage amid thunderous applause. During his undergraduate years, Leonard had once heard a professor say that the very best villain in the world was not one who wanted to rule the world but rather one who firmly believed he was the right man for the job. Such a man, the professor had said, could only exist in real life, never in literature or fiction or drama, because no audience would have ever believed in such a character.

Leonard slipped the glasses back into his breast pocket. The crowds, the speech, the sentiment: something about the man had embodied a zeitgeist, and Leonard wondered if it had been solely that man's doing.

The books he'd been reading had mentioned the man's imperialism, the man's nationalism, and the man's belief, true to his word, about races. Hitler, Leonard read, had sought to "purify" race, not by improving educational or social reform, but rather by eliminating those populations he viewed as inferior—including Jews, homosexuals, Romani, Soviet prisoners of war, and people with disabilities—in a massive genocide the books referred to as the Holocaust.

Could that man be the difference between the two realities? And if he was, Leonard wondered, how?

There were two possibilities. The first was that someone had traveled back in time to give Hitler some knowledge or weaponry. CIRTN had prevented several such interferences, including one in which a misguided traveler had ventured back to early millennial America to introduce gunpowder to the Native Americans and vaccinate them against disease several centuries before Columbus got irrevocably lost. Leonard knew, though, that interference didn't have to come in the form of bold action; even just the knowledge of an enemy's position might tilt a war.

The other possibility was that Hitler himself was the time traveler. That he'd traveled backward from Leonard's reality to pre-WWII Germany and then taken advantage of his own knowledge of the future.

Leonard sighed as he closed the books. He rubbed his eyes and pinched the bridge of his nose. He looked at his watch; although it apparently no longer connected him to the Safe, it still at least kept time. Close to four. He'd been studying several hours.

He tugged on his earlobe, trying Race again.

Still nothing.

He considered what he needed right then. To contact Race. To share the information he'd gathered.

Food. A drink. He got up from his table, went to the counter.

"Help you? Another coffee?" asked the cute, tattooed barista.

"There's a restaurant on the top floor, right?"

"Windows on the World. But the bar above it is nicer. More casual and less expensive. Food's still good."

"Greatest Bar on Earth?" Leonard asked. In his reality, the bar was his favorite not just for having the balls to call itself that but also the ability to live up to its name.

"That's the one."

"Thanks," Leonard went back to his table, picked up his leather notebook and headed out of the café. He wondered if the Operations Center's computers were still focused on the towers; if so, there was a chance that the added height might increase the likelihood that his implant would work.

As he headed down the stairs to the first level, he thought, then, of Jennifer and of her brother. Gabriel, whom she had said worked at Cantor Fitzgerald. Upstairs. Leonard didn't know if Gabriel would be able to help, but having an ally would be good. Especially someone more familiar with this alternity.

20

Chance tried to gauge Cassie's reaction. She had looked away as if something south had caught her attention, but nothing in the world moved. Everything was still.

"I'm not proposing we save him," Chance told her.

"I know," she said.

He ran his thumb over the jewels on the rosary ring, the intricate pattern—

Hail Mary, full of grace.

The Lord is with thee—

As a child, Chance had mouthed those words every Sunday. He had slicked down his hair and put a surplus over his cassock and served Mass throughout his years at Saint Benedict's, where his teachers had taught him all about the rosary and transubstantiation but nothing about geography and life and grief. Classes had begun with the Pledge of Allegiance and continued with the Creed—

We believe in one God, the Father, Almighty,
Maker of Heaven and Earth—

and the recitations of children who didn't understand to whom they were declaring their faith. He'd graduated from that school the same day he'd been confirmed, but rather than feeling new strength in his faith he'd whooped instead, tearing his clip-on tie from his collar and chucking it behind him in search of a perfect summer day before he began high school, where the gods were jocks and prom queens and faith was popularity and coolness. In high school, he'd discovered he excelled in history and English classes, which had come as a surprise because the parochial elementary school he had attended had ignored geography in favor of Catechism. He had discovered, then, the world was a bigger and more complicated place than they'd taught him all those years before in the quest instead to save his soul.

His mother, Miryam, had gotten sick not long after Chance had turned seventeen. What had seemed to be severe indigestion had turned out to be esophageal cancer, and doctors hadn't been able to prevent those rogue cells from spreading with the kind of startling ferocity only terminal diseases can manage. First to her pancreas, then her intestines, colon, lungs, and finally her spleen. It all happened too quickly for Chance to remember more than a few scant details among identical days in hospitals: specialists and therapies. The tiny blue dots on her body. Her light, straw-like wig.

One night, toward the end, when he'd begun to accept that none of the treatments were working, when he'd begun to accept the dread of losing her, he'd remembered the ring she had given him when he had been confirmed. He had searched his room that night until he had found it at the bottom of a drawer, beneath a stack of baseball cards and a long-forgotten, leather key fob he'd once made at camp.

He had held it in his fingers, watching the gemstones reflect the tiny light of his desk lamp, and he had felt both clarity and doubt like never before. One thing Chance had inherited from his father was his inquisitiveness; while his mother had been religious, had believed in the communion of saints and the holy Catholic church, Chance had been most curious about the man behind the religion, the truth behind the stories. Had he risen from the dead? Had he been born of a virgin? Had that virgin had an immaculate conception, free of original sin, and what does original sin even mean? What kind of God decrees that knowing the difference between good and evil is a sin?

Still, Chance felt in that ring, in those small stones, some connection to his mother, some tether to her. He had discovered, there as a teenager in his bedroom, that his fingers had grown since he had last worn it, and so the following day, at the hardware store where he'd worked with Bram Nazor, Chance had bought a length of the sort of ballchain soldiers wear dogtags on, and he'd strung the ring around his neck.

Prayer, too, has muscle memory, a spiritual reflex like a pull in the gut. Perhaps by habit, Chance had begun to finger the ring, to twirl it, to edge its corners against the balls on the chain, and he often found the prayers coming in tiny phrase fragments—

Make me an instrument of your peace;

Grant that I may never seek so much to be consoled as to console—

His father had never commented on it, but two weeks later asked Chance if he'd like to attend mass the following morning. It had surprised Chance, who had only ever known his father to go to service on Christmas and Easter to appease Miryam, but still they had driven to the small church nearby. Chance hadn't been there since he'd graduated from its small, associated grade school, and it felt smaller. The moments to sit and to kneel and to stand had grown unfamiliar, and the wafer felt like thin cardboard on his tongue. Through the journey there, the ceremony, and the drive back, neither Chance nor Dennis said a word except in rote response to the priest.

Chance hadn't been back to church since.

"So, what," Cassie said, turning back to meet his eyes. "You want to disprove it?"

"No. I just want to know."

His mother's death had broken him once and for all from Catholicism if not from faith itself, but then he had chosen to attend Fordham University in Manhattan for two reasons: it was known for its law school and its undergraduate programs in philosophy and history were equally strong; and because it was his mother's *alma mater*, the Jesuits had offered him a substantial scholarship. Those two considerations trumped the religious affiliation that had at first dissuaded him; by that time, religion had felt like an old suit, too short in the cuffs and without enough room in the crotch.

Fordham, like many Jesuit institutions, required all students to complete six credits of theology study, which was how Chance had met Fitzgerald *roshi*, a Jesuit priest who had been one of the first Zen Buddhists ordained in America. Fitzgerald had been a strong, virile man with white hair and quick eyes, and had required his class to read not only the Bible, from Genesis to Revelations, but also other works of literature, including More's *Utopia* and Dante's *Inferno*, relating them to their theological themes—

"You realize that this is all assuming he actually existed," Cassie said. "That he wasn't just a figment of the collective overactive imaginations of a handful of writers who stole from the myth systems of all of the popular religions of the time in a shameless attempt to get everyone to convert to theirs."

It was one of the few aspects he didn't dispute. The miracles and parables, the chronology and the outcome, perhaps, but not the existence of the man himself. "I think he did. I don't know about all the rest, but I think we can pretty safely assert that, around the year 34 or 35, during the tenure of Pontius Pilate as governor, a man named Jesus was crucified."

"So you want to go back to see if he came back?"

"You believe it all?" he asked her. He knew her parents had raised her in the Greek Orthodox system, but she had studied science and was about to take a prestigious fellowship at Princeton. "Sight unseen?"

"Isn't that the point of faith?"—

When Chance had taken that theology class with Fitzgerald *roshi*, he had tried hard to earn an 'A,' but all his papers seemed to earn 'B's and 'B+'s. He tried harder with each successive paper, including one memorable one in which he had compared the Ten Commandments and most of Deuteronomy to a constitution for the Jewish people newly freed from Egyptian rule, but consistently fell short. He had visited Fitzgerald *roshi*'s office; most of his professors worked in cramped rooms over-filled with textbooks and criticism, bookshelves seemingly stacked in other bookshelves, but Fitzgerald *roshi*'s office had been sparse, with a computer monitor and a single bookcase. The desk was simple, the floor hardwood and undecorated. Just on entering, Chance had felt some degree of serenity fill him.

Chance had brought with him a paper he'd felt he deserved better than a 'B' on. Fitzgerald *roshi* had examined it with pursed lips before handing it back to Chance. "It's not that you're a bad student. It's that you're not trying."

Chance hadn't moved to take the paper. He'd just glared. "The papers I write for this class are longer than any of the papers I write for my other classes. They have more citations. I spend more time researching them. I spend more time writing them, and I'm not trying?"

"I don't dispute your work ethic," Fitzgerald had told him, letting the paper settle to the desk. "But theology is not about work. God is not about books and research and citations. You hand in well written, well balanced, meticulously researched papers, but they've got no soul. They're all up here," he'd brought his fingertips to his forehead, "But they need to come from down here," he'd lowered his hand. Chance had thought he was about to put his palm over his heart, but he didn't; he touched instead two fingers to his stomach.

"Faith comes from your gut, Chancellor. You can't think yourself to it, and it's not like it comes from your heart. The heart is the human realm of romanticism and hope and idealism, and it is easily broken. The gut is not. Your gut doesn't bend or fold. You always have feelings there, and those feelings are your Faith. So start writing from your gut. Start writing something you feel. The most important thing I could possibly teach you is to stop worrying about some damned number on your transcript and start writing about something you believe in."

Unfortunately, something to believe in, without hesitation, without question, without doubt, was the one thing Chance had never been able to find. He could still feel those words and their truth inside him, down where it had hurt when he'd watched the World Trade Center fall, down where it still hurt that he'd lost his father. The same place where he'd felt so strongly he wanted to try to save his father, the same place within him that wanted to go back and find out what had happened to Jesus.

The same place that still just wanted something to believe in—

"And what if the Gospels are wrong?" Cassie asked him.

Chance looked around at the still world, the silent street, and he thought of all the wars he had studied at Fordham, all the history and dates and places he had attempted to absorb. The Crusades and the Spanish Inquisition, the Church who had persecuted the likes of Copernicus and Galileo. "I wasn't thinking about all that. Like I said, it's not like I want to disprove it."

"You just want to know."

"You're really not even just a little bit curious?"

"Of course I'm curious, it's just—."

"I'm not proposing we change anything. The wars and the Crusades and all the other stuff . . . When I studied them, it was always like studying another world I never felt any connection to. I don't want to change them, even if Jesus never really came back. Even if it's all based on a handful of exaggerated stories. All I want to know is if the stories were exaggerated in the first place."

"And what if they weren't?"

"You mean what if he really did die on the cross that our sins might be forgiven, and then on the third day rose again in fulfillment of the scriptures?" Chance asked her. The words came easily to him, but without conviction.

"I mean what if the Gospels are right?"

"What do you think's going to happen, Cass? You think God is going to smite us? Some giant lightning bolt is going to shoot out of the sky to strike us down? The hand of God has only ever intervened when Stephen King hasn't known how to end a novel, and other than that it seems like we're mostly on our own, just trying to do our best. Which is why I want to find out."

Cassie started walking again, so Chance followed after her. "You really don't mind risking further exposure to an intense quantum electrodynamic field, which might ultimately give us both cancer? It's really that important to you?"

"My mom—my mom always believed, Cassie. She believed all the stories they told her right up to the very end. But those stories were never enough for me. But if it's true, if it really happened—well, maybe my mom's okay, you know? I can't save my mom, but I can find out if those beliefs were true, and maybe that would mean she's okay."

Cassie hesitated. "If I agree to this, I want something in return."

He waited for her to continue.

"Like you said before we saved your father, you didn't have much to lose. Not in Manhattan, and not here. But I can't go back to the life I was living, and I was on track to becoming a professor myself, and I was doing a lot of great research, but I can't anymore, because now there's no place for me. But I could build something somewhere else. So if we're going to start over, I want to go to Munich. I'll got back to Jerusalem with you to find out if that tomb was really empty if you'll come back to Munich with me."

Though Germany was at the bottom of his list of European countries he wanted to visit one day, he had to admit the idea had its appeal. He knew European history well, and he had enough of a natural facility with languages that he didn't think he'd struggle too much. "And what then?"

"What do you mean? We'd figure something out. We'll have the time machine, and I hate to suggest it, but we could rob a bank to get enough money to start,"

Cassie continued walking. The library was just up ahead, not even a mile away. Chance didn't say another word as he followed her through that paused world.

But he thought them. He thought of sharing a cramped apartment in Munich with her. He thought of learning a new language with her. He thought of *drinking* German lagers and eating schnitzel, of walking down *strassen* and through *gartens*. He couldn't help it. He'd had a crush on Cassie since before he had learned to pray, and his heart had the strongest muscle memory of all.

*

Chance had once read that the single sense most connected to memory was smell, and walking into the Givingston Public Library brought Chance home. It was the fragrance of books that had been on those shelves since before he had been born, the brand new scent of just-arrived novels from Neil Gaiman and Michael Crichton. Nothing had changed: not the grey-pink, thin-pile carpet, not the hideous but comfortable armchairs, not even the librarian behind the check-out desk. Mrs. Gertrude had helped Chance fill out his first library card when he'd turned six, and she looked remarkably the same even though she'd changed the frames of her glasses and her hair had streaked with grey.

Chance smiled when he saw her even though her stillness unnerved him.

"So the first thing we'll need," Cassie told him as they moved past the circulation desk, "Is the coordinates. Latitude and longitude should be easy, but I'm a little worried about the temporal coordinates. The machine doesn't use dates, so we're going to have to do some math to calculate how far back we're going."

Chance put his hands up. "I'm not sure you want me doing any calculations. I suck at math. I can't even balance my checkbook."

"I'll take care of that part. What you can do is figure out where we're going. Latitude and longitude. Hours, minutes, and degrees. So our first order of business is a detailed map of Jerusalem. Then a better idea of when Jesus was crucified."

Chance looked at the shelves, spine after leather spine. "You're going to have to stop the time machine. Card catalog's all computer-based, and we'll probably need Google."

Cassie pressed a button on the time machine. Immediately, Chance felt the air change, its pressure somehow lighten. He hadn't realized he could perceive the difference until it was gone.

"Why, Chance Sowin," Mrs. Gertrude exclaimed when he and Cassie walked back toward the front of the library, heading for the computer room. "My, it's been ages."

"It has, Mrs. Gertrude. You look just like I remember you."

Mrs. Gertrude blushed, touched her hair. "How have you been? Did New York treat you well, or do I have to have a talk with it? We were so worried about you last month. Your father told me you were working there, in the towers."

"I was riding the escalator up when that first plane hit. Felt the whole building shake. They rushed us out of the building pretty quickly, and then—well, it all happened so fast. I don't think I expected them to come down," he said. As he said it, he felt Cassie squeeze his hand. It surprised him, and he looked down at it, then at her.

"So are you coming back home?" Mrs. Gertrude asked.

Chance swallowed. "I—," he started, but his voice quit on him.

"He just got back. But if you'll excuse us, we've got some research to do," Cassie said. She pulled Chance toward the computer room as she said it, and Chance let her lead the way.

"Sorry. It all just came rushing back," he told her. The memory of dust made his throat close up, his eyes water. The memory of the metal tremor shivering down the escalator he'd been ascending still made his neck prickle and his body shudder.

She gave his tricep a light squeeze. "Of course it does. It's always going to."

Chance eased into the closest seat. He sat forward, elbows up, fists bunched together and lips pressed to his knuckles. "But I knew people who didn't make it. A couple weeks ago I found out that a guy I graduated college with had just started a gig with an investment firm. He was only a couple weeks into the job. He—," he was about to say his classmate had jumped, but the word stuck in his throat as if barbed. "I know people who were worse off than I was."

"But that doesn't mean it can't have hurt you, too. Everyone felt it, no matter where they were. And you were there. Like you just said—I mean, shit, Chance, I had no idea you were actually in the building when it happened. I knew you were working downtown—."

"I was just temping at a law firm," Chance said. He'd been at Drinker, Biddle, and Reath for several months by then.

"No law firm officed in the World Trade Center could possibly be less than extraordinary, and even if it weren't, you could have been a clerk at the bookstore. It's still a job in the most exciting city in the world, and it's not like people who lost more or were closer or more affected have more right to feeling hurt and scared than anyone else. Just because you made it out alive, safe and sound, doesn't mean it's not allowed to have hurt you. It's obvious it affected you."

"Obvious?"

"You moved back home, didn't you?"

"I wasn't happy there."

"You didn't wake up two weeks ago and suddenly realize you weren't happy. What you said earlier, about wanting to make a difference, that's why you were so intent on trying to save your father. That's why you want to go back to Jerusalem and find out about Jesus. You want some answers. You want to know. You want some certainty."

"Is that so bad?"

"Only if you think you can't be happy without it."

"What about you? Is that why you agreed to this?"

"Ten years from now, seeing you disappear without me would've kept me up at night. Like you would have regretted if you'd stayed in Manhattan instead of setting out to find something new that made you happier."

Chance considered that. She was right that he hadn't been happy for a while. Not unhappy, exactly, but for the better part of the past year he'd felt dissatisfied, like the certainty that something better waited out there for him had made him restless. He'd known, too, that even if something had been out there waiting for him, time would not. Time never did, present circumstances excepted.

*

In college, one of his history professors had assigned Chance a book called *The Hidden Jesus*, by Donald Spoto, and he was happy to find a copy on the shelves. Because of his clear and level assessment of historicity and factual analysis, Spoto had been the one authority with whom Chance wouldn't have disputed a single detail regarding the life of Jesus of Nazareth. Along with some judicious Google fu, Chance worked out that they should try to arrive on the Mount of Olives, just outside Jerusalem, in the small hours of April 9th in the year 30.

"That's pretty precise," Cassie said like she didn't believe it when he told her the date, but he showed her the book and some of the search results he had found.

"And now Munich," Chance said as he began to browse the Internet. "Any particular spot?"

"Someplace public. Someplace we'll be able to disappear immediately if we have to."

"Do you want to go now?"

"No reason to wait."

"No, I mean, like, modern Munich," he told her. "I mean, if we have a time machine—."

"If we go back a ways, I could help make some breakthroughs, physics-wise. But it's difficult, because, let's face it, Germany didn't have the greatest twentieth century. Between how it faired after World War One, and then the wall didn't come down until the eighties . . ."

As she said it, Chance got goosebumps. His head swam with images: of red flags with big, black swastikas in white circles, of militant marches, of labor camps.

"Chance?"

"Sorry, what?"

"You seemed like you went somewhere for a second."

"No, I'm—well. I had a thought—."

"Oh, here we go—."

"I just thought of Nazi Germany. Those big flags. *Schindler's List.*"

"That's what I was saying. We'd have to be careful."

"But what if—we could change it."

"We already talked about this. There are too many—."

"But you just said you could help make some physics breakthroughs."

"I was trying to plan how we might keep a roof over our heads."

"But it would change things. You obviously know enough about physics—."

"I wouldn't go that far. I'm just starting on my PhD—."

"In 2001. So you know way more than anybody in the last century would. Hell, if we went to that time, with your background in physics, we'd have to be careful not to end up helping them build the bomb. And just our being there would change things, wouldn't it?"

"So what, you want to try to stand up to the Nazi army? Ask them to kindly stop invading other countries? And you know we're going to have a hard time getting official documents, which means they could just as easily throw us into a concentration camp. They didn't just do that to Jews, you know, and you're not exactly blond."

"What if we could prevent it from ever getting that far? What if we could keep any of those things from happening? The Nazis. The concentration camps. The invasions. What if we killed Hitler before he could do any of those things?"

21

Leonard left the Borders WTC, exiting back into the lobby with its towering, tapering windows so enormous he could see entire buildings beyond them. The sun blasted through them, making chrome gleam and large shrubs in silver pots look so green Leonard could have believed he was watching them grow. Their small limbs danced in the breeze of the hundreds of workers bustling through the building and the tiny residual Brownian motion of subway car rumble.

This building had always felt alive to Leonard in a way no other had. Leonard had seen more stunning architecture, swooping arches and towering ionic columns so white they appeared carved from bone to support booming industry in pursuit of newer gods, but this was different in a spectacularly vital way. These gorgeous windows seemed to allow the possibility of reaching into heaven; the express elevators carried their passengers up story after story as if in pursuit of the greatest ever told. These walls breathed with the life of a City that might as well have been another universe entirely, and actually were for Leonard.

He intended to seek out an office directory before he noticed the large, black marble desk with the enormous 'Information' sign. An older woman with silver hair and a blue blazer looked at him over small, half-moon spectacles that only her nostrils prevented from slipping down her nose. She informed him he could take the express elevator up to the Sky Lobby on the 78*th* floor, then a local to Cantor Fitzgerald's offices on 101. Leonard thanked her and approached the elevator bank, where lines of people queued up to ascend the tower. The far wall was a large, gold, metal pressing of the Empire State Building, too large for Leonard to believe it might have actually been gold, while from each sidewall, two American flags reached toward each other above all the people waiting for their chances to ride. The elevator cars were nearly the size of the subway car he'd taken downtown in the first place. After waiting in line, Leonard joined the other 20 or 30 people riding so high so fast his ears popped four times along the way. The elevator stopped at 78 and everyone disembarked for the Sky Lobby.

The windows weren't nearly as tall as those on the ground floor he'd just left, did not reach nearly so high, but they didn't have to. All around Leonard, Manhattan seemed to exist in aspiration to greater heights, as if it knew that its reach far exceeded its grasp but it was determined to try its hardest to touch Heaven anyway.

He remembered the view of the World Trade Center CIRTN's computers had extrapolated onto the screens. If the implant in his temporal lobe was going to work anywhere, chances were it would do so there, but a quick tug on his earlobe yielded no response.

Leonard crossed the lobby to local elevators, where several people were already waiting. Leonard thapped the button for the 101st floor when he got on. The elevator stopped twice to let people off as it ascended, and a few people walked out ahead of him when it stopped on 101, and then a couple others stumbled into him when he stopped. His breath left his body with enough force that he worried about ever getting it back.

Cantor Fitzgerald's lobby was tastefully decorated, ultra-modern touches on a basic corporate design, a blue-and-white logo emblazoned the wall behind the desk of the receptionist. She was speaking on a headset and tapping on a keyboard. Her hair was dyed hard blonde, and a single wisp fell toward her black, chunky-framed glasses.

She looked up when Leonard didn't move. "Can I help you?"

The same eyes. The same angular jaw. The same voice.

Leonard wanted to respond but couldn't make himself. All his thoughts had stopped.

"Sir?"

Leonard opened and closed his jaw before finally he managed to take a breath and get his voice to work. "Jennifer?" he asked.

22

Cassie opened her mouth but closed it without making any sound. She put her pencil down, stared at it, but still didn't speak, her body language more deliberate, more visceral, than it had been when Chance had mentioned Jesus. He wondered if it was because the idea was more immediate in a way visiting Jerusalem was not; Cassie might have described it more accurately than she had realized when she had called it research. He hadn't meant that they should save Jesus or try to change anything at that time, and yet the moment he thought of Hitler brought a moment of desire for action and execution.

Confirming the veracity of the resurrection and its repercussions seemed more in the realm of history and things he'd studied, the Crusades and the trials of Galileo and Copernicus. One of the few things he knew about the Spanish Inquisition was that nobody expects one.

Not so World War II. Not so fighter planes and atomic bombs, concentration camps and gas chambers. He hadn't just studied those things via secondary texts, and Spielberg's epic didn't account for his entire visual memory of the second World War. Some of it, perhaps, and he wouldn't ever forget the image of Liam Neeson watching that girl in the red coat, nor of Tom Hanks' shaky hand holding his compass, but neither could Chance ignore the grainy memories of black-and-white video: bomber formations and blitzkrieg attacks. Reifenstahl's footage of the happy, hopeful young men who had beat their drums and held their Nazi flags gleefully aloft at the Nuremberg rallies.

The naked, emaciated men and women huddling together for inspection and roll call. The enormous labor camps in which the char and soot of cremated human bodies flurried through the sky like snowflakes.

There is a difference in life between what we discuss and what we know. The first photograph Chance could call to mind was of a tall, gaunt president with a mole and a beard; before that honest man there were only words and portraits. Only Declarations of Independence and the course of human events, only stories of kites and lightning, Columbus and chocolate, a lot of hearsay, superstitions, and myths and very little in the way of evidence.

Photography and recording technologies had changed that. Objective photographs of people recorded by the unerring camera lens lent to history a reality that portraits and texts had lacked, substituted depiction for imagination. Chance wasn't entirely certain Jesus of Nazareth had ever existed like the stories described, but he knew he could kill Hitler. He had seen the photographs and video. He had heard the *Fuhrer*'s voice.

Cassie leaned back in her chair. "You realize what would happen if we did it."

"You've told me a lot about what *might* happen. You've told me you're scared. You keep saying that we're going to turn the universe inside out, but so far nothing's really happened. We saved my father, and everything's still here. We didn't unmake the universe."

"You know it's more complicated than that. What if we stop Hitler—*kill* Hitler—and somebody worse comes along? Somebody we can't stop? Isn't that what just about every science fiction novel in the world is about?"

"I'm pretty sure *Stranger in a Strange Land* wasn't about killing Hitler. Neither was *The Time Machine*, for that matter."

"That doesn't answer my question. It's like *al Qaeda*. Even if we killed bin Laden, he's just a figurehead. We kill Hitler, and the Nazis still exist."

"But Hitler was different. He was imperialistic. Bin Laden seems pretty happy in his cave or wherever the hell he is, but Hitler wanted an empire. The Nazis would still exist, but prevent Hitler from becoming Chancellor and you prevent a lot of the sudden momentum his rise to power gave the Nazis in the first place. And if we stay—."

"What, we can singlehandedly prevent the rise of the Nazi party?"

"I'm not talking about the Nazi party. I'm talking about one man. I don't know what would happen if we prevented him from coming to power, but I think it's worth a try, especially if we could save several million people whose only sin was believing only the first half of a book," Chance said, and then, when Cassie opened her mouth as if to respond: "I've heard people argue that America and the UK and other countries are just as much to blame for the Holocaust as Germany was, because they could have stopped it from happening but didn't. Because they had the opportunity to end it but didn't take it."

"So now the Holocaust is going to be our fault, too?"

"I'm just saying we might be able to save ten million lives by killing one man. I know we'd end up near the beginning of Nazi Germany. I know that being in Germany at that time would be pretty fucking awful. But I also know there's a good chance we could save a lot of innocent people and change the entire world in the process."

"But what if we can't? What if we end up there, in the middle of all those uniforms and swastikas, and we can't change anything? What if we got stuck there and we had to help them just so we could survive? I mean, sure, we have a time machine, but what if it breaks or stops working? Forget ending up in a concentration camp ourselves; what if we had to help them run the camps to survive? What if we had to call roll? Or stamp their documents?"

That thought stopped Chance. It seemed so clear, in a fundamental way, but he had studied the Holocaust, and one of the issues that had come up was that most people would say they wouldn't ever do such a thing, but no one could make that call out of that situation.

He thought, then, of Geisel. Of that elongated pistol pointing at Cassie and how his gut had seemed to harden, propelling him forward.

"But if the time machine breaks, or only works once, and we're going to Jerusalem first, there's a chance we wouldn't be able to leave there, either."

"True."

"So we don't know what's possible and what's not. So why don't we plan that it will keep working? Why don't we treat this like the once-ever chance it is?" Chance leaned forward in his chair, typed the words

'Munich' and 'Hitler' into a Google searchbox, and a moment later found a list of hundreds of thousands of links, the top few of which mentioned the *Bierhall Putsch*. "What if we go to Munich early, before he comes to power, right?" He clicked on one of the first links and perused the first paragraph. "We go to *Feldherrnhalle*," he said, mangling the word beneath his tongue but plowing forward anyway, "Where all the cops go to meet his makeshift army, and we kill him before he gets arrested. Even if we can't, even if we fuck up, we skip ahead twenty or thirty years and settle in Munich. After the war. You can do your work at the Institute. Hell, if we go a little further," he said, as he clicked another link to another page on another site, "We could always go to Switzerland." He typed 'Geneva' into the searchbox.

"I could do more work in Munich. I know it better. I know the Institute."

"Maybe," Chance said, as he clicked another link to pull up another page. "But if we went to Geneva . . .," he began, but he trailed off as he shifted the monitor so she could see the screen.

Her expression changed when she saw it. Not to agreement, but when she saw the screen, her eyes widened as if she suddenly saw that what he was saying was a very real possibility. "CERN," she whispered. "That's—."

"When it was founded," Chance told her. He shifted the screen again; she might have been looking at it, but she was no longer seeing it.

"We could be there when the cyclotron went live," she said, but her voice was distant. Thinking aloud.

"We could be anywhere."

"But then why are we limiting ourselves to the past? What about the future? I know you want to find out about Jesus, but what if we go forward? A hundred years from now, when we'd both be dead, anyway—."

"But if what my dad said about uncertainty was true, wouldn't that be worse for us?"

"You're the one who keeps pointing out that we don't really know for certain either way."

Chance tried to imagine a bright, shiny future, but after the previous few weeks, he was unable to. He thought of the religious extremism, radical fundamentalists in every corner of the world. Islamic terrorists who blew up weddings and Christian terrorists who targeted women's health clinics. He thought of gadgets that were supposed to make his life simpler but only complicated things and ensured more stress, more chaos in an already noisy world. "I'm voting for Jesus. And Munich. It just seems like our best option."

"And by 'Munich,' you mean you want to kill Hitler."

"I think we should try."

For a long moment, Cassie said absolutely nothing, and remained still. And then she sighed, closed her eyes as she shook her head, and she spoke like she couldn't believe she was saying it. "I can't think of any other way to argue against trying to save ten million people."

"Well, then, that's what we'll try to do," Chance said.

*

Chance had always been more at home on the other side of theory. His mind had never worked well with thought and abstraction; he had always been better at doing, which was probably why having definite goals and destinations in mind helped him concentrate. He could focus less on a big, abstract picture and work out smaller details with greater accuracy: ancient Jerusalem. The Temple Mount and Golgotha, the Mount of Olives and the *praetorium*. He could picture the sites, correlate hours and minutes and degrees on a page to buildings and stories in his head.

The research seemed to focus Cassie, too, so that she seemed less inclined to argue with him about hypothetical physical consequences he didn't understand anyway and wasn't sure he believed in besides. She plugged each set of spatial and temporal coordinates into the time machine until finally she stretched back in her chair, grinding her palms into her eyes and groaning.

"Yeah, I'm right with you on that," Chance agreed.

Cassie sighed. "I don't know how much more we can really figure out, at least so far as technical stuff goes. So our plan is to visit the tomb in Jerusalem to see if it's empty, then come forward to Munich, then travel to Geneva. But we'll need some supplies, and we can't very well wear jeans to Jerusalem."

Chance nodded. "No, but I have an idea."

*

Their research complete, Cassie stilled time all around them again, and together they walked two miles to a strip-mall where a seasonal retail space was sandwiched between a Target and a Best Buy. The seasonal space was still a Halloween superstore, at least until the following day, when its managers would replace all traces of devils and schoolgirls with wreaths and Yule logs for the hearth.

Cassie chuckled. "Are you serious?"

"I'm just worried everything will already be gone," he said as he pulled the door open. Inside, lots of costumes were scattered helter-skelter, as though a small cadre of overenthusiastic trick-or-treaters had spontaneously combusted, leaving behind three garments full of cheap polyester, a plastic triton, and some candy corn.

"This might just be crazy enough to work," Cassie eyed the plastic packages. She took a polyethylene package from its hook. An image on its front depicted a

pretty woman in a simple white garment, a 'Roman
Maiden.'

"Not that one," Chance said.

"Those web pages said that Jerusalem was under
Roman rule."

"Roman dress was a tunic. Only the prostitutes
wore the kind of dress you're holding," he told her. He
glanced up at the packages until he saw one with a more
appropriate garment. The cloth was thicker and a little
coarser, the style more conservative, muted tan with
more layers. He pulled it from the shelf. "This'll be
better."

"And yours?"

Chance looked along the packages on the opposite
wall, all of which depicted men in various costumes:
devils and pirates, prisoners and policemen, superheroes
and cowboys. He was tempted by the Roman gladiator
costume, with its stiff-plastic breastplate and crimson
loincloth, but he knew that even though the costume
looked impressive there, under fluorescent lights in a
Halloween shop in New Jersey, its plastic and artifice
would be unmistakable in Jerusalem, next to the real
thing.

He did, however, like the idea of Roman dress, and
so he chose a deluxe toga costume from the rack. It
contained a simple tunic; a large, if thin, toga; and a pair
of sandals that were all straps and soles. "This'll take care
of Jerusalem. And Munich . . . I mean, 1923, we can wear
what our grandparents would have worn, right? We can
get that stuff next door. And we can change there, too."

*

At Target, Chance found plain clothing more easily
than Cassie did: just a simple pair of grey slacks, a white
shirt, socks and underwear. While she was perusing the
women's section for her own outfit, he sought out a
bedsheet, stepping around paused weekday shoppers as

he did so. They were all completely still, and seeing them gave Chance the creeps: the tall, thin woman in the jeans and athletic shoes who was staring at a hand-soap dispenser; a man walking with two little girls, one of whom had been caught mid-foot-stomp, her little fists balled and her face screwed up brilliant vermillion.

Chance passed them, found the linens and tore open a package that contained an off-white king sheet set. He pulled out a pillowcase and the large flat sheet.

"What're you doing?" Cassie asked from behind him. She was carrying a plain blouse and grey skirt.

He held up the Roman Halloween costume. "I didn't like the toga in here. Thought I'd go for something more authentic. And I figure we need something to carry everything in," he indicated the pillowcase. "Seemed as good as anything."

They used separate booths in the men's fitting room. Chance stripped to his boxer-briefs, for a moment considered whether he wanted to go without them; they were certainly anachronistic, but he decided to keep them. He tore open the Roman costume package, pulled out the tunic, toga, and the belt, placing each on the bench as he slid the sandals out.

They looked evil. No other word for them. Simple soles barely thicker than a few sheets of paper, and each with two long, dark leather cords attached to the heels so that they looked like some sort of podiatric spermatazoan. He figured trying to fasten them after he'd already put on the toga would only complicate things; each cord was at least three feet long, and he wound them up his ankle and around his shins, which only served to highlight the lack of muscle in his calves. He tried to space out the binding but thought it looked strange, and pushing all the binding down toward his ankle looked even worse. He cursed.

"You okay?" Cassie called from a booth over.

"Yeah, I'm gonna need help with my sandals." She'd know, he figured. Girls always knew about shoes.

"Okay," she said.

He was so absorbed in trying to figure out how to remove the sandal, now that he had the cord wrapped so securely around his ankle, that he didn't realize he'd heard her open her stall door until the door to his own opened.

He leapt as he turned. "What're you—?"

"I didn't—," she stared. She had already put on the taupe robe, but not the shawl. "You said you wanted help."

"I didn't mean now."

"I can see that." She didn't move.

He blushed, pulled the tunic from the bench, yanked it over his head. It fell halfway down his thighs, just enough to cover the bottoms of his boxer-briefs—though not by much—and he smoothed his hands over his chest and down his stomach. "All right."

"What?" she said.

"The sandals?" He pulled them by the cords from the bench, letting them dangle from his fist.

"Right," she said, staring at them. She looked at Chance, then at the bench. "Sit down."

Chance sat on the bench. She took the sandals from him as she knelt, and he lifted his right leg as she slid one of the soles under his foot.

"You take the cords, and you wrap 'em like so," she pulled them backward first, then forward, then again several times until she could knot them into a near perfect approximation of what Chance imagined a gladiator sandal would look like. "There," she said, standing.

Chance turned his foot. The binding stretched with his leg rather than constricting his muscles. "Nice," he said.

"Want me to do the other one?"

"I think I'll be okay with it."

"Right. Okay," she said, but she didn't move. "Sorry I barged in like that."

"No worries."

"Right," she said. "Well. I'll just wait out here, then. Let me know if you need anything."

Chance nodded, as she retreated from the fitting room, easing the door closed behind her. The magnetic latch caught with a tiny click.

Chance smiled, shook his head as he exhaled; had she really just checked him out? He certainly felt like she had, all hot and flustered and decidedly pink. He glanced into the mirror as he picked up the other sandal. Of course he had changed; everyone does. He'd begun to exercise more, first swimming before he'd moved on to weights. Once he'd packed quick muscle onto his compact frame he'd attempted to sign up for one of Fitzgerald *roshi*'s martial arts classes, but Fitzgerald had refused him admission until he had learned discipline through study of meditation, Zen, and Taoism.

Chance still thought of those years as the true beginning of his instruction. Law school had lost its fabled luster, but it had left nothing in its wake to replace it. Chance had realized he wanted more and better but had never quite figured out what.

But that wasn't entirely true, he realized, as he slipped his big toe through the small leather ring on top of the sandal and began to wend the cord around his leg. Finding the time machine and saving his father had inspired him, but more than that, Cassie and home tugged at that place in his gut where Fitzgerald *roshi* had once told Chance faith resided.

Everyone and everywhere may change, but some of those small details we so rarely appreciate remain immutable through all the years we know. Chance still felt that familiar urge for her, and just the thought of her incandescent blue eyes made him smile.

He stood and began to arrange the flat sheet into a rough, twentieth-century New Jersey approximation of a toga, secured at his waist and then pulled around his back and over his shoulder to drape over his left arm. He knew he couldn't expect the appearance to be perfect when he looked in the mirror, but he was satisfied, and so he opened the thin door and left the booth.

Cassie stood in front of the full-length, three-way mirror. She, too, was adjusting her garment, a simple robe fastened together with a shawl over her head and shoulders.

"You look great," he told her.

She smiled at him in the mirror. "Thank you."

He walked up behind her. The folds and the way she had draped it looked okay in the mirror, but it was obvious she hadn't yet gotten a good look at her back. He reached for the edges of her shawl. "May I?"

She nodded at him in the mirror.

He tucked it partly into the neck of the robe and pulled the opposite end so that it hung more loosely. "Turn around?" He pulled the garment around her neck and shoulders. The shawl surrounded her head and framed her face, but a few stray strands of hair escaped it. "You'll have to tuck your hair in," he told her as he slipped the loose strands under the shawl, but he found himself wandering off from his own voice, unconcerned about its destination—

The softness of her cheek under his fingertips.

Her eyes . . . he couldn't remember if he'd ever noticed the flecks of grey and green and gold in them. Surely he must have. Surely he'd been this close to her before.

Her lips, full and red, hurtled him back, five years and then thrice again, back to Cherry Coke and licorice twists and a single stolen kiss behind the snackshack. The same constant lips, curled at their corners into the enthusiastic curiosity that was Cassie's fundamental expression, amused and inviting—

Chance stopped. His neck strained forward without actually moving, aching for the memory of his lips on hers. He felt as though he had suddenly discovered not a hard, fast boundary but rather a great precipice with an enormous, seething sea churning thousands of feet below. The overwhelming temptation to just do it, just jump, just pitch forward and launch himself from that great height to plunge down down down into that beautifully furious ocean and loose himself in its depths, but he couldn't bring himself to leap.

Instead, he tucked her hair into the shawl and pulled back. Her eyes had closed. "There," he said, and she opened her eyes. "That should do it. Much better, I think."

She stepped back, too, touched the edge of the shawl around her face. Her distracted eyes found the mirror, and she turned. "So are we ready, then?"

He considered their private department store, their private world, and their plans ahead of them. He imagined Jerusalem, the fractured stone and the abandoned tomb, the women relieved of their grief, the brilliant sunlight, the grey-white gravel and the hot sand. He wondered how long it would take to get there, especially since they would be arriving at their destination nearly two thousand years before either of them had been born, much less faithful departed. "How long will it take?"

Cassie shrugged. "It's not going to be like going back a few hours. Especially since we're moving spatially, as well. Before, it was just time. I think this is probably going to feel different. We won't see everything moving backward. Which might be better."

"Should we eat first?"

"I barely kept my lunch down the last time."

"But there's no telling when we'll eat again. And some water. Can't argue with water, and we can stow a few provisions in our sack" he held up the pillowcase. They trekked across the store and ate a quick meal of diet nutrition bars and bottled water. "And we should be okay in Munich if we need anything, since you know your way around."

"I know my way around now. Not 1923. But we've got coordinates and our notes . . ."

"And anything else, we can figure out along the way." He looked around at the aisle endcaps. "Should we just do it here?"

"I think it'd be a good idea to sit down."

Chance looked down at the floor. "Let's go outside."

*

They left the store together, red doors shusshing open to let them out into the bright sunlight of a still afternoon-verging-toward-evening. The sound of the world had passed beyond silence into the specific sort of stillness that signals anticipation, as if the universe had sensed that something important was about to happen and was holding its breath.

They crossed the parking lot to a copse of trees, where Chance set the pillowcase down on the ground. He sat next to it, and Cassie sat opposite him. She pulled the time machine from the pillowcase, turned the dials and made some adjustments, then set it on the pillowcase between them.

"Ready?" she asked him.

Chance nodded.

"And you're sure? This is our last chance—."

"I'm sure."

Cassie smiled. Her right hand was still poised over the time machine, and she moved her left hand forward, too. "Give me your hand," she told him.

Chance took her hand. He watched his fingertips find her skin. He watched her hand close over his.

He looked into her eyes again. The conviction in them never wavered, and when he felt it, too, he sucked in a breath to tell her to go for it, because it was the right thing to do, they were doing what they had to, but he never got to say a word before—

he felt like his body had accelerated though he never moved. Immobile speed while the world seemed to blur, hazily, until suddenly

everything sidestepped darkness.

Color didn't bleed out or fade; everything just suddenly disappeared as Chance

lost all presence, compressing

to plummet

as though down the rabbithole.

When he had practiced meditation and studied Taoism, Chance had learned words like *enlightenment* and *transcendence*, but he had never experienced a feeling like either until the moment he felt like a star. It was the only way he could describe the sensation; he didn't feel light or energetic so much as he felt radiant like a mad filament. He didn't just understand relativity, or that energy equals mass times the speed of light squared; those were mere words to describe the moment Chance experienced the universe as energy, which knows no bounds, which has no limits, which never begins or ends. Synapses in his brain either up and quit on him or burst like supernovae as time ceased to exist, and Chance lived the life of the universe from the end backward.

Neither with a bang nor a whimper but rather the cold stillness of entropy, of dead stars and abandoned nebulae, borne back ceaselessly through cold rock and nuclear fusion, the universe sped inexorably to the ecstasy of sudden existence combusting forth from the quantum phenomena of the Big Bang, and Chance was everything, and everything was Chance. He was lightning through primordial ooze; the biological imperative to fight and fly and fuck, Prometheus delivering fire from Heaven to mortals still too bewildered to understand what to do with it. He was the revolutions of millions of planets hosting billions of lives around the sun orbiting around the galaxy and back again to the sun and the planets and the lives and then himself;

he was
he was
he was who was—
You know this.

23

Dennis Sowin's ears pop when Chance and Cassie vanish into the ether like mundane guardian angels. He presses his cane to the floor switch to make the bookcase swing aside, then crosses his office to the basement. By the time he arrives at the landing where the limp body sprawls, his son has reached the door to the basement, and Dennis looks up the stairs at him.

"Dad? Are you—?"

"I'm fine."

"What's going on?"

Dennis hesitates then, because though he had always assumed this moment would come, he hadn't thought it would come soon. One doesn't build a secret room to keep people from finding it but rather to keep people from finding it right now. Dennis moves carefully around Geisel's body, up the stairs and into the kitchen.

"I called the cops," Chance says.

"We need to talk before they get here."

And so Dennis Sowin will begin to tell his son about his research and the laboratory he concealed in the basement. He will not feel guilty, and he will not explain every detail, only enough that his son will understand what he did, and why, and that they might be in danger. Dennis will not realize soon enough just how much danger they are in, not until the doorbell rings and he opens the door to find Richard Hanley standing on his doorstep.

Hanley will already have his silencered pistol in his hand, and Dennis will find himself staring into its elongated barrel before, suddenly, the world will go black.

*

Hanley will step quickly around Dennis Sowin's body as it slumps to the ground, walking through the hallway and into the kitchen, where he will find Chance sitting with his back to the doorway. He will fire three shots, each higher than the last. The first will strike Chance through the spine and perforate his lungs; the second through his neck to burst through his throat; the third through the back of Chance's head.

Hanley will turn and walk down the stairs, where he will shake his head in disgust upon sight of Geisel's lifeless body. He will step around it to cross the basement toward Dennis Sowin's office. He will rifle through the drawers in the desk, pull them out and turn them over, examine the bookcase, searching each text for Dennis Sowin's research.

He will find nothing.

Frustrated, he will kick a shelf toward the bottom of the bookcase, and it will crack through the backboard, wedging through to reveal darkness.

When he sees that darkness, Richard Hanley will smile.

*

Richard Hanley will be handsomely rewarded for locating Dennis Sowin's laboratory and confiscating Sowin's research. The government will dole out the research in discrete quanta to various institutions so that no single one will possess enough to understand the nature of the greater whole, while at the same time revealing information to the public in slow but substantial increments: the first of which will come when Ford Motor Company wins the Higgs engine in an auction. The implementation of the new technology will relieve the world's dependence on fossil fuel, altering the economy as Ford himself did with the Model T and the assembly line.

As the world overcomes its dependence on petroleum, tensions in the Middle East and among several large-scale oil conglomerates will rise. Newscasts will broadcast footage of a murky cave in Tora Bora from which Osama bin Laden will condemn the United States' large-scale exploitation of the Muslim world. In Iraq, Saddam Hussein will sense an opportunity to increase both sovereignty and empire by invading Iran and Afghanistan. The UN will send peacekeeping troops to fight hot and blind in desert warfare punctuated by undulating battle-cries piercing the darkness of close-fought skirmishes in dank caverns.

Iraqi troops will flush bin Laden from that cavernous network and into American custody, and the UN will try him as a war criminal. He will be sentenced to death by hanging, and grainy video of his slow-swinging feet shot from a cell phone will circulate on the

Internet for months to come. Toby Keith will incorporate the footage into a music video that will dominate MTV for seventeen weeks.

In early 2005, Congress will authorize the use of the Higgs laser against Saddam Hussein and Iraq, to vaporize Baghdad. Kim Jong Il will regard this as a crime against humanity and launch two counteroffensive missiles targeted at Pearl Harbor and California, but both missiles will disappear mid-trajectory when the American government uses the Sowin device to pause time long enough to vaporize the warheads before they can do any damage. News reports will note both the appearances and disappearances of strange, unidentified lights in the sky over the Pacific Ocean, but the government will produce convincing evidence dismissing these reports as weather balloons.

Richard Hanley will approach his superiors about the connection of the Higgs laser and the Higgs engine to Dennis Sowin's research. In an effort to hush him, the government will offer him a new job with higher responsibilities and new power, one of which will be the ability to pause time around him using the Higgs device. Under direct orders, Hanley will travel by plane to Korea, where he will pause time to kill the country's diminutive dictator. Subsequent investigations will allege foul play but never name a suspect, much less resolve speculation.

Speculation: this is where grammar falls. Future perfect collides head on with preterite and present continuous, bursting sideways into new tenses like future progressive and past continuous—

you've been here before—
you've been everywhere before—
not to mention everywhen—

In the collision of days and the sudden excitement of surprised leptons and petrified quarks, the United

States government will sense an opportunity. A month later, a clandestine group will send Richard Hanley back to September 11th, 2001, onto American Airlines flight 11 to prevent its highjacking.

Two roads converge in a blue-shift universe, and instead of following one not previously traveled in favor of a new path, to paraphrase one of the world's greatest Yogis (Berra), when time comes to that crucial fork in the road, time will take it.

*

Richard Hanley will appear in the cramped plane lavatory at 8:13 a.m., just as Mohammed Atta begins to stand from seat 9D, extending a box-cutter's blade. Hanley will chop Atta in the throat, then draw his silencered pistol and fire four precise shots at four other men before he begins to speak, in a clear, calm voice: "My name is Richard Hanley, and I am a Federal Air Marshall. There is no need to panic. Everything is now under control."

Flight attendants will address passengers' needs as Hanley enters the cockpit. He will use the radio to alert the FAA of the other hijackings as the pilots land the plane at Newark International Airport. September 11th, 2001 will become known as the day the US government shot three hijacked passenger planes out of the sky before they could be used for the worst terrorist attack ever on American soil.

Chance Sowin will not run from the Towers as they fall, or move back home. Because Hanley brought the time machine with him, the government will not need to steal it from Dennis Sowin's secret lab—

But if the Towers never fall and Chance never moves back home and the government never steals the device, it will never use it to send Richard Hanley back to that airplane lavatory moments before the flight can be hijacked, which means that it will be. Which means that Chance will run cough and choke on the dust of dense-pile rugs and cheap fiberboard office furniture, and Richard Hanley will send Peter Geisel to confiscate Dennis Sowin's research and steal the equipment the government hopes to use—

*

What will happen is simple: time will explore those two paths and find they coincide. That one cannot exist without the other, that where one ends another begins. Time will twist to become a multidimensional Möbius strip.

The government, flush with possibility, will send Richard Hanley back again to 1998 to Afghanistan, where he will use the Sowin device over a subjective period of several paused months, to track down and then assassinate Osama bin Laden in the mountains of Tora Bora—

*

Al Qaeda *will lose its central figure, but Fajid al Zawqiri will assume leadership. On October 31ˢᵗ, 2000, at 8:45 a.m. EST, seven* al Qaeda *operatives will attempt to detonate small-scale nuclear devices in major cities. Given the timing of the attempt and a record-high for an administration approval rating, Congress will pass a bill to postpone the 2000 Presidential election.*

Clinton will accept with one caveat: a two-year time limit, after which a special Presidential election will be held in 2002. In January 2002, however, Kofi Annan will step down as Secretary General of the UN, which will offer the position to Clinton. Clinton will become the second president in history to resign, leaving the Executive Office to Al Gore—

When Clinton discovers that Hanley used the time machine, he will okay a plan to send Hanley to August, 1992, where Hanley will locate and remove Saddam Hussein from power before he can invade Kuwait. One of Clinton's first actions on taking office in 1992 will be to relieve Iraq of its debt to Kuwait from the Iran-Iraq war.

Clinton's debt relief will ameliorate anti-American sentiment in the Muslim world. Osama bin Laden will become a professor of history at an Afghani university, and al Qaeda *will never gain numbers. No attempt at an attack will occur on October 31ˢᵗ, 2000. The elections will not be postponed. Gore will win when he demands a state-wide recount in Florida—*

Sending Hanley back to September 11ᵗʰ will not prevent the attacks; it merely creates the possibility that they do not occur. The possibility that they did still exists, and so too will Bush's administration. So too will their invasion of Iraq and their reelection, atrocities at Gitmo and Abu Ghraib. The WMDs they used as their excuse for Iraq won't exist, but then, never did.

The administration will seek and achieve reelection. It will threaten Iran with the same laser it used on Baghdad. It will withdraw from the UN, using the defense that America is the only nation willing to go to any length to achieve security in the world, regardless of the price. It will continue to allow a false sense of security to supercede both democracy and freedom—

*

Ways lead onto further and stranger ways but never need come back, but following all those possibilities would be impossible. At this point, the best hope is to appreciate a dance begun as an *adagio*, slow and stately, on the strings of the universe.

At this tempo, we can keep up with the electrons in the universe, and one-two-three one-two-three, gentleman upstage and ladies down, know we our positions or know we our speed? According to Heisenberg, we can know only one or the other, but who knows if he ever learned how to dance? Imagine now a tempo change, from slow *adagio* to walking-pace *andante*, but in addition imagine that former never stops. Francis Scott Key Fitzgerald once characterized people who possess first-rate intelligence as able to hold in their minds two opposing ideas simultaneously while retaining the ability to function; being of the Jazz Age, as he was, would Scotty have also characterized first-rate dancers as able to dance to two songs at once?

A better question might be whether it's possible. A waltz and a foxtrot, but now *con brio* and vigorous soul, and one-two-three and step-glide-turn. Another instrument, another song, another voice and another dance floor. Here we bypass comfortable *allegretto* for *vivo*, and the easiest way to dance to all this music (all at once) is to keep it simple as the universe prays our feet don't fail it now while we take on new dances. These are new steps in exotic dances, this is the thrilling discotheque of a universe where music is life and life is movement, this is the lepton tango and the hyperspace bossa nova, the super-collider lambada and the quantum mechanical bugaloo.

This is no longer dueling banjoes delivering us from static; these are hyperkinetic Gibson Flying 8s shredding and shrieking against each other. This is a dance to seven songs with seven tempos. This is what it feels like to try to maintain the discipline and control necessary for the perfect form of a waltz while still allowing the freeform style of headspins and the Worm.

Consider now a single electron encountering that branching of time: a tiny quantum of energy, a compact point so fast that we can't know both its speed and its position at the same time due mainly to disproportion of scale (for young Werner Heisenberg might have been wrong had he been smaller. Not to mention quicker). That poor electron, to extend our metaphor, might not know which song to dance to and so might attempt to dance to them all, and while it might pull it off for a while, it won't last long. Eventually that electron, streaming with sweat and completely out of breath, is going to need a rest; if it doesn't rightly decide to sit out, it's going to collapse on the dance floor.

And if one is going to, they all will.

This is what happens when time changes. Those other timelines go beyond historical events and political affiliation to the most fundamental aspects of quantum physics no scientists have yet explored; when Chance and Cassie leave for Jerusalem, the tempo will change. Reality is merely a super-combination of the most probable arrangements of particles. In that state of exponentially increasing confusion, a single electron will succumb to stress and collapse into a waveform, which will begin a change reaction in which all those trillions of others will follow suit, so that all those infinitely branching universes will flatline, abandoning Chance and Cassie to carom back back back to Jerusalem while Leonard Kensington goggles at Jennifer behind her desk at Cantor Fitzgerald.

24

Leonard thought Jennifer squinted at him from behind her corporate pre-fab desk but couldn't be sure because tiny, twin reflections of her computer monitor shone on her chunky black spectacles and hid her eyes. "Do I know you?"

He didn't know how to answer. Some logical part of his brain, the one accustomed to far-flung travel and temporal coincidence, kicked in immediately: she was different. Her blonde hair. The dark blue polish on the slim fingertips that hadn't yet stopped clicking keys on the keyboard. The desk in front of her hid her figure from him, but her face seemed harder, the angle of her jawline more extreme.

But yet: she was exactly the same. The same voice, and when she wisped a strand of hair back behind her ear, she did so with a gesture Leonard had loved a thousand times.

"I'm not sure," Leonard said. He struggled to hotwire his brain. "You look familiar. Like maybe I've seen you before. But probably just from my last appointment here . . ."

She moved her head just enough that those computer reflections left the lenses, and she eyed him. "I'm a contract employee, sir. Can I help you? What's your business with us today?"

"Actually, I'm looking for Gabriel Matthews . . ."

Leonard didn't know what reaction he had hoped for, but the one he got was just fine. Her fingers left homerow, her whole body turned away from the monitor. "Did you—you said Gabriel?"

Leonard nodded. "An associate of mine, a colleague in investment, so to speak, mentioned Gabriel to me. Said he was something of a wunderkind with bonds, so I thought I'd see if I could meet with him." When Jennifer started to shake her head, he appealed: "I know it's not usual—."

"There's no one here by that name."

"Oh? You seemed to recognize the name."

"My brother's name is Gabriel Matthews. But he doesn't work here," she told him. Leonard knew the squint she gave him very well: skepticism crossed with appraisal.

"My friend must've gotten one financial company confused with another."

"What I find odd, though, is that you called me by name even though I don't have any idea who you are. Don't you find that a little odd?"

"My name is Leonard. Leonard Kensington. I'm—I'm in investment."

"Are you?" she asked. "Because given that pause, it doesn't sound like you're sure. I'm certainly not convinced."

What was he supposed to tell her? That they were both in an alternate reality where he was trying to research when, where, and how precisely it diverged from actual reality? That this was just an alternate time and place, and in reality Jennifer was not a temp at all but a coordinator at CIRTN?

"Okay, no, I'm not actually in investment," he told her. As he did so, the elevator dinged open behind him and a portly man wearing a tailored charcoal grey suit with subtle heather pinstripes brushed forward. He carried a brown leather briefcase that matched both his shoes and the color of one of the worst combovers Leonard had ever seen. He smiled a hello to Jennifer, greeting her by name as he marched past her desk to disappear down the hallway beyond it.

After the man had passed, Leonard said: "You're not actually a temp, are you?"

Jennifer's cheeks colored. "What makes you think that?"

"That gentleman knew you. Which means either you've been here a while, or I'm not the only one who hasn't been entirely truthful during the past five minutes."

The blush had dissolved from her cheeks, and she tucked a strand of hair back behind her glasses as if to lock her composure back in place. "Explain to me how you know not only my name but my brother's, too."

"It's a bit complicated," he said.

"I thought you might say that."

He looked at his watch. Four approaching five. "You almost done for the day?"

She glanced at her computer screen. "Twenty more minutes."

"I was on my way up to the bar on the top floor when I sidetracked to see if I could meet your brother. Since he's not here, and since I'm still rather hungry, not to mention could use a drink, if you'll join me instead, I'll explain everything to you."

"Everything."

Leonard nodded. "The long version."

"How do I know you're not just stalking me?"

"I'm not. I have better things to do," he said, as a woman in a power-blue suit strode out of the hallway, past Leonard to wait at the elevators. He stepped forward, toward Jennifer's desk. "It's a long story," he told her, keeping his voice low. "Look, meet me up there. What, fifteen minutes? Come on. My treat."

Jennifer eyed him, then closed her eyes when she said, "Okay," as if she didn't believe she was agreeing to it. When she opened her eyes, she added, "Dinner. And you'll tell me the whole story. And that's it."

*

Windows on the World. Floor 106. This is not the most exclusive restaurant in Manhattan, nor the one with the most delicious food, but there isn't a view like this anywhere else in the world. All the way up the North Tower, World Trade Center 1, where one glance out those windows will clear every other thought from your head, not to mention, to be clichéd about it, take your breath away.

Look:

Manhattan North, miles of tall buildings appear squat from this height, pinpoint topography punctuated by spires and interrupted at the midway point by the verdant rectangle of Central Park, where green leaves are not yet wearing the fall line but are certainly considering it. Western sunset gold-washes across the whole City so that the taller scrapers cast their shadows right, where further yet the East river bifurcates the Island from southern Brooklyn and further-on Queens. Halfway up, the Empire State Building gleams handsomely, and beyond it and just right, the accents on the Chrysler Building glitter like an Art Deco mirrorball.

Leonard approached an antique mahogany lectern that would have looked haughty anywhere else but managed to look understated there, overwhelmed by the City all around it, where the Manhattan sunset encroached through the windows, demanding attention and being quite shiny about it. A tall man with slick, reddish-brown hair and a brace-straight smile took Leonard's information but informed him it might be as long as half an hour before he could accommodate a party of two.

"That'll be fine." Leonard gave his name, then instructions to send Jennifer to the bar when she arrived.

The Greatest Bar on Earth might not have been precisely that, but it certainly earned a solid place in the debate. It overlooked the restaurant from the South-East corner, affiliated with the main attraction but a destination itself, complete with a mod-art sculpture that looked like a strange cross between a Japanese lantern, a Manhattan skyscraper, and a wedding cake, as well as a spacious dance floor and a talented live band. Concentric golden circles on the ceiling bullseyed right above the black-and-chrome, backless chairs at the bar, whose surface shone. The windows beyond, on the South and East, overlooked the Brooklyn waterfront through one set and Lady Liberty herself through the others.

Leonard paid a ten-buck cover to sit at the bar. A man in an immaculate white shirt and jowls above his tied bowtie greeted him and asked if he'd like a drink.

"Martini," Leonard told him.

"Lemme guess. Shaken, not stirred," the man said it with a caricature of an accent Leonard couldn't place.

"Um, no, actually, I'd prefer it stirred, if you don't mind. Gin—Hendrick's if you have it—with a hint of vermouth," he said, realizing that a martini in this reality might not be the same drink he enjoyed, suddenly fearful the tender might use vodka. Or worse. "Two olives."

"I know how to make a martini," he said, and proved he did: a splash of vermouth swirled in the glass, another over the ice. Hendrick's from its squat black bottle. Poured so high right in front of Leonard that the only thing that kept the liquid from spilling over the rim was surface tension, then two olives speared with a metal toothpick on the same napkin as the glass. It was so full Leonard couldn't pick it up without disturbing it, so he leaned forward to take his first sip, then picked up the olives and swirled them through the gin.

He thanked the tender.

"Start a tab?"

Leonard gave the man his smartcard. "That'd be great. And do me a favor. A pretty blonde is about to join me, so bring another when she arrives."

The tender left to run the card, and Leonard sipped his martini, eying the Monday supper crowd, already starting to fill out though the workday was barely over yet; the place was full of men in haberdashed pin-striped suits and women in gorgeous straight-hemmed skirts. Businessmen and their suitors, businesswomen and their clients, and golden sunlight so bright it was tactile: this is the place where deals are sealed. This is the place where currency moves, the economy of billions of people, and it smells like money: musky cologne like cigars and limousines, amber perfume dotted on elegant necks and inside braceleted wrists.

Leonard bit an olive from the metal toothpick as he tried to decide what he felt knowing that, by that time the following night, it would be gone. It didn't seem possible. Not these buildings, not this City. He realized, as he looked around, that he was recording the scene as if he meant to memorize it, as if—

"So I think I've decided that either I know you from someplace I've forgotten," he heard Jennifer's voice, and he spun on his chair, rose. She was standing there in her fitted black shirt and her tight grey slacks, but she'd let down her hair and unbuttoned her shirt cuffs. "Or you're hoping to run some kind of con on Cantor Fitzgerald and have chosen me as your unwitting but attractive accomplice."

Leonard smiled. "I wouldn't call you unwitting. Though I admit you earn attractive."

"Attraction is subjective, Mr. Kensington."

Leonard nudged the stool beside his with his foot. "You going to sit?"

"Are you going to tell me what this is about?"

"Have a drink," he told her, even as the tender brought the second martini, placing it just beside his.

She eyed it. "You ordered a martini."

"I hope it's okay."

"I prefer them dirty."

"Really?" Leonard asked. Jennifer had never ordered a dirty martini as long as he had known her. She disliked the extra olive juice, and indeed generally offered Leonard her olives. Leonard signaled to the bartender and requested another, this new one tarted up a bit. When the bartender moved to take back the one on the bar, Leonard waved him off. "No, it's okay. I'll drink it. Just bring another, provided my friend here wants to stay. What do you think, Jennifer?"

"What he said. Dirty it up," she said, and as she settled onto the stool, Leonard settled onto his own.

He drained the remainder of his martini, set the glass aside as the tender appeared with another, cloudier, with the olives in the glass. Leonard pulled the second drink closer to him as Jennifer appropriated that third.

"You like your martinis," Jennifer told him.

"Who doesn't like a martini?" Leonard asked.

"Nobody you can trust."

"And since I do, you can trust me," he said, lifting his glass, just slightly so as not to break the surface tension and spill, as she raised her own. "Can't you?"

"The jury's still out on that particular point, but let's just say that it is willing to hear the defense," as she clinked his glass with hers.

Leonard held her big green eyes behind her black spectacles as he sipped from his glass, and just as they each set down their glasses, the maitre d' appeared. "Mister Kensington?" he said. "If you'd still like a table, I'd be happy to seat you."

25

Indigo from blackness first in throbbing waves, inverted colors coalescing around Chance from a free-fall to become a city visible in several dimensions simultaneously: the enormous, dark dome in the center, more walls and barriers than he could make sense of and people coming and going upside-down and sideways like an M.C. Escher print. Startling trees with dark trunks beneath fraying bark sprang up all around him and Cassie, and a hundred men and their mirror images appeared at the same time, super-imposed over each other before merging into a single group of more soldiers than Chance had ever seen. Hard-packed dirt like sudden terra firma beneath Chance as time skidded around him like an elastic burn, and he worried he might fall off the ground.

He blinked back tears, fighting down his gorge while his stomach clenched so hard it pulled his body concave. When he finally managed to breathe, it was an electric gasp charged with inverted oxygen and backward air. The world in his vision seemed to pulse as if possessed of a universal membrane, stretching thin with reversed colors, men carrying something like neon-chocolate soft-serve cones.

Finally, finally, the colors reverted to normal with a sound of thunder. He felt as though he had been riding a speeding train the conductor had thrown into reverse; his body lurched forward until he found himself on his knees with his forehead on the ground as if he were supplicating before Mecca while attempting inverted plow. He groaned as his shoulder rattled in its socket, then again when he felt Cassie's weight heave into him, pushing him farther forward until he was splayed prone with a mouthful of dirt.

Commotion as time righted itself. Angry voices shouting unintelligible words, punctuated by jingle-jangling that sounded like heavy keys in ancient locks.

Chance groaned and pushed himself up to his elbow. He shook his head to clear it because it felt like it had just received an electric shock from a cattle prod. His brain tingled and refused to focus around a coherent thought. Just images: the leaf-strewn ground, the flickering light, the overpowering scent of ripe, green olives. The whole world smelled like the bottom of a martini.

He rolled sideways, plopped to his butt on the ground, and wiped his mouth with the back of his forearm. Next to him, Cassie moved as if she had just mainlined a discotheque and was struggling to feign sobriety. She pressed her palms to her forehead like she was trying to keep her brain in, and she whimpered, low, throaty, cut off when she swallowed it.

Chance wiped his eyes with the meat of his palm as he rose. He had already smelled the olives, but inhaling brought to him the heavy scent of bodies and the dung of grazing animals.

They were in a grove of black-silhouette trees. Beyond, moonlight silver on a squat, stocky structure with primitive walls and illuminated by flickering orange and golden flames, all filmed by fine mist, but of closer and more immediate concern to Chance were what appeared to be dozens of soldiers, their armor ruddy bronze by torchlight. Some wore helmets with proud Roman tufts like roosters' combs, but most of their faces were covered solely by dirty beards or thinning hair. Their attention focused like discordant lasers on the single, small man before them, his body slight and his head bowed in deference.

"Jesus," Chance exhaled.

"Yeah," Cassie whispered. "I think that's him."

Chance didn't catch her meaning. "What?"

Cassie nodded toward the man in front of the soldiers. "I think we're early."

Until that moment, until he took a long look at the man before the soldiers, Chance had failed to consider the monumental reality of their actions. That sudden epiphany finally made the world real, the last layer of tangibility from that n-dimensional space-time confusion to the Mount of Olives. Somewhere close by was the Temple Mount, ancient Jerusalem, that high-walled Jewish city under Roman protectorate. The trees in silhouette obscuring the view, the smell of olives, the mount and the press: this is Gethsemane.

This is the world before asphalt and pavement, before easy travel and convenient communication. This is the silence of a time before cars and planes, darkness unpierced by streetlamps or headlights. This is a year still measured from the proposed time of creation, a place still unaware that much of the rest of the world exists. This is an Earth still considered flat when considered much at all, whose inhabits still believe that the entire rest of the Universe revolves around them because they have little doubt they are the most important beings in it.

This is the agony in the Garden. This is a cohort of Roman soldiers sent to arrest a man who had only just retired from a Seder where he had broken bread with his friends. This is mere hours after one man said to—

take this, all of you, and eat it.

This is my body, given up for you.

This is the blood of a new and everlasting covenant.

Do this in memory of me.—

This is the man who uttered them: small and squat, thickset with the sort of muscle that develops by hard work over time. Short, coarse hair in tight curls above a prominent brow and a wide, punched-in nose. A bloodied face swelling. A rough garment thicker than a tunic but without enough fabric to be a toga, belted around the waist. Small hands, fingers folded together, wrists bound tight. Wiry, stray hair crept up his cheeks and down his neck while it receded from his forehead and crown. Jesus of Nazareth was shorter than Chance had expected, could have used a shave, and was experiencing male pattern baldness, and it was only because Cassie had suggested it that Chance took him to be the humble stonemason who had taught the world to call God our Father—

Who art in Heaven,

Hallowed be thy name—

But human be this body before those who mean it harm.

"We can't just pull him away from them," Chance said. "That would probably only make things worse. There are too many people to just whisk him off somewhere to hide him, and if he disappeared right now who knows what stories people would tell."

Cassie nodded. Chance didn't see her shut off the Samhain device, but he could feel it as the excitement left his body. It felt as though every cell in his body had exhaled. Motion returned to the world, twinkle to the stars, flicker to the soldiers' torches.

One of the soldiers pulled Jesus by the bindings at his wrist, so hard his slight body collapsed forward, but as it did so two others took up his legs to bear their captive between them like carry-on. As one, like birds in flight formation changing course, the soldiers bore Jesus through the garden straight toward Chance and Cassie. The closer they came the greater seemed their number.

"Cassie, they—."

"I see, I see," she said. She fumbled with the time machine, but before she could use it, that band of Roman brothers came upon them in a mesmeric cadence of heavy-treading, sandal-clad feet and long swords bouncing against armor. The three soldiers in the lead who bore Jesus' body between them paused uncertainly when they saw Chance and Cassie, and their armsmen bore up behind them as if awaiting command. The soldier carrying Jesus' wrists shouted, and four others broke off from the cohort at his sides; two reached for Chance while the others grabbed for Cassie.

Chance felt rough, grabbing hands on the sheet he wore, fingers taloning in the linen before the soldiers themselves pushed him to the ground. He grunted as he sank to his knee. A rock cracked into his patella, splitting sharp pain like electric current down his leg so hard it paralyzed his toes. The soldiers worked rope around his wrists, grabbing and twisting his arm and renewing the ache that until then had quieted in his shoulder.

Through it all, he never looked away from Cassie. She fought, too, until one of the soldiers slapped her across the face, stunning her still. The toned muscles in her arms held against the soldiers' grasp, her eyes closed and her jaw set in effort, and in her left hand she held the time machine, in her right she held the pillowcase.

"Cass," Chance said.

She hesitated in her strain, looked at him.

Chance nodded toward her hand. "Get yourself out of here."

"But we can—."

"Go," he said, his voice stern to the point of anger. She held his eyes as the soldiers pulled her hands behind her, and just as the shawl around her dark hair shook loose, she twisted forward—

a flicker like the orange torches had strobed. The two soldiers shifted sideways, stunned, at the same time Chance thought he saw Cassie a yard behind where she had been just an instant before, and then she was gone and the two soldiers stood there looking confused.

The two soldiers holding Chance started, and Chance took advantage of their momentary surprise to surge forward, twisting. The sheet he wore unfastened in the soldiers' tight-grip, but Chance just kept going, leaving the two soldiers grasping nothing but department store linen as he ran, hard and fast and far as he could. He didn't stop to consider where he was, nor where to go, just forward, up the sloping ground, even as he heard the commotion behind him, the heavy tread that indicated at least one or two soldiers had followed. He batted low-hanging branches away as the hard soles of his sandals pounded into the loose sand, and cool mist clung to the fine hairs on his arms and neck. He dashed behind a patch of brush on a small dune to his left, crouched in wait, new sweat sheening his skin, and he held his freight-train breath when the soldiers passed close by, their torches flickering the ground around him vibrant, dancing orange.

He waited. Tiny branches poked at his skin, and his arms and torso goose-prickled at the touch of the cool dirt, but he did not move until the sound of the soldiers and their arrest grew distant. When finally he could see only darkness moonlit silver, when finally he could hear nothing but cricket-chirp, Chance eased forward to confirm that no soldiers had remained, alert in this immediate darkness for small rustles and tiny movements, twig-snaps and hoot-owls. He could make out only grey branches and dark trunks of thick trees, but he followed the downward slope back in the direction he thought he'd come.

When he was certain the soldiers were gone, Chance began to call Cassie's name.

Nothing.

He pressed on, completely alone in a grove of trees that stank to high heaven of rotten olives and animal dung and he hadn't a clue where she could be. He couldn't see much, just trees as though the rest of the world had faded away into the cool night.

"Cassie?" he whispered, when he thought he was close to where they had arrived and first encountered the soldiers, but who could tell, really? Every damned tree and cluster of bushes looked the same, and each time Chance called her name, his voice rose both a degree of volume and an octave. He clutched himself as he walked, crossed his arms to keep warm, until finally he marked the spot where they had arrived, a small clearing he recognized when he saw his toga sheet on the ground. He bent to pick it up, and as he did so he heard a thud behind him.

He whirled to see Cassie's body on the ground, her dark hair a tangle, her skin pale moonlit in the darkness. He scrambled toward her even as she stirred, pushing herself up on her elbows. He knelt next to her, his hands on her shoulders, her arms.

"You okay?"

She groaned as he helped her up, grasping her head, her fingertips brushing past her hairline, as she nodded. "I skipped ahead a few minutes. It was the opposite of earlier. Everything got brighter, and all the soldiers started moving like somebody had pushed fast-forward while—," she cut off, sighed. She regained her feet, but she bent forward at the waist, her hands on her knees. "I waited until I saw you. I might have stopped it too fast. I just shut it off when I saw you, and I felt like I'd pulled a rug out from under me or something."

"But using the time machine again didn't hurt you, or anything?" he said, his hand on her back, ready to catch her if she fell again.

She straightened. "I think I'll be okay," she said, her voice trembling and a little breathy, as if it came with some effort. "What about you? What happened to your sheet?"

Chance went again to retrieve the sheet from the ground. "Dropped it when I broke away from the soldiers. I found a hiding spot for a few minutes, then came back to look for you," he said as he picked up the sheet and fastened it around him, shrugging into the makeshift toga.

She went to him, helped him adjust it. "There. Much better," she said, and then she looked away, around the small clearing. All around them, tall trees with thick, dark trunks pressed close. The full moon glimmered brightly through sprays of branches and bursts of leaves like botanic firecrackers, dimly illuminating the light sand, the big bunches of gnarled roots jumbling into the ground. "We did it," she whispered. "We really fucking did it. We're two thousand years ago."

"Except we're not," Chance said. "We're right now. And we're—we're on the Mount of Olives. We're in Gethsemane."

"Are you sure? I can't see anything beyond these trees."

"I saw the dome of the Temple when everything started to coalesce. It was blurry, but it was definitely the Temple. Which is in Jerusalem, which means this is Gethsemane."

"And that means that . . ." she trailed off.

Chance nodded. "I checked the coordinates six or seven times—."

"And I double checked them."

"And we were set on the tomb, and it probably would have been nearby. And if we're in Gethsemane—I've only ever heard of one man having been arrested in Gethsemane."

"But there must have been others."

"I've never heard of any," Chance said.

"That doesn't mean they didn't exist."

"That was way too many soldiers to have come for just anyone. That wasn't how they did it. They sent a handful of soldiers to arrest someone, not the whole damned legion."

"So you really think that was Jesus?"

Chance nodded. "But that means you were right, and we're early."

"Only by a couple of days."

"They're a pretty fucking important couple of days."

"Only to you and me. Really they're filled with hours and minutes just like any other couple of days. Which means it's a pretty narrow margin of error, considering it could have been off by years or worse, and considering that we based those coordinates mostly on the best and most educated guesses we could find. I'd say we're pretty lucky."

"So what would be unlucky? Stuck in Egypt twenty years ago?"

"God, Chance, what, did you think it was going to be like riding a subway to your downtown office? For Christ's sake, we just traveled back in time almost two thousand years because you had this burning desire to know what happened, and now you're complaining because we ended up a couple of days early? We're lucky that traveling backward in time two thousand years didn't end us. We're more lucky we still exist than we are we're still alive. Our particles might never have stopped in the first place."

Chance couldn't speak for a second. He hated the way her words made him feel. He hated more that she was right. "Sorry," he finally said.

"Oh, it's not—," Cassie started, then sighed. "Shit. I'm sorry. Look, I didn't mean to go off. It's just—."

"I know," Chance said. "It's just we're on the Mount of Olives and barely escaped being arrested alongside Jesus."

"You don't think that could have been anyone else?"

"Given where we are, and when, I don't think it's likely."

Cassie paused a moment, then: "He wasn't what I'd expected."

"No," Chance said, considering it, recalling the man's compact features, the muscular body on its thin frame, but he didn't know what he had expected. He'd known that the image he'd grown up with, the tall, white man with the wispy beard and the patrician nose, was more driven by popular culture and media than by historical accuracy, as much brand logo as Coca Cola's, as mutable and open to interpretation as Santa Claus. He thought of Peter O'Toole and Willem Dafoe, cinematic sunsets over crowns of thorns, and then of the compact man they'd just seen arrested. "That's why I wanted to come."

"And you still want to find out what happened?"

Chance thought of the soldiers and the man they'd captured. He nodded.

"Then we need to find him."

"The books I was using to get the coordinates mentioned the Sanhedrin. The Jewish high council. That's where the Gospels say the soldiers took him, to one of the high priests, Caiaphas. It would have been like a preliminary hearing before he went on to Pilate," Chance said, looking around. He found the pillowcase again, opened it and withdrew from it a photocopy of a map of Jerusalem, its spidery lines of demarcation difficult to discern in the moonlight. "Which would probably be our best bet. If we're on the Mount of Olives, we'll be approaching Jerusalem from the west, so we're going to hit this main gate, right near the Temple. Which they're not going to let us into, because we're Gentiles—."

"We could always just use the Samhain."

"Maybe, but we don't need to be there. And we don't know what we're doing. We didn't plan to end up where we are, and there's too much—we don't know the language, and we're dressed to get away with barely being seen but not to fit in. So I think our best bet is to get past this gate here," he pointed, "But not venture too far beyond it. We can skirt our way around the Temple and make our way to Pilate's. And hopefully everyone will be too distracted by what's happening with Jesus to notice a couple of people from Jersey in the background. Pilate'll be in a big damned fortress I'm pretty sure it's going to be impossible to miss, especially if we just follow the soldiers' trail back the way they came."

"You don't think we should worry about meeting them along the way?"

"I think they got enough of a headstart that they're probably well ahead of us by now," Chance said. He tucked the pillowcase behind a cluster of medium-sized rocks and overgrown shrubbery, and then, by the silver light of a moon furtive behind olive leaves and fig branches, he saw the loose-dirt path the soldiers had trodden, white between the big, dark trees on either side. He offered her his hand without thinking, and her fingers entangling his came as a surprise.

*

Together they followed the path down the Mount of Olives, with Cassie always just a step behind Chance, if not right beside him. He brushed aside sprays of young branches, stepped around roots shattering from the rocky soil, and clusters of palms raised into the darkness knotty stems that fireworked into shivering tufts. They walked for a while before the trees began to thin, then came around a bend in the path and saw Jerusalem ahead.

When he'd been a child, Chance's parents had brought him to Manhattan for a weekend of Broadway shows and FAO Schwartz. Their first stop had been a trip to the top of the World Trade Center, where they'd watched the sunset from the observation deck, after which they'd descended again to the street and then walked, hand-in-hand, halfway across the Brooklyn Bridge. The City had come as a revelation to a then six-year-old Chance; up until then, he'd seen the Manhattan only from its own streets, never from a vantage from which he could appreciate the whole City, so exciting and glamorous it glittered.

In the years since, Chance had visited Chicago and Los Angeles and Berlin, all cities with distinctive features, and in each one he had at some point encountered a vantage like the one that took his breath away then, standing before ancient Jerusalem. The city was tighter and denser than Los Angeles, not nearly so tall as Chicago, not nearly so deliberately modern as Berlin, but because it used torches as streetlamps, it shimmered like a desert dream. A wall the color of museum-displayed parchment traced around the city's perimeter like a stone hedge, and atop columns spaced at even increments, torches flickered like copper-colored, Earth-fallen stars from unfamiliar constellations. The Temple's dome gleamed by light of flame and moon and looked like a more ornate version of Washington's Capitol building, while just to its right stood a squat, square building whose only curves came from archways in its four boxy turrets. Slightly left but at a greater distance, three proud towers spired into darkness.

Above it all, brilliant stars shone like shotgun blast through a black velvet sky, all highlighted by the pale shimmer-swish of galactic swirl. Chance understood why those people believed so fervently in Messiahs and prophets, sons of God and miracles from on high; looking into that sky filled him with awe so intense the only way to cope was through Faith. Not belief in angels and demons and men in the bellies of whales, but the metaphysical tingle that comes from close contact with the galvanic energy of Life.

Beside him, Cassie gasped. "Yeah, we definitely didn't get the coordinates wrong."

He nodded toward the squarish building. "That'll be Pilate's palace. I don't remember what they actually called it, but it's named after Marc Antony."

"As in Shakespeare Marc Antony? Cleopatra and Julius Caesar Marc Antony? That's where they're bringing Jesus?"

"After the high priest," Chance said. Hand in hand, they followed a moonlit swath down the slope, descending to a large stone bridge over what appeared to be a dry riverbed of cracked Earth and parched stones. On either side and all around, primitive dwellings huddled together, clay and brick, and people entered them and left them with the furtiveness of prairie animals: hushed entrances, quick bursts of dramatic conversation, quiet exits. All the while, Chance was conscious of her fingers intertwined with his; part of him wanted to comment on it, but the rest of him didn't want to break the precarious spell that might have made their clasp possible.

*

As they approached the city, the details of its stone walls came into greater relief, great bricks glowing orange by flickering torchlight, looming and intimidating, and they found more activity, people bustling back and forth, gathering in tight clusters and whispering in hushed voices. They slowed as they approached the city, giving its busy inhabitants wide berth. "I'm surprised it's so busy. It's got to be like, what? Two, three in the morning?" Cassie said, her voice quiet.

"Depends how long after the Seder they arrested Jesus. And these are probably all the same people who came to greet Jesus when he entered the city. He was staying on the other side of the Mount of Olives, so this is probably the same road he was using."

"Maybe we should get off it.

"We should be okay. They're all going to the Temple. Just happens this is the main road there."

The closer they approached the city, the bigger Chance realized it was. He'd known Jerusalem was a thriving metropolis, full of commerce and religion, a marvel of architecture and faith, but not until he stood in the shadow of those great walls did he realize their enormity.

They came soon to a large, ornate gate where men and women in thick robes and heavy garments loitered close together; some had ascended toward the wall-carved opening. High above the archway where the stairs disappeared, an intricate carving of what looked to be a city shone like bone, and at the top of the stairs, a line of people had queued up in front of two guards in heavy armor. "Looks like the way in,' Cassie said.

Chance nodded. "We just need to get near that big building right there," he said, pointing. The four turrets of Pilate's fortress blocked up against the darkness, a great, squat building enormous from their vantage, walls illuminated flickering orange, the scale astonishing. "Start up the time machine, and we'll sneak around everyone."

*

They wended their way up the steep stone steps to a platform where they found several Jewish guards and two Roman soldiers frozen, the latter distinguished by their ruddy armor and arrogant helmets. They ducked around and between the soldiers to find themselves inside Jerusalem, the great faithful city of saints with pasts and sinners with futures. Whereas the commerce of Manhattan and the contemporary cities Chance knew was traffic in futures and interests, tradings of bonds and ventures into capital, Jerusalem's currency was the faith of its inhabitants, its market decorated accordingly. Manhattan and Los Angeles were decorated by giant, beautiful faces selling youth and sex; in Jerusalem, the great glimmering Temple Dome sold salvation, or at least offered hope of it.

The city within the wall was an epiphany. Even from afar, the torches had reminded Chance of coppery stars, but up close he felt their heat and energy, vibrant and exciting. The immediate area within the walls was a courtyard before stone steps and the great dome. Proud columns rose to bloom into detailed masonry, and even the ground was spectacular, stone and marble, veined with sandy lifeblood and mosaic tiles. All around, frozen people's features caught in expressions of curiosity and concern and speculation, and Jerusalem came alive in a way it hadn't before, citizened by a million paused people otherwise just like Chance and Cassie.

Before them, the great Temple's dome gleamed silver on gold, situated on an enormous platform that reminded Chance of the parks he knew in Philadelphia and Manhattan, Love Park and Union Square, respectively, with their great walkways and piazzas, but it was at least ten times as big. The moon shone white on all that rock, populated by more people than Chance would have predicted, a crowd that surpassed one he would have expected to find near Times Square at ten at night.

To the right, beyond tall, leafy trees, Pilate's fortress loomed like some hard combination of penitentiary and barracks. Chance nodded toward it. "That's where we want to be. We can find a spot to hide in those trees and wait until they bring Jesus out." He led her forward, found a spot among the trees close to the fortress, with enough visibility to continue watching its courtyard, and Cassie settled next to him. He realized as they stopped that he had begun to sweat, but after a few moments he began to notice the dry, sandy chill in the sage-scented air. He shivered.

"Cold?" Cassie asked.

"Walking here got my blood up, but now that we're here, the toga doesn't protect much."

"Here," she said, and she took his hand, pulled his arm forward, and then before he realized what was happening, she was sitting between his legs, her back against his chest, and his arms were wrapped around her torso, while her arms, in turn, wrapped around his. "Body heat'll keep us warm," she told him, then, a moment later, "I can feel your heart beating."

Of course she could. Because her maneuver had pressed her body deliriously close to his, and he was overcome by her warmth and solid substantiality. "It does that."

"You're nervous. Or scared."

"I can't believe I'm here."

"I know what you mean," she said, but Chance thought they were talking about completely different things. Because while Cassie meant that part of her still couldn't believe what they had done, still couldn't believe that they had used a time machine to save Chance's father and then travel backward nearly two thousand years, what Chance meant was that he couldn't believe he was sitting there with her in his arms. Chance had never forgotten about her, but with age and time and distance, life had covered over his feelings for her with memories of nights in bars and beds with newly familiar girls, days in offices and apartment buildings. He realized, though, those feelings had never disappeared, and being with her had brought all those feelings back, not just the longing, but also the fear of acting on it.

Her in his arms. Her shawl against his ear and cheek, her body beneath the folds of her robe soft in his arms.

She shut off the time machine, and life and energy and urgency hummed back into the city and its citizens. Solemn people loitering together buzzed with anxiety and vigilance, tight knots of men and women who had lived and worked with Jesus, passed him on the street, sold him grain or wine—people whose eyes Jesus had held, whose hands Jesus had touched, whose hearts Jesus had found. Flickers returned to the torches set high upon their columns, and horseback Roman soldiers patrolled silent, brooding sentry.

Chance tried to be aware of his surroundings, but he discovered that once Cassie had settled into his arms, he couldn't think around her. He was two thousand years ago and fate had conspired to find him at the heart of

Jewish tradition on the very night of the trial of Jesus of Nazareth, but the most important thing in the world to him was not the man inside the Temple, the rabbi who was, even then, beginning the long road to condemnation, but rather the girl in his arms. He knew that outcomes were uncertain and who knew where the events to come would lead them, but he also knew that there was no one in the world he would have minded sharing an uncertain future with, because if the moments it brought could be more like the present one, it could go on and on and on.

And if the future didn't contain any moments like it, there was no reason he had to let it come at all. He'd live his life backward if it was the only way to keep moments like that one happening. Back back back until the beginning of time and beyond, if he had to, into a dark universe with nebulae like pinpricks in velvet—

You've always wanted to be here.

You know her.

You love her.

*

Sunrise over Jerusalem, above great walls the indigo sky brightened first to gunmetal, then light grey streaked with salmon swatches of clouds like burning embers blazed orange by oncoming dawn. Chance and Cassie remained in the shade of the trees just outside Antonia Fortress, watching the people filling the courtyard just to their north, but something bothered Chance. He couldn't figure out what until he realized he was watching the sunrise and remembered that the crucifixion itself was generally believed to have occurred around noon.

The trial preceding it, then, would have occurred well before then.

The trial preceding it should have been occurring even as he sat there.

But it was not. From among the trees in which they had found shelter, Chance could see a handful of people loitering to either side, groups of men and women entering and leaving the Temple Mount to their left and other people forming small groups in the courtyard to their right, just in front of the fortress, but there had been yet no sign of Pilate, nor of Jesus.

Cassie noticed when he began to become restless. "What's wrong?"

He told her.

"Maybe he's not here."

"But that's the Roman quarters. That's the barr—," he started to say before he stopped.

"What?"

"That's the barracks, but Pilate was governor. He wouldn't have stayed there. He was the Roman equivalent of the emperor, and Herod's palace was on the other side of the city—."

"Which is where he would have stayed—."

"Which is where we should be—."

"Because that's where the trial would have been."

"Shit," Cassie said, standing. "We need to go."

"Yeah," Chance said as he joined her. "We need to get to those three towers we saw on the way here."

Cassie turned on the time machine, freezing the sun on its ascent in the sky, and together they left the copse of trees to traverse Jerusalem and make their way to Herod's palace, to Pilate, and to the trial of Jesus of Nazareth.

26

As the maitre d' led them to a round table so close to those floor-to-ceiling windows it seemed in danger of falling out of them, Leonard dreamed up a million different things to say to Jennifer and another thousand ways to say them, but just as quickly dismissed them all. CIRTN had strict rules about time travel; the first was that any intervention had to be agreed upon by the internal ruling body and all members of the international council, and then only carried out by a handful of qualified operatives.

Leonard was not a qualified operative. He had an impressive CV and the kind of experience that can come only from working for a decade over a millennium, but he chosen not to seek authorization as an operative, because he had never wanted the responsibility intervention brought.

Leonard pulled Jennifer's chair back for her, then slipped into the seat opposite. He admired the lines of Jennifer's jaw and neck as she appreciated the eastbound view of Brooklyn and the great, grey East river. He couldn't help thinking of her body against his, and he wondered if this Jennifer's body differed, underneath her clothes.

"You don't look at me like most people," she told him when she caught him staring. "Most guys, they look at me like that and I feel like I should charge them by the minute."

"Sorry. I didn't—."

"That's what I mean. When you do it, I don't feel like you're about to start breathing heavy. Which is why I have a new theory."

"Having a new theory implies you had an old one."

"I did. Two. One of which was that you hoped I would be your unwitting yet startlingly attractive accomplice."

"Oh, right. Though I don't remember the 'startlingly' bit."

"I upgraded. I figure, I've never seen you before in my life and you invite me to dinner at a fancy restaurant, I earn 'startlingly.'"

"Fair enough," Leonard said, as he read down the winelist.

"Which brings us to my new theory."

"And this is a theory about why I'm here."

"And why you invited me to dinner. It's an all-encompassing theory."

A waiter materialized as if straight from the Safe. "Monsier and madame drinks?"

Leonard snapped the leather folder shut. "The Bordeaux, I believe, if that will be okay," he looked at Jennifer.

"Sure, I like red," Jennifer said, which made the waiter vanish as quickly as he had come. "So, do you want to hear my theory?"

Leonard smiled. "I'm all ears."

"I think Gabe sent you," she said, and with that she sat back, crossed her arms, and regarded Leonard with the sort of self-satisfied look only a beautiful woman can pull off.

"Gabe—oh, your brother. Gabriel. But—what? Why would—," Leonard started to ask, and then saw what Jennifer was thinking, and in it, perhaps, a way to save her without actually having to intervene.

*

Dinner a golden blur of candlelight gleams and incandescent bulbs on silver flatware, immaculate white china with gilt edges, deep burgundy wine in sparkling crystal glasses, lush green leaves and black seared steak and creamy pink sauce over pasta. Conversation at first click-clack sparring separated by semi-awkward pauses before Bordeaux sips lubed it slippy into the flirtatious banter of a strange first date between one person who assumed she'd been set up and another who both knew and loved the girl across from him in another universe entirely. She was both very different and very familiar; though the ways we behave and the choices we make might change, who we are does not. The details change, the places and situations that surround the decisions of life, but life itself does not. Life itself seems to be unable to.

The Jennifer he knew in Geneva, the Jennifer he had met uncertain years before and fallen in love with, was different from this Jennifer with whom he was on a date in Manhattan, but yet they shared similarities, too.

This Jennifer worked here, this Jennifer lived close by, probably across that bridge, in one of the boroughs, in a rent-controlled fourth-story walk-up with views of the buildings next door on either side. This Jennifer wore her hair differently but had the same neck; wore different glasses but regarded him with the same eyes; wore different clothes but filled them with the same body, which she used to make the same gestures he knew: the punctuative finger-points, the dismissive hand-flickers. Her brazen one-liners—

"I know it's just such a cliché to temp while you're exploring your options, but at least I'm not waiting tables. Not that there's anything wrong with that."

"The problem with American fiction is that its next great storytellers are Gaiman and Rowling, and they're both English."

"God, I hate that fucking show. Seriously, the best thing about that woman is that she married Ferris Bueller."

The details might have been different, but Leonard knew her. He might never have heard these particular opinions but he knew how she thought. Underlying their interactions: a familiarity, chemistry unchanged by the different physical laws of an alternate universe. When Jennifer started to talk about books, he wanted to interject something about either Salinger or Lee, two authors who had always impressed him if only for the sheer number of books they continued to publish. He might have stuck to a safe topic, like what she thought of the Beatles and their post-reunion albums, but those sorts of first-date topics weren't safe there.

But Leonard felt uncomfortable not being entirely truthful with her. It's easy to lie to someone you don't know, but lying to someone familiar takes effort, and every passing moment made it more difficult. Every passing moment also made it more likely that his contact with Race and reality would be reestablished, interrupting him before he could figure out what to do, what to say to her. Several times, he considered simply telling her outright, beginning to end, the whole story, but he didn't even know where to start. Given that her reality had not yet discovered intratemporal travel, she probably wouldn't have believed that he was from the future, and he didn't even know how to introduce to her the idea of an alternate reality.

He was relieved, then, when, after the waiter had cleared their dinner plates, the conversation came back around to more personal matters.

"And what about you?"

"What about me?" Leonard said.

"Well, let's see. You have a British accent, but it's filtered through somewhere else, and not America. I'm guessing somewhere in Europe, maybe Austria or Belgium. It explains the cut of your suit and your mannerisms. And of course there's your haircut. Not many men can pull off bald with such aplomb."

"I do my best."

"You wear it like a choice you'd make even if you had hair, which means it's functional. Maybe military. Also means you don't have to worry about it when you travel, which I'd wager you do a lot of considering the way you conduct yourself."

"And you've picked all this up as we've talked?"

"I picked up half of it the moment I saw you."

"What else have you picked up?"

She took a sip of her wine. "You're hiding something."

Leonard wanted to ask her what made her say that, but just her doing so caught him well enough that he didn't: the more things change, the more they stay the same.

"And your distinct lack of a response indicates I'm right," she said.

Leonard drained his wine glass. "Maybe I'm just impressed by everything else you just said."

"I can do you one better," she leaned back in her seat, letting her arms cross, her legs cross. "Gabe didn't send you here."

"What makes you say that?"

Jennifer smiled. "He would have called."

"Maybe he wanted to surprise you."

"Not before. During. If Gabe had sent you over here, he would have called a half hour in. To see how it was going, and to give me a reason to excuse myself if it wasn't going well. And even more than that, you're not acting like this is a date. You're acting like you already know me and have for a while, and like you're preoccupied with something else. All of which, I have to tell you, is a little unnerving."

Leonard hesitated before he realized that might well have been the very opening he'd been looking for. He'd been wondering how to tell her about physics and time travel, but maybe the best way to tell her was to talk about what those things were really about. "Yeah, about that, well, the truth is . . ." The words stopped on him.

But she said nothing, just waited.

He took a deep breath. The world and the restaurant seemed to fade in favor of the woman in front of him. This woman he knew from a different world, a different reality, a different tomorrow entirely. This woman looked at him with the same curious, deep green eyes he had come in recent malleable years to love. This woman knew him, or at least should have. This woman deserved honesty.

"The truth is you're right. Gabe didn't send me, and this wasn't meant to be a date. The truth is that I'm acting like I already know you because I do. And I admit the details I know are different, like what you do and the clothing you wear and where you get your haircut, but I know you well enough to know those are really just details and I know more important stuff underneath."

For a moment, Jennifer said nothing. She didn't even move, utterly still, eyes on him, slightly narrowed. No sign of either incredulity or acceptance. No hint that she believed him and was going to leave or that she thought he was lying but was going to stay anyway. For one excruciating moment that seemed so damned long it had to have begun all over again, realities and alternates popping into and out of existence while Leonard held his breath.

Their waiter appeared. Their dishes had already been bussed and their wine glasses had been drained to the bottom of the bottle. "Can I interest you in a dessert?"

Leonard looked at Jennifer, who said, "No, no dessert."

Leonard swallowed. "I suppose not, then. Just—."

"Some coffee, though. Especially after that wine. Maybe a nice Irish coffee?"

The waiter looked at Leonard. "Sir?"

"I'll have mine Sicilian."

"Very good, sir," the waiter said and headed off.

Even after the waiter had gone, Leonard didn't say anything. He was still waiting for Jennifer to speak.

"I bet you're waiting for me to ask you what you meant."

"No, I'm just—."

"I'm not going to," she told him, leaning her long fingers against her cheek. "I'm not going to pretend I understood you, mind you, but it sounded like you were being completely honest right then. It sounded like you knew exactly what you meant and you weren't holding back, and it makes me want to be honest with you. Can I be honest with you, Leonard?"

"Always," Leonard said. Across time, across space, across realities. Always.

Jennifer nodded as if she had expected that answer, and really she had no reason not to. "You know those things I said while we were eating?"

"Which ones? The ones about Gaiman or the ones about Ferris Bueller?"

Jennifer shook her head. "No, this is not the time to be disingenuous, okay? We're being honest, and I meant what I said about your accent, and your haircut. Those things," she said, and she waited, then, until Leonard nodded. When he did, she continued: "I knew those things right away. I don't know how, and I can't explain it, but I feel like I know you somehow. You're setting off every warning bell I've got, but I'm ignoring them because I feel like I know you. You lied to me about my brother. You've been hiding something from me since the moment I saw you. And I don't know what to do with that, but I know it's the truth," she told him, just as the waiter reappeared with their coffees. He set one in front of Jennifer, a clear, crystal goblet with a layer of thick cream over chocolate-deep coffee.

In front of Leonard, the waiter placed a crystal mug full of caramel-colored coffee beneath a thin layer of froth. Leonard sipped it, warm and stinging with flavors of Amaretto and Dixie whiskey. After the waiter had again retreated, Leonard said, "I might know why you feel like you know me."

Jennifer shook her head. "I know you do, Leonard, and while we're being so candid and not holding anything back, I'd appreciate it if you told me why, the moment you stepped off the elevator, the moment I saw you, I felt like I knew you even though I've never set eyes on you before."

Leonard sipped his coffee. Even when the answer to his dilemma was staring him in the face, quite literally, still part of him hesitated. But he fought that part, and finally he said, "Look, can we go somewhere?" Because how do you tell your date that you know her from an alternate reality in the middle of the dinner crowd?

"Is that a 'can we go somewhere so I can avoid answering the question,' or is that an 'I know the answer to that question but would rather not tell you here, in the middle of one of the busiest hours in the most popular restaurant at one of the most famous tourist destinations in the world'?"

"It's certainly the latter."

"But you will tell me?"

"I'll tell you everything, but I can't tell you here or now."

27

Jerusalem on the morning of the trial of Jesus of Nazareth bustled. The upper city, with white columns and newly constructed buildings, loomed to the north over the lower city, parchment-yellow with erosion by time and wind. Chance and Cassie followed an uneven path toward the towers, ascending in places toward those newer structures, descending in others into places where jagged stones cracked through the walkways. Charcoal clouds smudged away the sun, leaving the world grey-washed and somber.

All around them, the city was in the midst of coming to life. People paused in public ablutions, hands plunged into stone basins, water sprayed up and around them as they splashed their faces clean. Many were already dressed and on their way in the same direction as Chance and Cassie.

Some of the walkways were punched into disarray by wayward tree roots and weed clefts, but much more appeared to be brand new marble, its surface sheened by dawnlight and its veins. Along the way, they encountered areas where bazaar stalls stood in quiet repose with white linen sheets and ornately decorated rugs hung down their sides, awaiting their merchants' returns to display again their stocks.

Chance's thigh muscles ached by the time they reached Jerusalem's Western wall, where layers and angles crowded against each other. The narrow path opened suddenly onto a sizable but strangely empty courtyard. Above their heads spired those three impressive towers, greater at the closer distance, intricately carved and wondrously gilted turrets that stood proud and reached for the wispy clouds above. Through a large, arched gate in the opposite wall, Chance could see a throng of people.

"I think we found where everyone went," Cassie whispered.

They crossed the gate to descend the outer steps, down into the valley beyond; in the distance, the land stretched emerald and taupe, rural hills and vales where shepherds would tend their flocks. Immediately, however, a crowd of people formed a huge, confused mass into which Chance and Cassie insinuated themselves. The people's attention was focused on a platform at the top of stairs set into the wall Chance and Cassie had just crossed, and upon the top step stood several men, one with a close-cropped Caesarian haircut, wearing a breastplate that gleamed dully in the fresh light of a new dawn. He was far enough away that, to Chance, his garments looked bloody, a patchwork of colors like scab-colored rust and gold-highlit crimson. His mouth open, paused mid-proclamation. His right arm was raised, palm facing downward, in a gesture that reminded Chance of the Third Reich's salute to Hitler—

"That's Pilate, isn't it," Cassie said, and Chance nodded because he thought it was.

Beside pillars to either flank, four Centurions stood next to the gesturing man, two right and two left, their helmets jutting high above their heads, and finally, between them, Jesus of Nazareth, short among the Romans, dwarfed by society and the government and the city all around him. Columns and pillars and proud towers rising into the dawn, but among them stood one man whose small body was draped with some sort of purple robe; from the distance, Chance could not make out any thistle-crown, the features of Jesus' face obscured by both facial hair and gore, swollen beyond recognition.

"Looks like we got here just in time," Chance said.

Cassie's fingers found the controls on the time machine, rumbling life and noise back into the world so hard Chance realized he hadn't been ready for either. The evening road to Jerusalem and its early morning hours had been quiet to the point of near silence, but motion brought cacophony, thousands of people and voices and motives. Over the crowd that had gathered in front of the Western wall settled the kind of hyperbolic bedlam most people associated only with Times Square on New Year's Eve or post-World Series riots.

The man with the Caesar cut and the blood-clot colored vestments, controlled the attention of the crowd, and beneath his steely gaze the terrible discordant cry of the people subsided to hungry anticipation. "*Ecce homo,*" the man said. Behold the man.

Pilate continued to speak, but Chance understood nothing more than his control over his audience. He understood nothing besides that Pilate held the kind of strict authority that came not solely with compliance but moreso with the subjects' knowledge that anyone who disagreed would find themselves nailed to a cross. Pilate stalked back and forth upon the stone-cut *praetorium* upon which he had established authority; beside him, Jesus of Nazareth stood quietly. Pilate strutted and shouted, pomped and circumstanced upon the stage, but Jesus of Nazareth stood beside him, resolutely still, a silent observer patiently awaiting fate he believed already decided.

Pilate addressed a long diatribe to the crowd that Chance only understood in terms of spittle and despotism. He engaged in a brief question-and-answer session with the dark-robed men at the front of the courtyard, but his conviction didn't waver, his message clear; he was the Roman governor, and Jerusalem was his city. If its prisoners did not beg his mercy, they provoked his wrath, which was, judging by his demeanor, voluminous. He punctuated every utterance with a pointed finger or sweeping gesture; like so many of the modern-day Italians Chance knew, Pilate spoke with his passionate hands and emphasized with his muscular arms.

When Pilate seemed satisfied he had made his point, two more Centurions emerged from the building behind them, bearing between them a large beam; Chance didn't mean to gasp when he saw it, but he couldn't help it. Images acquired through years of Sunday school: the scourging and the Stations of the Cross, the silhouette of the crucifix on purple felt banners with golden letters.

He felt Cassie's hand on his shoulder. She didn't ask if he was okay, just moved her consoling hand to his back, didn't move, didn't speak. Pilate barked a handful of short words before shoving Jesus, who stumbled forward so hard he staggered down onto the stairs.

"Wasn't there another guy? Did we just completely miss Barrabas?" Cassie asked.

Chance shook his head. "When you translate it, 'Barabbas' just means 'son of the father.' My theology professor told us that was Pilate's way of mocking him for teaching the 'Our father.' There's a good possibility the only important prisoner Pilate ever had was the one we're looking at."

The four soldiers fastened around Jesus' wrists the great beam they'd hoisted between them, even as Pilate swaggered two, then three steps, addressing the crowd as he descended. In one swift, cruel movement, he reached down, grabbed the beam with both hands, and yanked upward. Jesus grunted through clenched teeth as he struggled to his feet, then staggered forward when Pilate pushed his back, down the stairs one shuffling step after another. Chance could see, as Jesus moved closer, the glistening wounds on his body.

Before Jesus, the throng of people who had gathered parted. People with whom he had worshipped and prayed, but most of all people with whom he had lived and loved. People who, less than a week before, had greeted with open arms and unabashed jubilation Jesus and the ass he'd ridden in on, but who now moved quietly aside as the four Roman soldiers prodded him forward. Chance saw nothing but terrified faces, faces not without compassion but neither without trepidation. The people around him were not faint of heart, just scared of the governor. If they had encouraged Pilate, it was because they were afraid not to.

Chance had to swallow to keep from being sick when he saw Jesus' back; he thought, at first, that they hadn't actually removed Jesus' linen garments until he realized, no, that was shredded skin, peeled away, hanging loosely from his body. The Roman scourge contained bits of metal and bone woven into the leather cords, and he wondered if the small, white fragments he could see in the center of Jesus' back were bits of the whip that had broken off or parts of spine.

The two soldiers trailed Jesus, pressing him along. Twice they poked their swords into his buttocks, and then, when he still, apparently, was not moving fast enough, one of them pushed so hard at the beam of wood that it toppled Jesus over, who cried out in pain.

Chance couldn't just watch anymore. It was a miracle on the level of loaves and fishes that the fall hadn't killed Jesus, that the giant damned piece of wood strapped to his wrists hadn't snapped his neck. He had to do something, anything, and he started to move.

Cassie grabbed his arm. "What're you doing?"

"I don't know," he said, tearing from her grasp to push through the people in front of him, beyond them to the soldiers. When he got to Jesus, he bent and pulled him up by the armpits. Jesus groaned as he did so, and Chance struggled to keep from retching on the scent of blood and sweat, then struggled harder when he was grabbed from behind and yanked backward so hard he lost his footing. Shouting behind him, and he felt spittle against the back of his neck, could smell the cloying scent of freshly polished armor and unwashed cloth, before more hands than he could count shoved him down to the ground. He felt knees in his back, pushing the breath out of him and preventing him from getting it back, and then he felt a sudden, enormous weight across his shoulders and over his back.

At first, he struggled, but the soldiers held him fast and lashed rough cord tight around his forearms. Thick rope tight around his wrists, knotting the heavy beam across his back, and then they pulled on the wood, raised high the long beam so hard it strained his heart in his chest and sweat popped out on his head.

Cassie has pushed her way to the front of the crowd, but when he shook his head, she paused, staring at him. He flexed the backs of his shoulders, his traps and his lats, feeling the wood cut coldly into his skin. He pressed his left foot forward, steeled himself, bent his waist and crooked his knees as he balled his hands into fists, accepting the beam Jesus had carried across his own back. He sucked in a breath, and though it was not comfortable, though the wood grain ground into his skin, he realized he could hold it.

He could stand.

As he stepped forward, the guards shouted at him again. Their tone demanded response, but he couldn't parse their syllables enough to attempt one.

All around him, the same people in the crowd who had bowed their heads a moment before shouted in response. "*Yehoshua ex Kirioth,*" one said; another, "*Yuchanan ex Galilee.*"

"*Simon,*" several people shouted. "*Simon ex Cyrene.*"

It was the *ex* that did it, that finally brought the language to breathing life in his head. Chance knew *ex*. *Exeunt. Ex scientia vera. Ex post facto. Extemporaneous.* In Latin: out of, or from.

The soldiers had asked who Chance was, and the crowd was trying to tell them. In Latin. *Yehoshua ex Kerioth*: Joshua from Kerioth.

His first thought was of Anthony Hopkins' Hannibal Lecter, *quid pro quo*, Clarice, but that made him remember the legal forms he had processed during his stint temping at the law firm, all of which had contained such sporadic phrases. *Caveat emptor. Habeas corpus. Pro bono.* Buyer beware; you may have the body; for good. All the motions he had helped to draft had contained those phrases: whereas the plaintiff *et cetera*, pursuant to the defendant *ad nauseum*, so shall it be *ad infinitum*.

"*Sine nomine*," he said. I have no name. "*Nolo contendere. Pax vobiscum.*" I do not wish to contend. Peace be with you.

The soldiers eyed him.

He didn't have an endless supply of Latin words, so he had to make what few he had count. He flexed his shoulders so he could sink to one knee as he bowed his head. "*Pax vobiscum. Pax Romanum. Serviam summa cum laude*," he told them. Peace be with you. Peace be with Rome. I will serve with highest praise.

The soldiers sighed, and one said something that sounded like "*Surga*," but Chance didn't move until the soldier grabbed him by the hair and yanked him to his feet. "*Surga. Surga.*"

Rise.

"*Mea culpa*," Chance said. My fault.

The soldier shoved Jesus forward. "*Progredi*," he said, and Jesus, now unburdened, shuffled forward. "*Sequitur*," the soldier said to Chance, nodded toward Jesus, and so, when Jesus passed him on the path, Chance followed him, scritch-scratching after Jesus over loose sand and small pebbles to continue north, following a wall that traced along the Western boundary of Jerusalem. The crowd followed them, a great, seething mass of people whose number did not seem to change at all.

*

They came to ground that sloped downward. Jesus stumbled, put his arms out to catch himself but tumbled anyway, settling sanguine on the bank. Chance wasn't sure Jesus was going to get up; he wasn't sure he would have, under the circumstances.

Cassie surged forward from the crowd, pulling off her shawl as she moved. She helped Jesus to his feet and, once he had regained them, wiped his face. The soldiers rushed forward, and Chance wanted intercede but could not, not with that giant, heavy damned beam strapped to his back. He just wanted to keep them from touching her, from hurting her.

A long ago memory of Miss Lewte's Sunday school lesson: Mary Magdalene's first encounter with Jesus after he had left his tomb. "*Noli tangere*," Chance said. Don't touch.

The soldiers paused, looked at him.

"*Noli tangere*," he told them, more quietly now he had their attention. Because she was a woman, the Roman government wouldn't bother with the *praetorium*, the trial and sentence and crucifixion; the soldiers could simply stone her on the spot. He thought of another legal phrase from a nuptial clause. "*Est uxor.*" She is my wife.

The soldiers eyed him. "*Uxor?*"

Chance nodded.

One of the soldiers shrugged, while another ushered Cassie back into the crowd.

"Thank you," Chance said, forgetting his tongue, then, quickly, "*Gracia. Grazi,*" he figured one of the two was close to what he meant, and then he continued forward at the behest of the soldiers. The beam across his shoulders seemed to be gaining weight as he went, and the softer sand beneath his feet felt less supportive. He struggled for secure purchase as he followed the way of Jesus, whom the soldiers helped descend the valley bank and then continue up the other side. The soles of Chance's sandals scritched on loose pebbles and small rocks, but Chance tried hard not to hesitate or pause, just continue onward, but then his heel slipped. He struggled to keep his balance but found it impossible. He fell first to his ass before the beam hit the ground and cartwheeled his body half-backward over itself as he slid down the slope he was descending behind Jesus. By the grace of God, he did not break his neck; the hard wood jarred against it, and his injured shoulder shot serrated pain down his back and side. His right ankle twisted, pitching his body sideways and driving the end of the beam into the ground, and then his body came to rest with the wood stuck in the dirt and his body arched diagonally to support it. The leather cords around his wrists burned so hard into his skin his fingers had gone numb, while frigid pain creaked through his body, freezing him in place. All his muscles above his abdomen felt like bone, ossified and unable to move.

He slipped down the slope, but, by tensing his leg muscles, found footing again when he reached the cracked, dried mud at the bottom, pausing before he set his sights on scaling the other side. Because of the position of the beam on his shoulders, though, he found greater stability in climbing, the distribution of the wooden weight balancing down upon him, and Chance pushed on, forward, up, and so hard he nearly collided with Jesus as he overtook the crest.

His sudden stop made him look up. From the bottom, there, with his head lowered as he climbed, Chance hadn't been able to see the top of the small dune. Several meters ahead stood three thick, dark wooden poles looming into the sky. The two on the right and the left were bare, but the one in the middle bore a makeshift plaque on which had been marked four words: *Iesus Nazare, Rex Iudaia.*

The soldiers said something quick to Jesus, then went to Chance and spoke. When Chance didn't understand what they said, they repeated it, louder, but Chance's brain had shut down; he found he could only goggle at that pole. Pain burst behind his knee when one of the soldiers kicked it, and Chance sank down before the pole with the horizontal shaft of the crucifix of Jesus of Nazareth strapped to his back and holding his arms wide. He bowed his head because he couldn't stand to look at it.

The weight of the beam pulled Chance's body forward and downward, but the soldiers grabbed his hair and yanked his body back until the heavy wood pulled his arms earthward and his head lolled. He could see only white, the sky, could feel only the excruciating pain, the fear that shot across his chest and threatened to rend his pectoral muscles asunder. His injured left shoulder wrenched under his skin to grind bone against bone. His breath heaved and shuddered in his chest and he wanted to scream, to cry, but found he could not.

The solders cut the cord around his left wrist and his limp arm flopped against his side, the heft of the beam pulling his crumpling body over it. When the soldier cut loose his right wrist and pulled away the wood, Chance rolled on his side as his knees slipped from beneath him and an involuntary scissor-kick shuddered through his legs. Every breath constricted his throat and made him want to gag. He slipped backward down the slope, stopped finally upon his back, right arm draped over his face. The sky so bright, so white. He squinted, reached and grasped for numbness, for sanctuary, for deliverance and salvation—

Hands. On his face. His cheeks. "Chance. Stay with me, Chance."

Cassie.

Her fingers forced his eyes open: painful, blinding brightness. Her hand gripped his cheeks. "No, come on Chance. I need you to stay with me."

The darkness and chill washing through his body was so calming, so inviting, he just wanted to bathe in it, bask in it, embrace it, but he couldn't leave her, not here, not like this. He groaned. Swallowed. Started to roll to his right, but his left side—he cursed, his pain the only coherent thing in the world. His voice cracked when he said, "My arm."

When her fingers touched his shoulder he could feel them in his nerves. Cold sweat popped out on his forehead as she probed his shoulder. "It's dislocated," she said. "This is going to hurt," she told him, and he started to ask what she was going to do, but screaming white pain lightninged across his shoulders, through his arms, throbbing up in his wrists where he could still feel the echoes of leather bindings, before a low, rumbling ache like thunder settled deep into his back and shoulders and neck.

He lurched upward, forward, rolled to his knees until his forehead was on the ground, his left arm clutched close to his body. He pounded his fist into the dirt, splaying his fingers to dig them in, clenched and unclenched them through the sand. Back two thousand years, and for what? To carry a plank of wood a few hundred yards, to nearly pass out at the feet of Jesus?

He looked up, vision blurred by tears, and saw Jesus, sanguine over the beam. The soldiers crouched on either side of him, holding long stakes over Jesus' palms, and they raised high their hammers before driving them down down down, crack-clang. Two dark jets of wet blood arced out over their heads. Jesus cried out, so loud unto the heavens that Chance thought it demanded a response, but none came from the peaceful clouds accumulated over the Holy City, and the soldiers raised their mallets again. Chance screamed, but they continued their upswing as Jesus kicked his legs, his body writhing with seizure and with pain, and Chance pounded the sand again, screaming for them to stop, please, like he had wanted to scream for the World Trade Center not to fall, like he had wanted to scream at Geisel to leave Cassie alone: stop, don't do it, undo, undo. Every muscle in his body screamed with the debilitating knowledge that he was helpless to do a single fucking thing about it.

Together, the four soldiers raised high that humble beam of the carpenter, hoisting it toward the center pole while a fifth settled Jesus' feet upon a block on that pole. That fifth soldier took another stake and, as if it were routine, as if he did it every day of his life, drove it down through Jesus' feet to fix them to the block.

Through it all, the crowd made little noise: some bit their knuckles and gasped into their hands, and the ones who had wished against the penalty, the ones who believed it was too harsh but were afraid to speak against either the governor or the high priests—they bent and retched into the desert sand. The soldiers did not speak, only carried out their swift punishment as if it were a duty. As they stepped back to admire their handiwork, Chance felt Cassie's hands on his bruised and exhausted body, easing him forward and upward, to his feet. He sank against her, and when she said, "Come on, we don't need to be here," he nodded and let her lead him away.

As she turned him away from the scene, as she led him through the crowd, he heard the final words of the man on the cross, which neither implored deliverance nor demanded reason for having been forsaken.

Consummatum est.

It is finished.

*

Cassie led Chance along the wall, along the valley, eastward following the great northern wall of Jerusalem to their right. They left behind the crowd, and he shuffled along with her, his left arm stiffening close to his side. The ground was uneven, the sand loose, but they finally came to the bridge they had taken from Gethsemane, and they crossed it back again to find themselves on the Mount of Olives. The upward slope looked different in the daylight, the bark on the tree shredded in fine detail, the dirt paths tan among twisted roots. Leaves that had appeared only dark the night before stood in green relief, palm fronds and long, taupe branches with grey microfilaments peeling away from the bark like cornhusks.

They didn't speak until they found a spot near the top of the slope with a cluster of large rocks and small boulders where they could rest. "Okay?" she asked as she helped him off his feet, off his tired legs.

"I think so."

She checked his shoulder. "It's probably going to be stiff for a while."

He didn't need to test it to know she was right.

"Jesus Christ, Chance, what were you thinking?" she tore off her shawl, tossing it to the ground. "It's one thing to want to know what happened, but one minute you're standing next to me, and then the next you're on the damned ground and a bunch of Roman soldiers are—."

"I know what happened, Cass. But thanks for reminding me. If you weren't here, I might have forgotten—."

"If I weren't here, they might have turned around and seen your ass on the ground and decided to hang it up next to his."

"That wouldn't have happened."

"How would you know? Nobody knows what happened right now. You said you just wanted to see—."

"I didn't change anything," Chance said, his voice louder and closer to breaking than he had planned. He folded his right arm across his chest a moment, then decided against it and used it to leverage himself to his feet. "I saw his back, and I saw him fall, and I—I mean, shit, Cassie, did you see them? Did you see them hammer those giant nails into his wrists?"

"Of course I saw it. You do realize I was right there while you were doing it, don't you? You realize you plunged ahead and left me behind in that crowd, don't you?"

He realized, then, how lucky they had been. How his actions could have gotten them both into a lot more trouble. "No, I—it wasn't like that."

"It's exactly what it was like. We came all the way back to Jerusalem, and what do you do when we get here? You jump out of the crowd to play the hero."

"I wasn't trying to play the hero. I just couldn't sit back and watch it happen."

"So you just stepped forward to help carry the cross—."

"But it didn't matter. They called me Simon. And he's in the Bible, so nothing's really changed. Jesus still gets arrested and crucified, and as far as the rest of the world is concerned, at some point some random guy people called Simon carries the cross."

"But what if you had changed it? What if some random guy named Simon had stepped forward, and the Romans had crucified him instead? What if Simon had ended up on the cross, giving up his life for a man he believed was the Messiah? What if they—?"

"Look, I didn't plan it, okay?" Chance said. He looked at the dome of the Temple Mount, big and proud but obscured by haze and clouds. "I wasn't thinking about him as the guy people pray to. I just wanted to help him. I'm sorry if I wasn't supposed to, and I'm sorry if you wish I hadn't, and I'm sorry I might've screwed up the universe or whatever—."

"Oh for God's sake, do you really think that's why I'm upset? The paradoxes you might have caused? I know you mean well, but sometimes I wonder about you."

"What the hell's that supposed to mean?"

"It means I was worried about you. It means I saw you carrying that damned cross and I was scared you were next. It means I couldn't get to you to try to help. It means—."

"I get it," he said. He exhaled, looking back toward Jerusalem. Indigo clouds blotted the sky like stratospheric hematomas, and the leaves on the trees all around them shivered. A few fat raindrops fell from the bruise-dark clouds. "We should get back to our stuff."

They walked deeper into the trees, where the leaves provided inconsistent shelter from the rain and none at all from the chill wind. Branches shook and roiled as he and Cassie passed them. "You know where we're going?" Cassie asked.

"I think so."

They walked another minute or two in silence before Cassie said, "I didn't mean to blow up at you. I was just—."

"It's my fault. I let the moment get the better of me. I thought I could help him."

"You did," Cassie said.

"For all the good it did."

"I wonder if you haven't gotten so wrapped up in results you've forgotten what 'good' actually means. You know you did all you could, right? And not just back there. You were saying earlier how you wished you could have done something last month, when the Trade Center fell, but what could you have done? You're beating yourself up because you couldn't stop it, but who short of Superman could have? You need to stop focusing so much on whether what you did had the results you wanted and remember that you still did good."

"I did what anyone would've done."

Cassie grabbed his hand. "You did something a lot of people wouldn't have, and not because he was Jesus or someone made you, but because you thought you could help. That's worth a lot more than you're giving it credit for."

Chance looked down at her hand on his wrist. His eyes burned with tears he tried to hold back, but finally he found he couldn't. When they came, he tried to turn away from her, his shoulders twitching. "Just—just give me a minute. I don't—," he said, but that was when his voice broke away, and she pulled him back toward her, opening her arms to accept him into them.

"I know. You wanted to do more. You wanted to help more. But sometimes I think you want to do so much good you forget all the good you've already done. You're beating yourself up because you couldn't help that man avoid dying on the cross, but you're forgetting that you came back two thousand years just to be here. You forget that you show up at his trial, and what do you do? You step forward and you help him carry his fucking cross."

"But what difference did it make?" he asked. He felt a density, a dark pressure, pressing against him, constraining him.

"Stop worrying about what difference it made and start realizing the difference you just made."

"But I didn't. The world—."

"Forget the world, Chance. Forget the universe, and forget the physics, and forget gods and faith and religions. Because maybe you didn't make a difference in any of those things, but there's a man who just died, and you made a difference to him. He had a message that we should love each other, and in the very final moments before that man gave up his life for what he believed in, you proved his life and his message weren't hollow. If that man died believing his life was worth something, it's because you showed him."

"I think you're giving me—."

"Too much credit? More than you deserve? You just traveled backward in time two thousand years and carried the cross of Jesus of Nazareth. If anything at all, I think you're downplaying the monumental fucking reality of what you just did."

With those words, she cracked him open. The tears came hot but with some relief. Sunrays chose that moment to shine through the storm clouds above and palm fronds all around them, flooding their private grove with warmth and shimmer even through rainshower.

He wiped his eyes as he pulled back from her. "Sorry, I——."

"If you're planning to apologize for being emotional, don't," she palmed his cheek.

His head moved without his meaning it to, toward her fingertips, and then, when she watched him kiss each of her fingers in their turn, he pulled her face to his, her lips to his. Her lips: uncertain at first until they accepted possibility. At first surprise before she clutched him like she meant to, like he would have hoped, like she wanted him, too, and her hands found his shoulders, her nimble fingers through the hair at the back of his neck. Chance sometimes thought of kisses as unfamiliar territory— drunken lips stumbling against each other in the dark corner of a bar's booth, awkwardly brushing together at first like strangers on a train—but kissing Cassie felt like home.

His body clenched with desire deeper than merely possessing her; he wanted to take care of her, to hold her, to keep her safe. His arms wrapped around her wonderfully tangible body, so solid against him. He wanted her present certainty, and they culminated possibilities in defiant protest of uncertain flux. The world could spin around them and all of time could continue ever onward and ever backward in endless permutations from their present moment, but there and then Chance could kiss her, and that alone could be constancy enough. If the entire universe had come into existence and all of history led up to the moment of his lips on hers, it might well have been meaning enough.

When finally their lips parted, still he clutched her to him, his hands on the nape of her neck and the long curve of her back. He could feel her breath hot and close on his neck. He heard her lick her lips and swallow, her breath gentle breeze, and when she spoke, her voice soft and low and warm in his ear. "That was just like I remembered it."

Suddenly, Chance was twelve again. "Everyone else was swimming, but we snuck behind the snack bar to sit under the elm tree. You wore a blue bathing suit, and your cold tongue tasted like Cherry Coke. You smelled like coconuts."

She laughed. "I'm not the only one who remembers."

"Who forgets his first kiss?"

Cassie eased back, her smile the brightest thing in the world. "That was your first, too?"

Chance nodded.

She squinted at him as if attempting to cull something just from looking at him. "You never kissed me again."

Chance's thoughts stuttered. "No—I—but—."

"But you wanted to."

"'Course I wanted to. Always. But I—after I asked you out the one time—."

"When did you ever ask me out?"

"My sophomore year of high school. You don't remember?"

"What'd I say?"

"You laughed. You said we always go out together."

Cassie burst out laughing. "Did I really? That's hysterical."

"Well it wasn't back then."

"I'll bet."

"No, seriously," Chance said. The rain had begun to fall harder, and he took her hand to lead her further on. "You really never knew I had such a thing for you? I was—even my dad told me I needed to stop mooning over you. I was crushed when you said no—."

"But I didn't. 'We always go out together'? Does that sound like the sort of answer you'd get from a girl who understood the question? I had no idea. I mean, come on, me and my big old glasses, and my stupid braces?"

"When I saw the picture your dad had up in your living room, when I saw how much you had changed, I just thought, yeah, that's how beautiful I always thought you were," he told her. "But I was always scared. That maybe it wouldn't work out, and we'd break up, and then we never would've been comfortable around each other, trying to be friends."

"And we never would've ended up here, but here we are."

28

Check paid, Leonard descended the Tower with Jennifer, then traversed the concourse to exit into the kind of balmy twilight that can only exist in September. The moment they passed through the doors, Leonard tugged at his earlobe, but still found no connection. With dinner behind them and Jennifer next to him and twilight falling all over Manhattan, he felt both greater urgency and greater fear. Though he was acquainted with some of the concepts involved in the quantum mechanics of traveling through time, he wouldn't have known where to begin to attempt to repair his implant even had he been in a place where he was familiar with the technology. As it stood, he thought this current world was far behind the technological advances CIRTN had made; even if its gadgets, its phones and credit cards, were similar in principle, they probably were not in technology.

As it stood, all he was really certain of was that he needed to warn Jennifer. The doors opened onto a great expanse of bone-white plaza above which the twin towers of the World Trade Center loomed into deepening blue twilight. An enormous, irregular sphere the color of tarnished pennies squatted over a fountain in the center, around which a lip of bench formed a long circle, while fast-food restaurants lined the perimeter. Food kiosks and information booths dotted the courtyard.

It was as good a place as any. "Can we sit?" Leonard said, and they found a spot on the benchlip, far enough from most of the sightseers and businessmen leaving for the night, but close enough to be part of the energy. "You ever wonder if there's more out there than this?"

Jennifer looked out at the crowd, then, at the other people gathered around the plaza. A man with greying hair encouraged his pig-tailed daughter to toss a coin into the fountain. "You're not about to try to sell me on some religion or something, are you?"

"What? No. I'm—what?"

"Just, whenever you hear someone ask if you think there might be more to life, they're trying to sell you some God."

"No, that wasn't—I meant literally."

"What, like aliens or something? *Men in Black*, Will Smith and Tommy Lee Jones? You're not going to tell me you're from another planet, are you?"

Leonard looked out at the fountain. When he said, "I might as well be," it was more to himself than to her.

"Oh, Jesus, you're not a—are you a Scientologist? Because if I'm ever going to be audited, it's going to be by the IRS."

"What—I mean, yeah, of course I'm a Scientologist, but what do taxes have to do with anything?"

"What?"

"You mentioned auditing—."

"Isn't that what you do? The whole Dianetics thing?"

"I don't know what you're talking about."

"Scientology? Tom Cruise."

"The arch-bishop of Pacifica?" Leonard hadn't thought this reality had any Union-States. He sighed. "Look, that's a digression we don't need to make at this point. I told you I was going to try to explain what was going on, and why you felt like you know me. And I think you feel like you know me because, in another time, and another place, you do."

"What does that even mean? Another time and place? Like when I went to London last year?"

Leonard shook his head. "No, farther than that," he started, but dropped off before he went on because he realized he wasn't going to get anywhere down that line. He had to start from the beginning. All the way back. "Do you know Shakespeare?"

"The playwright? Of course."

"Just yesterday, or close to, I was in Elizabethan England watching a performance of *Macbeth* as part of a job I perform for the International Council for Temporal and Nuclear Research. I was trying to determine the actual authorship of the plays when my supervisor contacted me. Our computers monitor spacetime, and they detected an anomaly. That anomaly turned out to be you."

"Me?"

"Not you in particular. This world. You're living in an alternate reality, and I think the reason you feel like you know me is that, in reality, in the real reality, the original reality, you're my girlfriend."

"Right. Yes, of course," Jennifer said, though Leonard noticed she inched subtly away as she did so. "That's how I know you. I'm your girlfriend. From an alternate realit—."

"Not from an alternate reality. From actual reality. This is the alternate reality."

"And you're here because . . ."

"Someone in this reality built a time machine and decided to use it. They're going to change history and create a moment where this reality breaks off from mine. I need to figure out when that happens, because we need to prevent it." He was surprised by how relieved telling the truth made him feel.

"What'll happen if it does?"

"I don't know. We've never seen an alternate reality before. We weren't even sure they existed until we found yours."

"So where are they? Whoever's got the time machine, I mean."

"So far the best lead I've come up with was Hitler."

"Hitler?"

"World War Two? The Nazi party—."

"I know who Hitler is. But why come to New York, then?"

"I'm just here to do the research."

"And take me to dinner."

"That wasn't planned. I probably shouldn't even be here right now. I should be trying to figure how to get back in touch with my supervisor—."

"'Get back in touch'?"

"I got cut off from them when I got here," he said. As he did so, the streetlights all around the plaza clicked on as though finally deciding that fast-food neon and business office fluorescent couldn't provide enough illumination in the encroaching evening. "I thought the extra height would help, and they were watching this building when I left."

"Why?"

Leonard looked up at the two Towers, two enormous squares blocking into indigo. Some of the windows blazed golden, occupied by men still trading funds or crunching numbers, people talking to Tokyo or Singapore or Hong Kong. Manhattan never slept because neither money nor business ever do. For that matter, neither does life. "Because it wasn't here."

"It wasn't— . . ." Jennifer started, but her confused voice trailed off as she looked around at the plaza, the people still bursting around the fountain, business managers finished with their days and ready to begin their nights. Happy-hour drinks at local pubs or trains up to Grand Central and then on to Westchester or Connecticut or New Jersey. "Here?"

"When we found your reality, they—I suppose they were looking for landmarks. I never asked, but that's what I'd have done. This one wasn't here."

"What, like they didn't build it? They used the Chrysler building, or MetLife—."

"No. It had been here. But by the time we found you, it wasn't. It was gone. All that was left was a dustcloud about a mile across and a couple of beams of light."

"But it's right—," Jennifer started to say, but stopped herself. "So, wait. You're telling me that, in addition to being a man from a different reality, you're also from a future where these two buildings don't exist."

"I know it's probably not easy to believe—."

"So what happened to them? A bomb?"

"Planes."

"Weren't they designed to withstand that sort of thing? Earthquakes, natural disasters . . . you'd think a plane crash would be on the list."

"Not just crashed. Somebody used them in an attack."

"Of course. An attack now. Committed by Hitler and the Nazis—."

"Not Hitler. That's why I was suspicious of him. If Hitler ever actually existed, in reality, he lived and died a quiet life I'd never heard of."

"So who committed them?"

"If they looked before I left, they didn't say."

"So when exactly would this attack—."

"Tomorrow."

That stopped Jennifer. Perhaps she'd expected him to mention a date years, or even decades, from their little bench. Through all his travels through time, Leonard had discovered that's what 'the future' means. People who plan for the future plan for next month or next year or next decade, not next week, not tomorrow. The future is not just a different day, a different tomorrow. People expect the future to come on wings like thunder, but damned if it doesn't pass like smoke.

"Tomorrow," Jennifer said. "So how far exactly— when are you actually from?"

Leonard thought of the werewolf mask Jennifer, his own Jennifer, had worn. "Halloween. So six weeks from now."

"This year? And I suppose you probably don't actually have any proof?"

"No, I don't—," Leonard began, then stopped when he remembered the Oracle still in his pocket. He withdrew the white device itself, pulled the glasses from his breast pocket.

"What's that?"

"You wanted proof," he said, offering her the glasses. "Put these on, and look up."

Jennifer regarded them skeptically before slipping them on. She turned her head, craning her neck to take in the towers. "Okay . . ."

When Leonard turned it on, he could see on the device's LCD the image Jennifer saw. He pressed the button to advance the image, and it appeared like timelapse: the night deepened, windows blinking on and then off again, until rosy-golden dawn appeared from the East. Leonard would have said the sunrise lit the building aflame had the metaphor not been spectacularly grotesque considering—

He'd forgotten that the audio connected through his cranial implant, and the impact of the plane shattered through his skull. He sank to his knees, grunted when his legs struck the hard concrete, and put out the hand that wasn't holding the Oracle to steel himself. He sucked in a breath even as he heard the great splintering rush of the towers' collapse and the frantic screams it would prompt. Jennifer stood, raising her arm as if to shield herself as she turned away. Leonard grabbed her hand. If he could hear the rushing of that enormous cloud of dust, she could see it, roiling toward her, over her, around her—

"It's just the glasses. It's not real," though he didn't add the next single thought: "Yet."

Jennifer clutched the glasses from her eyes, her fingers tightening so hard Leonard worried she would snap the frames. She pulled her other palm to her eyes. "What—was that?"

Leonard eased the glasses from her hand. "I told you. Tomorrow morning—."

"No, I mean that—it looked so real," she said, the back of her hand against her mouth. "You—you're really telling the truth."

Leonard didn't speak, just rose and returned to the bench.

Jennifer exhaled as if she'd been struck. She stared up at the two towers as if trying to reassure herself they were still there. "We could—we need to tell someone."

"No, I can't—."

"But it's—do you know how many people work in this building?"

Leonard swallowed. "It's not my place," he said. He almost didn't want her to hear it.

"Not your place? What does that even—."

"It's not my place. I do recon. I only came down here to use the bookstore and see if my connection would work from higher up. It's—."

"Not your place. Right. You said," Jennifer told him.

"Look, it's not . . ." Leonard was about to say it wasn't like he didn't want to, but he realized that wasn't true. The realization tightened his gut; traveling had become very much a job, a series of missions and objectives through time, with no real difference from any other career. "I never—," he started to tell her he had never intervened, hesitated, then: "CIRTN—that's the organization I work for—has rules and regulations. I'm not supposed to—."

"And this organization—CIRTN—it never intervenes?"

"Only in special circumstances, like when—."

"Someone is about to attack the World Trade Center with a couple of planes?"

"If CIRTN won't change our past, I doubt it would change yours—."

"But it's not the past. It's tomorrow."

"Time doesn't work like that. If CIRTN decides to intervene, it would send someone else after I came back with my report."

"If you came back," Jennifer said. "You just said you were cut off."

"There's that."

"And you said this was the first alternate reality you've ever encountered."

"It's the first anyone's ever encountered."

"What if this was a one-way ticket here? Because it could be, right?"

Leonard realized he hadn't wanted to consider that, as though not thinking about it might prevent it from becoming true. "It's possible."

"So if you're stuck here anyway, you might as well try, right? If you can't ever get back, they'll never know the difference, right? So you could——."

"It doesn't work that way. I only came back to figure out where your reality diverges from ours, because changing the past like someone is about to do could be catastrophic. Not in the lives it might save or the disasters it might prevent, but in the way it affects the universe. And before you ask, no, I don't know exactly how it would affect the universe, but I know it wouldn't be good."

"But how do you know? How——?"

"Einstein said we should prevent it."

"Einstein?"

"He was a scientist——."

"I know who Einstein was."

"When CIRTN first began, before it was even CIRTN, he said that it was possible to see through time but that we should try to preserve it, because he said spacetime is like a hyperdimensional construct of spiderwebs."

"Then why tell me all this?"

"To——," Leonard was about to say 'to save you,' but didn't. "Because I love you."

"So now I either think you're crazy and this is where we say goodbye, or I do believe you and leave anyway because I think you're a coward for not doing something about it. And if I believe you and don't go to work tomorrow, doesn't that mean you changed the past?"

"I don't—," Leonard said but stopped, because he suddenly realized that one of the reasons he'd withheld from Jennifer was not just because he hadn't known either what or how to tell her, but also because inaction was so deeply ingrained in his training. Leonard did recon; he didn't intervene, never interfered. He wasn't sure how to feel about the revelation; "We didn't really examine the events, so I'm not sure what happens to you."

"But doesn't that—."

"It might, all right, yes? Bloody hell," Leonard said. "I didn't—I haven't been thinking well. I'm stuck in an alternate fucking reality and can't contact the people who put me here, and then I go to the one place I probably shouldn't have and find the only person in the world I wouldn't have wanted to see there, and I don't know what's happening. So yes, maybe even just telling you changes destiny, and maybe I just screwed up the universe, but I couldn't not tell you, anymore than I can actually do anything about what's going to happen. And I probably shouldn't have. I probably should have turned around the second I saw you, and I probably shouldn't have ever said a word."

Jennifer considered that. "Then maybe you shouldn't."

Leonard just looked at her, nodded. "Maybe not."

He rose as Jennifer picked up her purse and stood.

"Thank you for dinner," she said.

"I'm sorry—."

"Don't," she shook her head, put her hand out. "It was nice to meet you up until five minutes ago."

Leonard just looked at her long, slender fingers; he didn't realize he had moved his hand until he took hers.

"I hope you make it back home," Jennifer said, then let go of his hand and strode back toward the doors they'd walked out of only a few minutes before; to Leonard it felt like a lifetime ago. Click-clack echoes of her heels across the concrete, before she pulled open the door and walked through, never once looking back.

Leonard felt like all his energy left his body when he sighed, and he sat, heavily, back on the bench. It felt colder and harder, the air chillier the world darker. He thought of the Safe, of his life, of the Jennifer he knew and loved. He wondered if she was all right, back at CIRTN. He wondered if she would go to work tomorrow.

He might have kept on wondering had he not been trained against doing so; he had more urgent priorities than sitting on a bench and mooning over an alternate-reality version of the woman he loved. He needed to figure out how to get in touch with Race. He needed to figure out how to get back home, or at least get his implant back in contact with CIRTN.

He needed a physicist. Someone he could talk to about the Safe and the Schrodinger Chamber and who might than be able to, if not replicate them, at least understand their conceptual underpinnings to help him figure out a way to contact home. CIRTN forbade introducing advanced technology to primitive societies, but it might be the only way to get home—

"You! On the bench! Stand up and put your hands on your head!"

He'd already been rising, and he put both hands atop his close-shorn skull, turning slowly to face them: a group of dark-uniformed cops, all drawn guns and hard stares. Jennifer stood next to one, her arms crossed, and one of the officers approached Leonard, producing handcuffs as he did so. He circled around and clamped one cuff over Leonard's right wrist.

"You have the right to remain silent," the officer told him as he pulled Leonard's arms down.

Leonard chose not to. "You called the police?"

Jennifer shrugged. "I had to. I'm sorry."

"Anything you say can and will be used against you in a court of law," the cop told him.

Leonard gave half a thought to attempting escape, but he saw all those guns and instead let the officer cuff both his hands together and lead him back toward the World Trade Center.

29

Their supplies weren't wet as Chance had feared; Cassie had possessed foresight enough to cover the pillowcase with some stray palm fronds and long-dead branches. The first thing he pulled from it was a bottle of water, twisting the top and downing half its contents before he offered the rest to Cassie, which she guzzled with one long pull that made her slender neck undulate. He wanted to kiss it.

When she had finished, she handed the bottle back to him, and he stuck it back in the bag. "Hungry?" he offered a protein bar.

She shook her head. "So, the way I figure it, we have three options. Either we find out what happened, in which case we either wait or try to jump forward a few d—."

"Given the way we got here, I'm not sure trying to jump forward is a good idea."

"So we either find a place to camp out for a few days, or we go on ahead to Munich."

"I vote Munich."

"But I thought—."

"I wanted to know what happened. But what you said earlier—I think you're right. He died for something he believed in so hard that he ended up on the cross, and that's more important than whether or not he came back. The more I think about it, the less I think it matters what happens in the next few days," Chance told her. "So if you just want to get changed and go to Munich, I'm okay with that."

"You're sure? Because if you want to find out . . ."

"I don't need to—but I'm just wondering, we meant well coming here, but we fucked pretty much everything up. From the coordinates on. I mean, if you wanted to just go to modern Munich—."

"Munich doesn't exist right now. For a few more centuries, too, if I'm not mistaken."

"I mean modern, like, 2001 Munich."

"I only plugged coordinates for here and 1923 Munich into the time machine. And home, but that's just because that's where we left from. We're also a few days earlier than where we expected to be. Which might affect when we arrive."

"So this is going to be a shot in the dark coming up."

"It's a little late to be worrying about that. Considering what we've been through so far, I think we can handle just about anything the universe decides to throw at us," Cassie said. "And you still want to try to— stop Hitler?"

"Why don't we wait to see where we end up, and then decide from there?" he said, then watched her adjust the time machine. "What's it going to feel like?"

She shrugged.

"But you——."

"I jumped ahead a few minutes. We're talking nearly two millennia. I haven't a clue."

"So we can't prepare for it."

"We could try. Probably wouldn't matter."

Chance nodded. "We should change first."

*

He noticed in retrofit that the medium shirt he had chosen was tight around his biceps and across his chest and back, but the slacks fit well enough. He unbuttoned his cuffs and rolled them to his elbows, tied his shoes, and ran his fingers through his thick hair. Cassie ducked behind a large boulder, shucking the robe and shawl for a slim grey skirt and a simple white blouse under a charcoal wool blazer. Incongruous among the olive trees but more familiar to Chance than the world around him.

Chance slung the pillowcase over his shoulder. "Should we sit again?"

"Didn't seem to make much of a difference before. Maybe if we just——," she said, and for a moment they executed an awkward semi-dance of half-gestures and quarter-advances. Some primitive part of Chance reacted to her closeness as if she had gravity unrelated to either mass or density; he could think of nothing except how close she was. Her skin. Her cheeks and her lips and the individual strands of blonde hairs among black. Her eyes downturned to the time machine, the controls of which she manipulated with her right hand, pressing its buttons and turning its dials with her thumb.

"Is this ok——," Chance never finished the sentence, because the world bled away from him as he spoke. Everything around him filled with light so strong it seemed to press into and through him as if he were tanning from the inside out, colors disappearing as detail fell away. The world bleached brilliant white like crisp linens and favorite memories and dreamlike potential, reality like gossamer pulled into indeterminate strands as they

s   t   r   e   t   c   h   e   d
all across
the   universe,
blurrrring forward through millennia,
time and space warping around them, freezing them in a perfect moment.

Rome fell.

Alexander achieved and squandered greatness.

Genghis Khan came to and then lost power.

Muhammad heard the voice of Allah and early Christian soldiers fought crusades.

Shakespeare wrote his plays and Beethoven composed his symphonies.

Columbus sailed to discover a new world where millions of people already lived.

All of existence fluid and changing but they together remained constant, so strong and powerful they became immutable until finally vague details began to emerge from the brilliance, blurry features as years and worlds slowed to coalesce all around them,

motion-blur forests of green-brown streaks segued to smudged buildings as sketched by the hands of drunken architects until finally—

so bitter cold it took Chance's breath away. A grey sky filled with seething clouds the same color as the gun-metal dark pavement. They were in a large public area he would have called a quad in college; before them was a giant building the color of old corn whose enormous, near-black cupolas loomed over the square and which stretched expansively left and right, while to their left was a smaller structure the color of bone, with three large arches, beyond each of which were greenish statues. A biting wind flapped a black-red-yellow German flag, and the square pulsed with policemen in harsh green uniforms and headgear that resembled safari helmets.

As the buildings gained their density, as the European square gained material, as the world coalesced around them from a whirling dervish of spacetime, the tiny hair follicles on Chance Sowin's neck leapt to the same attention as the policemen he saw all around, because he had only one thought:

We've been here before.

Cassie pulled him backward, against the wall opposite the giant yellow building. No one noticed them; the officers were preoccupied with their activity, and what small crowd had gathered was focused entirely on the officers. The officers shouted German through the square, while the people gathered murmured to each other, harsh whispers full of cracking fricatives from the backs of their throats.

"I think we made it to exactly where we'd planned to be," Cassie said. "That smaller building to the left, with the arches, is *Feldherrnhalle*, and that big yellow one across the way is the *Theatinerkirche*. A church. The *Putsch* marched right down this street—."

"*Ludwigstrasse*," Chance said. "We studied it in one of my history classes. The Bavarian state police stopped them, which means that's who the guys in the safari helmets are."

Being there was different from reading about it. The massive square bordered statues of lions and soldiers, with, overlooking it all, the kind of church built by people who still believed grandeur could impress God. The square was filled with people watching the dark-uniformed officers standing ready.

Chance had known all those things, that Hitler would narrowly escape when his makeshift army marched upon the *Platz*, but he had never known the cold, never felt the seething energy, the tension. He rubbed his biceps. The air was the sort of frigid that penetrates the skin and settles into the bones, and he could feel it tightening his shoulder, but on the other hand he felt none of the ill effects that had sent him reeling when they'd arrived in Jerusalem.

When he commented on that, Cassie agreed. "I think it's because we came forward, instead of moving backward. Technically, we all time travel into the future at a rate of one second per second, so we just increased that speed, rather than moving backward against it."

The people who had gathered watched with the same electric fear as the crowd that had gathered outside Pilate's palace, anxious but thrilled. The policemen stood with eyes fixed straight ahead, staring at nothing, ready for war.

Jagged lightning bit down the clouds far beyond *Feldherrnhalle* and thunder rumbled in its wake, and then the gun-metal skies opened to pour down strong, steady rain. The white shirt Chance wore soaked right through, and water droplets beaded on Cassie's blazer before the wool began to darken with moisture.

"Maybe we should get out of the rain?" Chance said.

But Cassie shook her head, her attention riveted by the historical maelstrom unfolding before her. "We're where we wanted to be. Shouldn't be long," she said, her voice low and distracted.

*

Ultimately, Cassie was right. About everything.

Hitler's homemade march came neither suddenly nor quickly but rather like a distant thunder rumble without the warning of lightning precursor. Chance felt them first, low bass like a rock-concert sub-woofer until the concrete surfaces of the streets and the brick exteriors of the buildings began to echo footsteps like roaring applause so loud it seemed like an armada approached.

It came up *Ludwigstrasse*, a teeming mass of dark khaki so dense he could see no details, no features, a single movement of harsh, synchronous energy. He pulled Cassie closer to the building they'd fallen back against as the troops approached, the faces and bodies of uniformed men emerging from the murky swarm of soldiers, row after row pressing inexorably through the sheeting rain. The *Putsch* outnumbered the Bavarian police by at least ten men to one.

The police officers came to life and began to mobilize, moving as one to coalesce into a quick mass of rifle-aiming, German-spewing green. Most formed tight clusters in formation in the center of the square, their arms raised and their eyes squinting down the barrels of their rifles, while their ancillary comrades flanked to the sides in a sprinting crouch.

One man in the very middle shouted orders into the storm:

"*Mehr manner zu linken seite!*"

"*Wartet auf mein kommando!*"

Chance was about to ask Cassie what his words meant, but then he saw—

Even with a helmet, even without the narrow moustache above his lip, his small stature and beady eyes were unmistakable. Chance had seen that face too many times in history texts and on documentaries not to recognize Adolf Hitler when he saw him.

His breath caught. Imagining the man had been one thing, beholding him another entirely. His rigid posture and his determined, steely eyes were unmistakable: this is Adolf Hitler, helmet beaded by pelting rain, cheeks flushed and forehead gleaming, face a countenance of deliberate fury.

Beside him marched a larger, burlier man with thick cheeks and a body his uniform strained to contain. Behind them both, grunts buzzed with nervous energy, but those two marched silently and solidly and deliberately, eyes straight ahead as if they meant to claim not merely the *Platz* and Munich, not merely all of Germany and Europe, but both the world and its future as their own.

The sky above them flashed, raindrops falling down on the world like liquid diamonds, and far in the distance beyond the *Putsch*, the thunder rolled as if to state that the furious Nazis had all of nature behind their cause.

Chance forgot to be cold. His shirt clung to his skin, his hair matting limply against his scalp, and raindrops streamed down his forehead like marathon sweat, but his body burned hot and urgent. He clenched his jaw to keep his teeth from chattering, and he couldn't take his eyes off Hitler. "We can't let him live," he said, more to himself than anything else.

Beside him, Cassie surprised him by agreeing. "No."

Together, they began to move toward the south, closer to the *Ludwigstrasse* intersection. All around Cassie and Chance, German *volken* had emerged from the cafes and shops, men and women their age who watched the march as if their lives depended on it. Their frightened eyes betrayed soul-poverty, but Chance couldn't tell, either by listening to them or looking at them, which side they had pinned their hopes for survival on. All watched the Bavarian police and the *Putsch* troops with equal intensity.

They came to a corner at the far end where two Bavarian police officers stood. One controlled the crowd with quick, efficient bursts of speech, but the other crouched one knee to the ground, sighting down a rifle.

Down along the *strasse*, a big, black sedan idled.

The *Putsch* was nearly upon the square.

"*Still gestanden!*" the man shouting orders over the State Police officers called as if he expected all of the world, the storm and the crowd and Munich itself, to heed him.

The big man next to Hitler spoke. He screamed to be heard over the urgent rain. "*Nicht schiesen! Seine Exzellenze Ludendorff kommt!*"

The crouched officer hesitated, moved his gun slightly to look over his sights.

"What'd he say?" Chance whispered to Cassie.

"He just told them not to shoot because Ludendorff is coming."

Chance watched the man shout again, watched Hitler stand silent next to him, his jaw defiant, his eyes blazing with furious pride. "That's Graf, isn't it? Hitler's bodyguard?"

The crouching police officer had glanced up, but lowered his sight along his rifle.

"The police officer. With the rifle. Tell him to aim for Hitler."

Cassie looked at the crouching man. "*Offizier, schiest den kleinen mann zuerst.*"

The officer controlling the crowd looked at her. "*Was haben sie das?*"

Just then, the head police officer called out again. "*Standplatz!*" he shouted.

The tension in the *Platz* exploded with bullets and rifle shot as men on both sides fired. Muzzles burst like tiny lightning, and men cried out as if smitten from above.

Graf dove over Hitler, driving him to the ground even as he himself took a shot in the shoulder. He winced, clutching his arm as he rolled over Hitler, urging the smaller man forward.

Down the *strasse*, only a few yards from where Chance and Cassie stood, the black sedan's muffler whispered white smoke into the air.

The people around them teemed. The shouting police officer tried to control them, to calm them, but they quickly overwhelmed him, pushing forward against the crouching officer, who held aim until their weight pushed him sideways even as Graf pushed Hitler forward in a low, darting run. They pressed straight for the spot where the officers stood, where Chance and Cassie stood, where the black sedan idled and belched white smoke into the storm-clogged air.

As they moved and darted, as they fled, Hitler pulled from his coat a small gun with a narrow barrel, and he fired it into the crowd. The sound of the report seemed tiny, a mechanical cough, but still Chance heard a woman scream.

The crowd control officer fumbled with his own gun, but Graf barreled into him, knocking him sideways. His pistol skittered away.

Hitler darted forward.

Chance heard the sedan's engine shift out of park, saw its brake lights flash.

He also saw the police officer's rifle on the ground.

Even despite his injured arm, Graf shouldered people out of his way, clearing a path for Hitler. Together they pressed into the tiny bedlam on the corner, pushing toward the sedan.

Chance reached for the rifle. Hitler saw him do it and kicked at his fingers even as Graf yanked open the sedan's door, but Chance dove, twisted his body to grip the rifle even as he tumblesaulted between Graf and Hitler, and then he spun it around and bashed Hitler in the face with its butt. He felt the reverberation through the stock even as he twisted, pivoting to slam it into Graf's gut, torqued it around again to bash Hitler again across the head hard enough to knock off his helmet. Graf grunted forward, his head thudding against the sedan's door frame, then crumpled sideways to fall to the pavement.

Chance continued to spin the rifle like vertical roulette, until its butt lodged firmly into his shoulder, barrel downpointing into Hitler's eyes. He squeezed the trigger for a single-shot not nearly as momentous as it should have been. Part of him expected it to feel as singular and spectacular as atomic detonation, but it was not: the rifle cracked like a whip-snap as the butt chunked into his shoulder, and Hitler went down quick and sudden with no struggle whatever.

Chance bit through the didn't pause, pumped the rifle's barrel one-handed as he spun around to blast Graf through the chest—

and then he stood, panting, heart thudding in his chest. All around the sounds of rifle bursts and angry shouts he contributed his own to. His lungs seethed, and tears streamed down his cheeks. Furious energy clenched through his whole body so hard he didn't understand what to do with it until finally he looked at his trembling hands and realized he had to let it go.

He dropped the rifle. It clattered to the pavement, metal and wood against concrete.

He gasped. His breath came in bursts, and each one wanted to shatter.

His first coherent thought was of Cassie.

He turned. "Cass?" he asked, but his voice shuddered in his chest and broke before it made it beyond his throat. He took a deep breath and tried again. "Cass?"

"I'm—over here," her voice came like relief, and he followed it beyond the crowd to find her leaning back against the wall. The rain had plastered her hair down, and she clutched her arms around herself, her body shivering. "You okay?" she asked when she saw him.

Chance looked back in the direction of the sedan, already hidden by the raucous crowd. "I think so. I think—I killed him," he said, even though he didn't think that at all.

Cassie nodded.

"So now we—I guess—now what?"

"Now you figure out where to go from here."

"I think we should just get out—."

It happened so fast. One minute she was leaning against the wall, shivering, and the next she'd slid down it as her legs gave out on her, sinking to the pavement. He rushed to her, and as he got closer, he saw the spatter of her blood against the brick, saw how pale her skin had gone, felt how tightly she'd clutched her arms around her body.

"What—," he said, but then he saw the dark hole in her dark blazer. "Shit, you're—," he started, but he never finished his sentence as her body shivered into his arms. "Is it—?" he said, and he meant to ask how bad it was even as he unbuttoned her blazer, but then he saw her entire abdomen slicked crimson. "Oh, Jesus, no. Oh, fuck, Cassie, no. No," he said, and he said it over and over and over again, but still she continued to bleed.

30

This is not how a world will change—it is, rather, how one begins.

Let there be light:

From *strasse* to *Platz* to *Munchen*, eschew Passau and Nuremberg to keep in focus a small group of friends and family who will mourn the death of Adolf Hitler—because here it is worth remembering that long before he became *der Fuhrer, jung herr* Hitler was a frustrated artist whose paintings displayed, perhaps not ironically, a certain lack of perspective. That group of friends and family will grieve his passing, but greater Germany, as the *Reich*, will regard Hitler as a footnote, a decorated but otherwise unexceptional soldier who marched with Ludendorff on *Odeonsplatz*.

Europe in turmoil during the twenties because not much will change. Lenin will die around the time Israel conflicts with Palestine. A young revolutionary named Iosif Vissarionovich Dzhugashvili will succeed Lenin as General Secretary of the Communist Party of the Soviet Union not long after he adopts the name Joseph Stalin. In Germany, celebrated Great War hero Paul von Hindenburg will become the first president. In China, Chiang Kai-shek will succeed Sun Yat-sen even while conflict with Japan heats.

A brief history of a twentieth century our universe avoided:

Increasing public support for the Weimar coalition in Germany will allow former Prussian president Wilhelm Marx to win the 1932 election; he will appoint Karl Jarres as Chancellor in 1933, and the first political action of the new administration will be to help Italy's King Victor Emmanuel III depose fascist dictator Benito Mussolini. Freedom will reign throughout Italy, and Churchill will propose a European Alliance within the League of Nations.

Sensing opportunity for growth and a way to provide relief from the Great Depression, Franklin Delano Roosevelt will propose an alliance with Central America and Canada as well as a new direction for the League of Nations. The United States will join the North American Union, and FDR will be its representative when the United Nations establishes a global headquarters in Manhattan.

Aware of his own failing health, however, FDR will propose Indiana governor Henry Schricker as the first Prime Minister of the NAU; Harry Truman will accept when Schricker declines. Leery of a Democratic party with too much power, the nation will elect Tom Dewey as its next president in 1944, establishing a precedent for bipartisan leadership between the US and the NAU.

Later, when Adlai Stevenson wins presidency under Prime Minister Earl Warren, they will together propose a reformation of the United States into Union-States, decentralizing the Federal government and increasing power in the new members—New England, New Holland, Atlantica, Delta, Columbia, New Canaan, South Canaan, Dakota, Pacifica, and the People's Republic of Texico.

Upon learning of the Soviet space program, the NAU, in cooperation with the UN, will recruit the world's leading scientists—among them Einstein, Planck, and Rutherford—in a top-secret project known as the Geneva Campus, where they will collaborate on cutting-edge research into the consequences of relativity and its meaning in the universe. The Soviet launch of Sputnik will encourage the UN to increase activity at the Geneva Campus with the help of the world's leading physicists—Oppenheimer, Szilard, Meitner, Fermi, Feynman, and two Bohrs—to focus attention away from space and instead upon the secrets of subatomic particles.

Before conflict between China and Japan can escalate into war, the UN and the NAU will intercede, and the Manchurian Proclamation will take its name from the country whose independence it establishes as a member of a new Eur-Asian Union. Diplomatic relations between Mao Tse-tung and Chiang Kai-shek will proceed with some caution.

Unhappy that the newly formed EAU did not remove Japanese imperialists from power, Korea's Kim Il-sung will ally with Nikita Kruschev and the Soviet Union. Together, both will lend support to the Indian resistance to British occupation and support Palestinian efforts against Israel. In defiance of the EAU and UN, they will establish the Indo-Russo Korean Union.

In 1962, NAU Prime Minister John Fitzgerald Kennedy will receive a report from Atlantica president

Richard Nixon concerning the installation of an IRKU missile base in Cuba. In retaliation and without considering diplomatic relations, PM Kennedy and UN Secretary General Dag Hammerskjold will begin the Quantum Age when they train the Einstein-Feynman generator on Cuba. A quantum electrodynamic pulse will render every electronic and mechanical device in all of Cuba inoperational. No missiles will be fired, and the age of non-violent warfare will begin.

It will not last. The NAU and the UN will work with IRKU leaders to establish peaceful terms for coexistence. India will gain independence, the USSR will dissolve into member-states, and Korea and Palestine will both gain membership in the newly reformed Eurasian Russian Union under the condition that the technology implemented in what will become known as the October Crisis be centralized on neutral territory, in Geneva, and under a neutral ruling body that will be the scientific equivalent of the UN; a group of renowned and respected scientific researchers from all countries working together in the best interests of the world.

The Geneva Campus will become the *Conseil Internationale pour la Recherche Nucleaire*, and New England president Robert Kennedy will encourage his brother to pledge billions of dollars to the new international entity. By the 1980s, with the help of Feynman, Born, and Sowin, and the support of funds earmarked by PM Ronald Reagan and Atlantica president Martin Luther King, Jr., CIRN will have become CIRTN. As part of the ERU, CIRTN will collaborate closely with the NAU's Brookhaven laboratory in upstate New York and adhere to UN control. Its energy research will alleviate the world's dependence on fossil fuel when it discovers a way to siphon almost infinite energy from, literally, a grain of sand.

In the late 1990s, when CIRTN announces the development of the Schrodinger Chamber, PM William Clinton, Pacifica president John McCain, and New England president Al Gore will suggest the original Constitutional Convention in Philadelphia as the inaugural installation of SecondSight. The only opposition will come from PRT president George W. Bush, but subsequent investigations will reveal Bush's ties to Saudi Arabian terrorist faction and he will be summarily impeached. Tourists from the world over will flock to Olde City to watch the Founding Fathers scribble their names on parchment, while in Europe they will watch Beethoven mock-conduct his Ninth. When London applies for an installation at the Globe, CIRTN will send its best researcher, Leonard Kensington, back to Elizabethan Southwark before it calls him back to Geneva to send him, instead, to an alternate Manhattan, which is where he is, while several universes over—

That's right: Chance and Cassie just created his—

PART III
TOMORROW AND TOMORROW AND TOMORROW

"WE LIVE IN DEEDS, NOT YEARS; IN THOUGHTS, NOT FIGURES ON A DIAL. WE SHOULD COUNT TIME BY HEART THROBS. HE MOST LIVES WHO THINKS MOST, FEELS THE NOBLEST, ACTS THE BEST."
-F. LEE BAILEY, ATTORNEY

"WE SHARE THE COMMONALITY OF DREAMS, WHICH WE NAME TOMORROW."
-RAY BRADBURY, *YESTERMORROW*

31

The officers escorted Leonard through the lobby and across the concourse, down stairs and through a chrome-handled glass door into a nondescript office area with thin, taupe carpeting; beige walls; and labyrinthine corridors. They led him down a hallway between undecorated wooden doors, then into an grey office bare except for a folding table and a wooden chair, which they pushed him heavily into. He sat so that his arms, cuffed behind his back, fell over the chairback, as two officers cuffed his ankles to the chair's legs.

Then they left him.

Leonard wished he might be unable to believe Jennifer had betrayed him, but betrayal is a matter of trust, and the truth was he'd never built any real trust with the Jennifer in the alternate universe in which he was stranded. The Jennifer he knew, the Jennifer he loved and who loved him, was who-knew-how-many hyperdimensions across the universe, and the Jennifer with whom he'd eaten was merely a stranger with whom he'd had dinner. His trust in her was emotional residue from another time, another place, another future.

That the cops hadn't tossed him immediately into a cell indicated they probably meant to interrogate him. They had confiscated everything he'd been carrying, which worried him. His identification might hold up to casual inspection, but it wouldn't fool a computerized database of names and locations on which he'd never existed in the first place.

Then there were his other supplies. His smartcard, the serious gun, the Oracle—

The door opened. Two men in dark suits entered, one tall and predatory with the sharp appearance of a bird of prey, the other shorter but better built. The tall man carried a sleek black attaché case, and his suit fit like he'd gone to a tailor, while the shorter man's fit like he'd filled it out himself. He carried nothing.

"Mister Kensington, I'm federal agent Richard Hanley, and this is my partner Peter Geisel," the tall man introduced himself. Geisel nodded.

Leonard nodded to the men. He said nothing. He had the right to remain silent, and he planned to exercise it for the time being.

"Mister Kensington," Hanley began, "It has come to our attention that you recently made some interesting claims concerning certain events that may occur in the very near future. Can you tell us about that?"

Leonard continued to say nothing.

Hanley looked at Geisel and gestured his head toward Leonard. Geisel stepped around the table and delivered a quick, tight blow to Leonard's solar plexus. A punch that knew what it was doing: Leonard's breath whooshed away so hard he couldn't get it back for a second before the new pressure dissolved to let him breathe again.

"I worried you might make this difficult," Hanley set his attaché case on the table and quick-unlocked its clasps like cocking twin guns. He opened the lid and withdrew from within the case the items the officers had taken from Leonard. First the Oracle, then the serious gun and his smartcard. "We ran your identification, Mister Kensington, if that is your real name."

Still catching his breath, Leonard met Hanley's predatory eyes before he decided that cooperating might put him in a better position. "It is."

Hanley nodded. "Now, as I said, you made some rather extravagant claims—."

"What makes you call them extravagant?"

Hanley paused as if surprised by the interruption. "You must admit—."

"I mustn't anything," Leonard said. "I was completely honest with Ms. Masters."

"But why was that, Mister Kensington?"

"How do you mean?"

"I mean that, by Ms. Masters' account, she'd never met you before. If you truly believe what you told her—and I've no reason to doubt you do—you must admit the information would be either sensitive or implicative, which leads me to wonder why you might share it with her if you'd never met her?"

Leonard wondered how much Jennifer had told them. For a moment, he weighed against telling the agents what he knew, but then reconsidered. He'd worried about telling Jennifer because he'd wanted her to believe him; about the appearance of his credulity to these two, he couldn't have cared less. "Because I have met her before," he said, then, when he saw the look on Hanley's face, "She didn't tell you everything, did she?"

"That probably depends what you mean by everything."

"I mean everything. Temporal anomalies and time travel and alternate universes and physical paradoxes I only came here to prevent," he said. "Everything."

"She only mentioned the attacks."

"The planes."

"You don't deny it."

"It's going to happen. Tomorrow morning."

"How did you come to this information?"

"The parts she didn't tell you."

"You mean the—how did you put it?—the time travel? Alternate universes? That you came here to prevent these attacks yourself?"

"Not prevent them," Leonard said. "I—," he started, but then stopped when he felt his implant vibrate.

He didn't realize how scared he had been that it never would again until spectacular relief flooded his system so hard he nearly laughed when he exhaled. Race. CIRTN. Home.

Jennifer. The real Jennifer, the one he loved, the one who knew him. The Jennifer who never would have betrayed him or turned him over to these goons.

"You what, Mister Kensington?" Hanley said.

Leonard considered his position: arms bound behind his back. He shrugged his shoulders toward his ears, but just brushing his earlobe wouldn't establish the connection to Race. Hanley nodded again to Geisel, who stepped forward and wound up for another punch.

"No wait," Leonard said. "Sorry. I—." If he could get his hands free, could he— "I wasn't trying to prevent them. I was just—," he said, his eyes flicking between Hanley and Geisel and the door behind them and the

Oracle and the serious gun on the table, when he had an idea. "It'd be easier to show you."

Hanley looked down at the Oracle and the serious gun. "You mean your toys," he picked up the Oracle. "This has something to do with it?"

"Except it won't—it's biometric," he said, surprising himself.

Hanley eyed him. "Biometric."

Leonard's skull kept buzzing. "Only works with my fingerprints," he said, shrugging like an apology.

Hanley seemed to consider that, then nodded at Geisel. "Just his hands."

Geisel stepped around Leonard. Hard metal pull, quick mechanical ratchet, then release. Leonard let his arms relax, rubbed his wrists and flexed his fingers in front of him, in plain view. "Thank you."

"Only so you can give us the information we need."

Leonard nodded. As he did so, he rubbed his neck, quick-tugged his earlobe like it was just another stretchy-scratchy motion. "Absolutely. Like I said, it's biometric."

"What's biometric?" Race's voice boomed through his head even as Leonard's fingers closed on the watch's band. He didn't bother trying to get it onto his wrist, just pressed the button on the side—

nothing.

"Fuck," Leonard said.

"What?" Hanley asked.

"Are you all right? Give me a status," Race said.

"I think—it might be broken," Leonard said. He shook the watch near his ear. "I don't think it's working."

"What is it?" Hanley asked.

"What's not working?" Race asked.

"Just my watch."

"Sounded like you were upset about more than just a watch," Hanley told him.

"Had it for a long time," Leonard said.

"It's okay," Race said. "It still works—we lost you the moment you started the Safe."

"What about the others? This, for instance," Hanley picked up the serious gun.

"Just a—nanoscope."

"A nanoscope? What are you talking about? Where are you?" Race asked.

"A nanoscope," Hanley said, like he didn't believe it.

"A nanoscope. Measures quantum waveforms. That's why I came here in the first place. I figured the waves at the World Trade Center would be more concentrated because of its height," Leonard said. With confidence, and as if surprised Hanley didn't know what a nanoscope is. Because, Leonard knew, when in Rome, act like you own the place. "Probably won't work down here in the sublevels, though."

"World Trade Center sublevels," Race said, but as if to someone else. Probably one of the computer scientists in the Operations Center, running CIRTN's quantum resources to help Leonard escape. "Just give us a minute. Are you stuck somewhere?"

Leonard reached for the Oracle. It might only buy him a moment, but all he needed was to use the moment well. "But this little baby, shouldn't matter if we're stuck down here—."

"Yeah, he's stuck, people. Come on, let's get him out of there," Race called to all of CIRTN's Operations Center. To Leonard: "Just try to get unstuck, okay?"

"What is it?" Hanley asked.

Leonard indicated the glasses. "Put those on, and I'll show you."

Hanley picked up the glasses, held them in front of himself for a moment, then slipped them onto his face.

Leonard swallowed. He glanced once more around, at his equipment on the table, the door and its chrome handle. Geisel stood close by as if coiled and ready to strike, steel-blue eyes laser-focused on Leonard. Leonard considered trying to get Hanley to give the glasses to Geisel, but decided it might sound too suspicious to risk.

He took a deep breath, looked down at the Oracle. He touched the screen to bring it to life, then chose first "pause," then increased the opacity to maximum—

He drove his toes down hard as he jerked his whole body backward, upending the chair as he pushed his calves down its legs, freeing his ankles. Geisel rushed forward, but Leonard torqued around, feet windmilling, fixed his legs around Geisel's and then used the hard, concrete floor for leverage to twist Geisel hard sideways. Just a stumble was all Leonard needed to quick-chop Geisel in the neck.

He grunted with the effort.

"Are you okay?" Race asked.

Leonard skittered forward, thrusting his whole body under the table even as Hanley pulled the glasses from his eyes, and he crunched up to kick his feet into Hanley's crotch.

"Just getting unstuck," he reached into Hanley's blazer to pull the agent's gun, twisted to turn it on Geisel but discovered he didn't need to; both agents struggled on the floor, one grasping his crotch, the other his throat.

"We can't see you because you're in the sublevels, so you need to get out of the building. We should be able to find you then."

Leonard swiped the Oracle glasses from the floor, grabbed his equipment from the table, stuffing everything into his suit pockets as he pressed against the door's jamb, pulled it open a crack through which he scanned the long, fluorescent-lit hallway. It looked empty. He crouched to slip through the door, easing it closed behind him. The corridor ended in blind turns in both directions. "And then you'll get me back?" he said, hugging the wall as he moved along the hallway.

"No. Munich."

"Munich? Bloody fuck's in Munich?"

"The coincidence."

"You found it?"

"Just a second before we found you," Race said.

Several yards ahead of Leonard, a group of uniformed officers turned the corner, guns drawn. "Hold it right there," one said.

Leonard put his hands up. He counted eight cops in all. He turned, only to see another four cops turn a corner behind him. He squeezed the trigger on his serious gun, but nothing happened. "Cops. And my serious gun didn't work."

"Something about the different reality, Darren said. He's working on it. It's been chaos with our whole system. Major—."

"Hate to interrupt, but can you do something, rather than telling me—."

"Hang on. Darren says he can—what?" Race asked, but the 'what?' wasn't for Leonard.

The cops, as one, approached him, closing in.

"If you're going to do something, bloody well do it now," Leonard said.

"Darren says run."

"What?"

"Run," Race's voice boomed through his head, jumpstarting Leonard's feet without impedance from Leonard's brain.

Gunfire behind him the instant he moved, but given strange echo. He glanced over his shoulder to watch a bead of lead slug shoot through the air, and he ducked sideways to let the bullet pass, watching it leave a shimmering, wavering wake behind it.

Another echo, and another.

More.

Bullets sailed all around him, a sudden gunmetal ballet of hot lead and sizzling air. Leonard twirled forward, pirouetting around the bullets, dodging sideways here and twisting forward there. He ducked under one, lifted his leg over another, pitched his body to the wall and swallowed as a third passed him very closely by. A sound like a hail of party-noisemakers made Leonard throw himself to the ground even as too many bullets for him to count converged on the wall where he'd been standing, and then he somersaulted forward when he heard two more gunshots like ricochets. The immediate air filled with the vapor trails of tiny missiles, and Leonard noticed that the effect decreased as he scuttled forward, each successive bullet faster than its predecessor.

"I don't know what he just did, but Darren says it won't last."

"I noticed," Leonard said, moving more quickly as the bullets came faster, taking greater care to dodge and using more spontaneous movements. Almost a dance, hyperkinetic Twister under a hail of bullets, right hand carpet, left hand wall, both feet in the air and bend-twist-cartwheel-crouch until he found himself in front of the cops and used what little advantage he had left to split his legs apart and push forward, sweeping two of the cops down at the ankles. He twisted to his feet behind them, reached out and slammed two capped heads so hard together their bodies slumped beneath them, then turned and ran from the remaining four.

Around the corner, down another corridor and around another corner, at the end of which a set of stairs led upward like relief. He broke into a sprint, the sound of pursuit, shouts and anxious footsteps, close behind him.

Up the stairs—

The usual speed and rhythm of Manhattan's early-evening, last-minute commuters had slowed, though Leonard noticed it doesn't ever really stop, even when hindered by hypertime machinations several realities removed. Leonard pushed forward through the crowd, ducking around men and women alike, fighting elbow-first for a straightaway. They were all descending toward the train platforms, so Leonard had to fight up urban stream, back toward the concourse. He skirted around a tortoise-slow businessman, jumped a turnstile and hit an escalator, which he ascended hard and fast as someone behind yelled slow motion—"ssoommeebbooddyy ssttoopp hhiimm"—voice like a 45-rpm record played at 33.

Race's voice: "What's going on?"

"Almost there," Leonard took the peak, hit the concourse. Up ahead, big glass doors gleamed like freedom.

Two cops stood between Leonard and the doors, their guns drawn.

"Just get out of that building, will you?" Race said. "I don't know how much longer Darren can push the Safe."

"I'm working on it," Leonard grunted as he leapt over a business woman's pull-briefcase. "Cops aren't the only thing going slow. Hang on," Leonard said, and instead of continuing onward toward the doors, he changed his course to sprint directly at the closest cop, who fired a single shot. With quicksilver reflexes, Leonard ducked and rolled, sprung up to swipe aside the hand with which the cop held his gun, but Leonard didn't stop. He grabbed the cop's shoulders and pulled as he

jumpped

A sound like a muffled sneeze.

Leonard twisted mid-air to allow the slow-mo bullet to sail harmlessly by, knees bent to land hard running at the doors.

Push.

Push into the evening, into Manhattan darkness.

"Right. Out," Leonard said, even as he pushed the button on his timewatch, and everything changed. The Manhattan pursuit of police officers behind him shifted in a temporal ricochet,

giving way:

a pixellated dervish shot around Leonard as if chasing its own tail. A new world coalesced around him, buildings and streets and people solidifying into three dimensions. Steel grey sky the same color as the sudden pavement beneath him. Driving, insistent rain. A crowd to his left: a mob of a thousand or more men marching toward a large square where police officers in green uniforms and safari hats stood to fire high-powered rifles at them, gunfire filling the air to drown out any sound of thunder. "Munich," Leonard said when he saw the giant, yellowish building looming high above him, its maize sides so bright they seemed to glow against the seething dark sky.

"1923," Race said. "Ludendorff's march on *Feldherrnhalle*. Historical footnote."

"I saw something about a German man named Hitler."

"Put the Oracle glasses on."

Leonard pulled them from his pocket and onto his face. He could see through the lenses, but transposed over everything in front of him was an image of a young man who appeared to be in his mid-twenties. He was holding a rifle like a bat, and he looked like he'd been in the rain a while; his white shirt clung to his body, his black hair to his head. "We don't know who he is, but he's the one interfering. He's there. We put you as close to him as we could," Race said.

Leonard took a quick mental snapshot of everything around the young man: a black sedan, a group of people. Beyond them, a brownish building the rain stained darker. A streetlamp. He tore the glasses from his face, looked around as he ducked farther back from the street. The police had ceased fire but stormed forward, and the clash of dark khaki uniforms reduced the square to chaos. To Leonard's right, a large structure with three archways seemed to be the mob's destination, but the police seemed intent on not allowing them to reach it; some wrestled the marchers to the ground, pistol-whipping them and then cuffing their hands behind their back.

A man in the center of the square, still overlooking the chaos, barked out over the bedlam, stentorian voice like thunder. *"Drehen sie sich um oder sie warden verhaftet!"*

Leonard couldn't remember the last time he had used his German, but even if he hadn't understood, his implant translated for him: turn away or you will be arrested.

Some of the men in the mob shouted angry responses so fast their German fricatives blurred together. Several broke away from the crowd, ducking sideways in favor of back streets, passing Leonard along the way. He made no move to stop them.

Finally: across the square, the brownish building he'd seen behind the young man. On the other side of the crowd.

Leonard cursed—

"What? What is it?" Race asked.

"Nothing," he said, plunging into the chaos of the square. Men squeezed together; the front line had stopped short of the square itself, and so the ranks of the march bunched more closely until packed. Desperation and confusion and fury crackled through them, and Leonard took advantage to press forward, forcing tongue memory as he went. "*Bewegung dich*," he told them. "*Aus dem weg*," shouting now, shoving anyone who didn't move: out of his way.

Someone grabbed Leonard's collar. "*Was machen s—?*"

He never finished his question: Leonard spun to crack his elbow into the man's jaw, then hand-chopped his collarbone, and the man slumped to the ground even as another reached forward. Leonard caught his arm at the wrist and bent his hand backward until the man howled and sank to his knees, then kicked the man so hard in the face a gout of blood arced backward. Several other men had moved forward but hesitated.

"*Aus dem weg*," Leonard said, and the crowd parted before him; Leonard hurried through until he found the pavement on the other side, where a small crowd had tightened to focus their attention at the ground. Two men lay on the asphalt, rain spattering down on their pale skin, darkening their clothing; one a large, rotund man with hands like rounds of ham, the other a smaller, slimmer man with dark hair but no face, just a gaping, bleeding maw.

"*Wer hat das gemacht? Wo sind sie hingegangen?*" Leonard demanded from the people standing around him. Who did this? Where did they go?

"*Es war ein mann in weis. Er und ein madchen. Sie verschwanden*," a woman said, shrugging. A man and a woman. Who had disappeared.

"*Scheissen*," Leonard said.

"Do you see him?" Race asked.

"No. Woman says it's a guy and a girl, but they disappeared."

"Disappeared? Ask her what she means."

"*Was bedeutest du?*" Leonard said.

"*Sie verschwanden. Gegangen.* Poof," she said.

"Poof," Leonard said.

"Poof?" Race asked.

"Poof," the woman nodded.

"But they didn't—they're still—Darren's got an aerial. He says you're next to a street?"

Leonard glanced toward the corner, saw a pair of black skidmarks, and took off after them. His heels clapped the pavement, and he struggled to maintain his balance on the treacherous, rain-slicked cobblestones like bumpy ice, sprinting around pedestrians—"*Aus dem weg! Aus dem weg!*" The rain had become a downpour, liquid hammers and nails against window glass and steel fire escapes and fabric awnings, sluicing down his head and soaking him to the quick.

"They're up ahead, to the . . . your left, I think," Race told him, and Leonard picked the first building corner he saw on his left, skidding around it so hard he bumped into the opposite wall. He pushed himself off the brick and continued on even as Race said, "No, wait, sorry, your right," before he also added, "Can we reverse the view so I can keep Leonard on his feet, people? And can we do it yesterd—wait, what?"

Leonard slipped when he tried to reverse his direction so quickly his heels lost traction, sliding several inches and almost planting ass first to the pavement. He caught himself, spinning his arms, even as Race said, "Okay, Darren picked up their machine, and he says it doesn't work like ours. Theirs generates a field that speeds them up and slows time around them. He says he can balance the difference, but he's not sure how it's going to feel for you."

"Why does that sound like it's not going to be comfortable?" Leonard asked, even as his whole body shuddered as if electrified with strange pressure that seemed intent on turning his every cell completely inside out. His muscles tensed hard enough he thought they might compress his body like a physiological stellar implosion, his legs buckling to send him to his knees as if in anguished prayer. He groaned, but as suddenly as it had come, the feeling passed, his body washing over with relief as he put his hands to the pavement. He wiped his eyes. "Fuck."

"You okay?" Race asked.

"I—I think so," Leonard said, running his hand over his scalp, wiping away sweat and rain, and as he did so he realized the drops weren't falling anymore.

He raised his head. Raindrops like tiny crystal beads suspended in the air. Nothing moved. Even the usual background hiss of silence had disappeared.

"Bloody hell'd you do?" Leonard asked, his voice a whisper.

"Balanced the difference. Slowed time around you."

Leonard eased to his feet, still astounded by the uncanny stillness. Without a breeze to guide them, flags' fabric hesitating, waiting for wind direction; in the crowd and the mob, men's faces had frozen in grimaces of fear and anger and determination. "Jesus," he said. "It's—it's amazing."

"I'm sure it's a nice special effect, but we don't have time for you to appreciate it. Leave that alley the way you came, and put the Oracle glasses back on."

Leonard fumbled the glasses out of his pocket as he ran, dropped them but spun-caught them one handed and mashed them onto his face. The whole world went black and white, as if he'd sprinted onto the set of an old movie. "Okay," Leonard huffed.

"On the ground."

Leonard looked at the pavement. It glistened wetly greyly like brushed steel in the rain. "What am I looking for?"

"You should be able to see his footprints."

"What're you kidding me? You want me to track them by their footprints in the rai—?"

"His footprints should be highlighted. Anything he comes into contact with should be. And your gun should work now."

Leonard scanned the ground, looking left, back toward the square, back toward the beginning of the street, then the other way. Finally he saw a single set of footprints glowing DayGlo yellow like a highlighter emphasizing the sidewalk all the way to the corner, then turning to round it. Leonard kicked into a dead run and took the turn wide, crossing the street as he did so, half-jumping and slipping across the rain-slicked hood of a paused car as he did so, all the while keeping alert for those highlit footprints—

Until: movement.

Among the frozen passers by and the suspended raindrops, the incongruous movement took just a second longer to register. The young man in the shirt so wet its color now matched his pale, soaked skin, running hard but like he was burdened. A quick yellow glow surrounded his body.

"Got 'em," Leonard said, kicking his speed to a sprint. "You, moving! Stop there!"

32

Chance kept whispering "no," even though he realized it wasn't going to make everything okay, that he couldn't deny reality. Just saying "no" over and over wouldn't warm Cassie's body in his arms, wouldn't erase the crimson streak from her abdomen.

He pulled her body close while, back in the square, the Putsch met the police. Close by, the crowd surged, and all around fell a hard rain, but his attention focused on Cassie.

"Is it bad?" she asked him. Her voice strained.

Chance eased her blazer open. Dark crimson edges marked the small hole on the left side of her abdomen, a few inches above the waistband of her skirt, but the problem was the other side, which Chance couldn't see but could feel with his right hand at the small of her back, fingers slick with too much hot, thick blood. "I'm not a doctor," he fought to keep his voice steady. "How do you feel?"

"Cold," Cassie said. "Feels like I'm not going to last."

Chance shook his head. "No."

"You keep saying that."

"I'm not going to let that happen."

"I'm not sure we have much of a choice," Cassie said. She took a deep breath that sounded like it had tried to be deeper. "Hell of a ride, though."

"No, that's not—this is not how it's going to end. I will not let that happen. We have a time machine. I could keep you from getting shot. I could kill Hitler before . . . ," Chance started to say, but trailed off when he remembered the first thing he had thought of the first time they had paused time; that it had seemed as though the world were holding its breath.

"We can't just go back and revise just because we got it wrong the first time. It's bad enough—."

But Chance was staring at that bullethole. "What if we don't? What if I pause time, just for me, just so the whole world stopped—and then I could get you—," Chance hesitated, his attention caught by fighting in the square, the soldiers and the police officers still clashing, still shouting. "Where's the nearest hospital?"

Cassie swallowed like she had difficulty doing so. "They're called *Krankenhauser*. There might be one on the other side of the *Platz*, but I don't know."

"Then I'll find one. They'd be marked" his fear had given way to goal-oriented problem solving and task managing. Cassie was hurt, but if he did this and this, in that order, in a specific amount of time, he could save her, and saving her was all that mattered.

She pushed the time machine toward him. "Just push that button," she told him, and then she coughed, weak and liquid. A spot of blood appeared at the corner of her lip to trickle toward her chin, and she groaned as she brushed her fingertips against her face. She stared at the trace of blood on her fingers like it surprised her, then swallowed. Looked at him. "Oh, God, help," she said, like she was realizing she should be scared.

"You're going to be okay, Cass," Chance told her as he shut off the Samhain, then re-pressed the button, freezing down the rain, pausing the chaos, the whole universe, because it wouldn't take her from him. He wouldn't let it. He gathered up her body in his arms; she was lighter than he had expected, but he would have held her close even had she not been. Years in scouts had warned him against jostling any injured person's body too much for fear of broken bones or worse, and so he veered away from the chaos of the square. He turned the first corner he could, trotting through suspended raindrops like bead curtains, torn between moving faster, to save her, and the knowledge that it didn't matter because her heart wasn't beating anyway, not with the rain paused, not with the world and the universe halted in their forward progression. He sped along the nearly deserted sidewalk; everyone seemed to have either gone to watch the march or sought refuge from the rain. His only thought was how to find a—what had she called it? *Krankenhauser.*

He needed a map. His first instinct was a gas station. Any sufficiently trafficked road would have one, and he noted several cars on the *strasse*, but he didn't see one as far forward as he could discern. He considered both directions when he reached the corner, then started down the one where the cars seemed more plentiful, but still found no sign of gasoline. He wondered if 1923 Munich had the equivalent of telephone books. When had enough people begun to use telephones to justify directories in places of business? He remembered the image of housewives pulling the cone from the wall in 1940s television shows; would a restaurant have a pay phone with a phonebook he'd find a map in? Across the street, he spotted a café with a cluster of outdoor tables and chairs deserted in the rain. Its door displayed an 'Open' sign, and Chance started toward it, sidling around a car as he went, speeding with hope, anticipation, possibility, Cassie felt lighter, his steps more nimble—

"You, moving! Stop there!"

33

Coincidence: Leonard Kensington standing on a paused *strasse* in *Munchen*, Germany, aiming his serious gun at Chance Sowin, who is standing just in front of the café, among all those rain-deserted tables. When Leonard shouts for him to stop, it will not be the command itself but rather its sudden breaking of the absolute stillness that makes Chance turn. Pain will jigger up and down Chance's neck and around his shoulders as he turns to scan the street, the pedestrians, even the cars, until finally he sees the tall man with the bald head and the ballfield glasses, in the man's hands what appears to Chance to be a stun gun.

"You—you're," Chance stumbles on the words as he realizes how dull it might sound to point out that Leonard is moving.

"Agent Leonard Kensington, of CIRTN. You are in violation of regulations established by the Feynman convention and—hang on," there Leonard will pause as Race's voice booms through his head:

"You've got him?"

"Certain? What—who—?" Chance stutters before he realizes he doesn't care. All he cares about is getting Cassie to someone who can help her.

"I've got him, Race. He's carrying someone—I said stop," Leonard says as Chance begins again to move away. When Chance hesitates, turns again to face Leonard: "Who's she?"

"She needs help."

Leonard inches forward, serious gun still in front of him. "She's hurt."

"Gun shot," Chance says. He wants to ask how the man can move, why he is not paused when the rest of the world has stopped so completely, but he is preoccupied with more urgent concerns. He starts to turn. "I need to get her to a hospital."

"I told you to stop. I don't want to have to—."

"Look, I don't know what you're talking about, but right now, all I care about is getting this girl to a crankerhouse—."

"The only place you're going is back to CIRTN—."

"I don't know what you're so certain of, but I know I'm not going to—."

"Not certain. CIRTN. The International Council for Nuclear and Temporal Research."

"Nuclear and Temporal—," Chance whispers, then stops when the chill shivers down his neck. The same chill he felt as he walked across his lawn and saw the door busted in. The same chill he felt when he first stepped into his father's secret laboratory—

You've been here before.—

Just as Chance has. Just as Leonard has.

You've seen this.

Chance falters. "You—you're from the future."

"Same as you."

"No," Chance says. "Not the same as me." Chance doesn't breathe, can't.

This is inevitability. This is how worlds collide—

"What?" Leonard asks. "Look, just don't—," he stops when Race's voice booms through his head—*Stop talking and bring him back*—then, "What?"

"We're not from the same future," Chance repeats as he feels thoughts supercollide, slamming one against the other to achieve excitement, and he can hardly keep up—the tall man is from an organization that sounds like, but is not, CERN—the hairs on his neck prickle.

Because it's not just how worlds collide; it's how one universe creates another, how one reality causes more. These are the consequences of one young man who just wanted to make a difference and only wanted to save his father. By doing so—by traveling back to yesterday, by traveling to 1923 Munich to kill Adolf Hitler—this is how one young man and the girl he's known since he was a boy not only changed their own history but created a new universe entirely.

"Fuck," Chance whispers as he realizes the enormity of his actions. Up until that moment, quantum uncertainty and alternate timelines existed only as abstractions, but Leonard pointing his gun makes everything concrete reality. Just as seeing Jesus made Gethsemane so real, so too does seeing Leonard make Chance realize the consequences of his actions: "I just created yours."

The moment Cassie started the time machine was the moment reality became visible to CIRTN because it was the very moment that created it. The instant Cassie said—

"I'll help you," and it felt for all the world like a sudden new universe had flashed into existence with an entirely different set of rules and laws and physics, in which time and space were not just the same thing but malleable and flexible and words like "yesterday" and "tomorrow" had no real meaning at all—

was actually precisely as described. A moment that created new worlds, the inciting incident in a chain of events that began on Halloween 2001 and culminates here, in 1923 Munich, just a few blocks from *Odeonsplatz—*

Where Leonard struggles to come to terms with what Chance just said. Leonard, who has a full-fledged biography, who played cricket in knickers and wore a jacket with a badge on it. Leonard, whose parents loved him and whose friends wondered why he was going to accept CIRTN's offer, doesn't want to wonder whether his reality could really be the alternate reality solely because he already knows the answer.

This is the knowledge not that you don't exist but rather never have: Heisenberg uncertainty, a dense pit in the stomach that makes you want to turn inside out. A rage against the universe for giving one young man— who can't be more than, what, 26, 28?—the ability to create reality, to change the past, to let there be light on the only world you've ever known until this very moment.

Leonard's grip on his gun falters. "Race," he says, "Race, I need you. He says—he says he just killed a man and created—is that—is that possible?" he asks, frantically, even though he already knows Race's answer—

"Dear God, I think it might be."—

even as Chance starts to turn again, because he doesn't need to stick around while Leonard wrestles with some existential crisis. He's got his own personal crisis, and he's carrying her.

Without thinking, perhaps even without meaning to, Leonard fires his serious gun.

Across Chance's turned back flashes a sensation like an axe-blow, quick and shattering, as the sky flashes deep purple as inverted lightning. Air whooshes out of Chance's lungs as the rain begins again to fall fall fall, and Chance stumbles as Cassie's body seems to double, perhaps triple in weight to knock him off balance. He struggles to hold his arms steady but they let go, shuddering with electrostatic tingle, as he sinks to his knees.

Cassie—suddenly unfrozen—cries out as she hits the ground, and Chance falls nearly on her but forces himself sideways, comes to rest on his back with the rain falling down down down upon him.

"Chance?"

Great weight atop his chest, or more accurately inside it, heart like a black hole sucking all his air into it. His lungs feel like they've turned to bone, and the rain falls into his open mouth, filling his windpipe, but finally he hacks it all up, a great, wracking seizure. Out with all that bad air, all that negative air, before his body curls into the fetal position as he sucks in good air, better air. "I'm here," he struggles to move to her.

Cassie, for her part, is still. "What happened?"

"I did," Leonard says. Standing over them, staring down his gun.

"He's from the future. He tried to shoot me," Chance says. His back aches with the after-effects, tiny tremors like electric ripples shuddering through his body.

"I don't think he tried," Cassie says, as Chance feels her fingertips on his back—not through his shirt, but against his skin. He realizes he can feel the rain, too, sluicing toward his waistband. He shivers.

"No one's ever—," Leonard is about to say no one has ever survived a serious charge, but the sentence dies in his throat when Chance lunges up at him, driving his shoulder into Leonard's waist to tackle him sideways. Leonard bends around Chance, twisting sideways to slam Chance against the sidewalk. Dirty-bomb pain explodes through Chance's skull as his cranium strikes the concrete before tiny white starbursts smash together in the air in front of him, quantum collisions that leave behind anti-consciousness.

Chance struggles against both the darkness coalescing around his head and Leonard's grasp, pushing his palm against Leonard's chin as his fingers close around Chance's neck. He chops Leonard just below the ear, hard enough to knock him sideways; Chance scuttles backward as Leonard tucks into a tumblesault from which he emerges in a defensive crouch.

Cassie struggles along the sidewalk, toward the café's brick façade.

"Don't move, Cass. I'm coming," Chance calls to her as he blocks Leonard's first punch. He jounces backward, feels his back press against one of the café's outdoor tables, and he swings the first chair he can grab as hard as he can. Leonard twists like limbo, raising his foot to catch the chair's leg with his ankle. When he scissors downward, Chance's firm grasp of the seat jerks him forward. Leonard takes advantage of Chance's momentum and smashes his elbow into Chance's nose.

Hot tears spring to Chance's eyes as cold rain washes bloodgush down his lips and chin; he stumbles backward, clutching his broken nose, and Leonard foot-flips the chair, grabbing its back to swing its legs around his head in an arc. Chance ducks to avoid it and can't keep his feet, hands to the coldslick sidewalk, but he spins to cartwheel his lower body to first sweep Leonard's right knee and then crack his foot down on Leonard's ankle. Surprised pain zippers up Leonard's leg as he crumples to his knee, and then Chance chops him hard under his arm, where a nerve shudders pain like white lightning across Leonard's side as he sinks to the ground.

The chair clatters to the sidewalk. Chance's chest heaves, his breath coming in furious spurts, but he turns to run back to Cassie. She sits against the brick wall, clutching the time machine. "I thought I told you not to move."

"Who was that?"

"We did it, Cass. He was from a different future."

"What'd he want with us?" The blood on her shirt looks darker. The stain has spread.

"I didn't bother asking," Chance takes the time machine. "Still work?"

"I—think so," her voice weak, soft.

Chance steps back, presses the button and turns the dial until he can feel the energy field through his body. He nods. "It works. Let's get you to a hospit—."

She sees Leonard struggle up behind Chance, but Chance's pressing the button cuts her warning off just as Leonard sucker-slams him from behind.

What follows is the sudden coincidence of universes. Before that moment, there were only collisions and ricochets, but the moment Leonard and his Safe-generated field encountered the Samhain's energy, both attempted to merge. Worse than the impact is the sudden jolt of energy that knocks both Chance and Leonard to the ground. An electric singe bristles through Leonard's jaw like a popped breaker, leaving only silence, and his skin prickles like a charge has left it. He pulls on his earlobe as he struggles to rise from the ground, but no answer comes. "Race? Are you there?" he says, but no response, and something about the finality of the way his implant shorted makes him think it wasn't temporary.

Chance springs from his back, rubbing his eyes as he sits up. They don't seem to be working correctly, and even if they are, his brain apparently doesn't understand how to process the information they're receiving. The world has reversed, storm-grey clouds bleached to bone, from which black rain falls like acid through a phosphorescent sky flashed by an jagged indigo lightning like a slice through a tie-dye troposphere. Chance squeezes his eyes shut, attempts to shake his head as he scrambles sideways toward Cassie, whom he sees also in the same backward colors: black hair glowing light, brilliant teeth indigo, bright eyes darkly shimmering. Her body like night, black blouse, blood like a bright splotch over a tiny bullet-hole moon.

"Chance?" her voice is high, somewhere between fear and wonder, when she sees Chance and Leonard, both of whom appear like photographic negatives surrounded by golden aurae. She understands instinctively what has happened: the collision of two time machines. "Are you—Look out!" she shouts, because as Chance struggles to his feet—dropping the Samhain, which clatters to the ground but remains functional—Leonard picks up a chair leg he wields and swings like a baseball bat. Chance rolls sideways, twisting, can't duck in enough time to fully dodge but still manages to catch the wood, noting as he does so that Leonard still looks normal to him, that Leonard doesn't seem inverted.

Chance pulls hard enough on the chair leg to draw Leonard closer, then bashes his elbow into Leonard's eye—

Another jolt. Colors right themselves. Gunmetal sky and dark grey pavement, but the rain falls upward. The world backward: cars reversing up the strasse with their mufflers sucking in exhaust—

Chance uses the chair leg to windmill Leonard's arm over and around his head, planting a foot into the same knee he'd kicked before—

Jolt, and backward time slows, blurrrrs before righting itself, raindown again.—

Leonard's leg bends as he sinks to his other knee, as Chance lifts the chair leg over his head, twirling it like a baton to clamp it around his neck. Leonard's pulls against Chance's grip, but Chance plants a knee into Leonard's back—

Jolt, and time squeezes together, bunched up and compressed forward quicklapse, rain as from buckets, cars at dangerous speeds—

Chance pulls harder, harder. Leonard sinks sideways. When the foot of the chair leg strikes the sidewalk, it jitters out of Chance's hand, but he slips his arms down, grasping Leonard from behind—

Time slows again to normal—

Chance tries to get his elbow around Leonard's neck, but Leonard slips down and presses forward. The world continues to jolt and change around the fighting men: when Chance grabs Leonard's ankle—*everything inverts all over again*—Leonard flicks his ankle and twists to chop just on the bulletgraze on Chance's shoulder, which flares with sudden, exquisite pain. Chance stutters backward, clutching his arm but still managing to deflect Leonard's next blow—*time slow*—grabbing Leonard's elbow and then aiming a kick high.

When Leonard catches Chance's leg and twists, Chance leaps to let himself be thrown, landing on his knee a yard away, steadying hand to the pavement, pain in his shoulder burning like embers. When Leonard rushes him, Chance tucks, focusing his body to thrust his elbow forward, and when he feels Leonard's torso—*colors invert, as time goes backward and the rain rises up again*—Chance pushes to his feet and pulls Leonard up and over him, crashing him into a table.

Leonard pulls a chair from behind him, sweeping its legs in a broad stroke Chance avoids by skipping backward and sucking in his stomach. Leonard finishes the arc by raising the chair above his head to drive it downward, but Chance knuckles it head on, wood splitting around his fist. He grabs two falling bars by the bottoms to wield one in either hand as Leonard drops the chair to pick up another, but Chance thrusts a bar through the chair back and twists it out of Leonard's hands, yanking the chair high and backward over his head even as he smashes Leonard in the face with his other hand—

time down again, raindrops falling on his head—

Chance curses the drops: the longer they fall, the less likely he will get Cassie to a hospital to save her. He realizes he needs to stop fighting, now, and move on.

He spinkicks Leonard in the solar plexus—*inverted colors but time stays forward, raindrops iridescent in a sky like a tanning-booth smile*—leaps and twists. The air seems thicker, he jumps higher, harder, his body lighter, and he shatters Leonard's jaw with his elbow—*time down again, inverted raindrops*—as he cartwheels over Leonard, landing behind him but keeping momentum, torquing as he grips skull—*color return to the world, the right colors in the right orders, but the world in pause*—and crooks his elbow around Leonard's neck, flexing his bicep and all the muscles in his forearm while he pushes Leonard's cranium forwardforwardforward until Leonard's body falls slack and Chance lets go, stumbles toward Cassie, weaving as though drunk, toward the time machine still on the sidewalk next to her.

34

Cassie's eyes had closed, and paused raindrops had
beaded on her face. Her blouse had soaked
through so that he could make out her white bra
beneath, almost transparent save for where it was
crimson with blood.

Chance gripped her body, squeezed her shoulders,
clutched her wet cheeks. Her skin was so cold. "No,
Cassie, come on. I need you to come back to me."

Cassie's eyelashes fluttered. "You're okay."

"Stay with me," Chance said, reaching for the time
machine.

"Too late."

"No, it's not. I can—," he stopped, because he
realized, then, as his finger sought the button to turn on

the time machine, that its LCD still glowed. "It's still on."

"So was his. He must have been using some other method to manipulate time, but however he did it, whenever he touched you, his time machine affected the Higgs field the Samhain was generating. Basically, you canceled each other out."

"So I'll reset it—."

"It's already done. Doesn't even hurt anymore."

"But I can still—what do we do?"

But Cassie's eyes closed, then, and when she exhaled, softly, slowly, her body shifted. All its energy, all her life: gone.

His trembling fingers shivered on her cheeks. "No, you can't, you can't," he said, his voice cracking and breaking away, while manic energy coursed through his body, his muscles, his brain. He pressed two fingers to her neck, fighting impatience to find a pulse, a flutter, anything, anything at all.

Nothing.

She was gone.

"No," he said, again, like he could change it, like he believed he could fix it, and he pulled her from the wall, easing her body down to the cold-slicked grey pavement. Old first-aid methods guided him into problem-solving mode: airway, breathing, circulation—two fingers, chin up, a breath, then another. Her chest rose, fell, but didn't rise again. He cut his finger on wire in her bra when he tore open her blouse to free her chest, her flesh pale, breasts lifeless, nipples small and hard. He found her sternum, two-fingers up, clamped his hands one over the other, locking his fingers and elbows to PUMP, one-one-thousand, two-one-thousand, and then on three her ribs crumpled under his hands. The first-aid classes he'd taken had never mentioned that, and he very nearly lost it right then, but he knew he had to keep it together if he wanted to keep her with him, so he bent to breathe twice into her mouth.

He felt himself start to move faster, compress harder, urgency and anxiety piggybacking on the adrenaline slamming through his system, and he fought to keep control. Rainfall soaked through his shirt while the cold seeped into his body, and the world moved on, kept going, and somewhere, someone was screaming.

He didn't realize at first that it was his own voice. He was too occupied by trying to restore life to her body, because she couldn't be gone. Couldn't be. He couldn't do it without her, and when he bent again to breathe for her, light buzzed through his head, washing through his vision, making his brain feel like it was twitching and jitterring as his muscles had. His body shuddered, and he sank to his ass on the cold, hard sidewalk.

This is loss: this can't be happening. These towers can't fall. My father can't die. The girl I love will breathe again. Loss is rarely instantaneous because it takes so long to accept it. Loss isn't running from the dust; it's waking up the following morning and being surprised when you realize it wasn't, in fact, a dream. Loss isn't losing the girl you love but rather wondering if she knew your feelings you never told her.

Chance squeezed his eyes shut, fist clenched to his mouth, and then he reached to pick up the time machine as he scuttled back against the side of the building. Staring at it in his hands, the display still neon blue, he felt temptation. What if he just went back a few minutes? What if he just kept that one bullet from hitting her?

They'd never have to know, she and his former self. He could disappear into the—

He could only describe it as an anti-flash. Imagine a great bolt of lightning from the inside of the storm cloud, static electric tension and then a blinding flash all around, and then consider the opposite. The universe's lights seemed to flicker as if something had, for a moment, diverted all its power.

In its wake, a changed world. Cars disappeared one second to the next, and the sky cleared its clouds to make way for sunshine and birdsong. People hustled and bustled about, and they didn't have to step over Cassie or Kensington or the detritus of Chance's confrontation because it all vanished, blinked away so suddenly it was more like it had never existed at all.

Chance stared out at the world. This new world. He stood, shielding his eyes from the sudden sunlight as he looked down the street—

And then another flash. This one bright, more intense. The sky darkened again, the rain reappeared in the sky. The man from the future was still gone, but Chance was certain, that time, that details had changed, that the world had shifted—colors inverted, as if the world had jerked backward and time itself had lurched into reverse—

Chance found himself staring at a wall. He turned, scanned the street, and across it saw a ghost-version of himself backward fighting a ghost-version of the man he'd just killed.

While Cassie looked on.

He shouted her name, excitement and relief flooding his voice—

But a flash and he was back where he'd started from, in front of the café. Sunshine in Munich, but no other man, no fight, no Cassie, and he swallowed the dread that crept up into his throat. His gut tightened. He had thought that Cassie had overstated the possibility of truly altering, truly damaging, spacetime, but, he realized, as the universe blinked and shifted and disappeared into and reformed out of uncertainty all around him, this must have been what she had feared.

They had created a feedback loop, two universes supercolliding head-on like particles in an accelerator, and they would keep doing so—

"Oh, God," Chance said as he realized then the enormity of it. He remembered the other complication, why they couldn't return to their own lives: they had created another in which they hadn't existed, because, if his father never died, they never would never find the machine to use it, which meant they would never go back, back, back, first to save him, then to Jerusalem before finally arriving in Munich—

But if they never went back, he couldn't be standing there, which meant they had to—

He remembered his father's admonition about quantum uncertainty, trying to exist in two realities at once, and he wondered if that was what was happening. Quantum uncertainty occurring on a universal level, while all of existence attempted to simultaneously occupy two realities. Time bounced between the moment Chance killed Hitler and the moment he left the future with Cassie, and all those years in between were attempting to give up certainty for potential. Which meant that, if it was allowed to continue, the universe might blur, so confused it could no longer differentiate the singularity of events, which would, then, all begin to occur at once.

"Oh, Jesus," Chance said as the universe blinked and recoalesced around him, because God didn't seem to be listening and at least he'd seen Jesus. He looked out at the world, terrified that it was going to blink itself out of existence, and him with it, and he realized what he must do. To fix the continuum, to prevent the universe from becoming stuck in uncertainty, he had to go forward to keep them from using the time machine in the first place.

As he understood that, he realized something more: he would save her. If they never time traveled, Cassie would never die in his arms.

Chance looked down at the time machine, reset the geospatial coordinates to the numbers Cassie had designated 'home.' He didn't even look around one last time before he pressed the button, simply did so, and then he

s   t   r   e   t   c   h   e   d

again across years and decades

a mad blur from 1923 to 2001. People lived and died as he took a breath, wars were fought, presidents killed, missiles launched. A man set foot on the moon, and nothing seemed impossible, because nothing ever is—

32

A shiver slithered up his neck as he blasted onto Bradbury Lane—night. Streetlights stained the darkness orange. His father's SUV in their driveway, the house's windows dark. He started toward the lawn, then stopped when he considered causality.

He could destroy the time machine to keep them from using it, but then, how could he be standing there, facing his house and holding it? That wouldn't close the loop; that would just create another possible way for events to occur, another reality, another set of potentials that time could or could not follow. He tried to remember what his father had said before they'd left him in his lab, tried to remember what Cassie had told him in her living roo—

He gasped at the thought of her frantic eyes: "Because he didn't. You did."

You've been here before.

Was it possible that wasn't the first time he'd convinced Cassie to travel back in time with him?

He didn't think it was a question of possibility, not with the universe fuzzing uncertainly around him, a kaleidoscope of quantum neon and a scent like shorted electronics. Could it really have been inevitable, since the moment he'd crossed his lawn to see that busted deadbolt, since the moment his father had pressed that ring into his palm, that he would end up there on Bradbury Lane in the small hours of Halloween? Could it have been unavoidable that the universe and reality would flicker all around him, at some times like an old fluorescent tube struggling toward luminescence and at others like an aging engine trying again and again to turn over?

But if Chance's only hope is to keep himself and the girl he loves from using the time machine in the first place, if his only hope for preventing quantum uncertainty from overwhelming the universe is to ensure that he and Cassie never travel into the past—

So long as he carries the cross and kills Hitler, so long as he stands on Bradbury Lane and thinks of her words—

"Because he didn't. You did."—

He will be unsuccessful. He will tell Cassie again and again not to use the time machine, and failing that, he will walk across the street, to his house, and he will descend the stairs into the basement as he pulls the rosary ring from his pocket. He will jam that ring to its hilt into the lock, and he will bust into his father's secret office, where he will find on his father's workbench a time machine exactly identical, in every way, to the one he will be carrying, but as he reaches toward it, he will—

return again to Bradbury Lane, where what should be his house will not be, where an indigo sky above him will sputter lavender like lightning as the world shifts and changes around him, herky-jerking backward before its progress slows and skips and jumps like a badly buffered video streaming over the Internet.

This is a temporal paradox, a universal game of three-card monte with reality—

round and round it goes, and where it stops—

The universe like a delirious carousel, quantum mechanical fireworks like luminous flowers in spectral darkness. Time is just biology's unsuccessful attempt to render reality finite, limiting it to mortality, but the universe is mad, mad to live and desirous of everything all at the same time—

You've seen this.

Round and round he goes: Chance crosses his lawn and crosses his lawn and crosses his lawn. Chance will watch his father die and pass out himself, and Trish will drive him home drive him home drive him home. He will see Cassie's portrait, and he will remember her hair and her eyes—

kissing her, and her lips, and the golden sunshine and the green grass and the spangling, sparkling water—

and the time machine.

When they find it, they will debate whether they should use it, never realizing that's tricky misdirection and that the real question is how many times they already have. How many times has Chance snapped Geisel's neck? How many times has Chance carried the cross of the man who would become Christ? How many times has that stray bullet struck Cassie, and how many times has Chance fought Leonard, and how many times has Cassie died in Chance's arms? How many times has Chance found himself on Bradbury Lane, the time machine in his hand, and gone up to Cassie's bedroom to convince her not to use it, and how many times has he tried to destroy the time machine to prevent the universe from collapsing on itself? How many times has Chance come again forward come again forward, to this very evening, to this very street? How many times this wild dark long year has Halloween come not just early but over and over and over again?

Chance will ask himself all those questions before finally he will settle on the only one that really counts. If he has returned again and again to Bradbury Lane, how can he make this time the last? How can he make this time different?

You know this.

Just asking that question, however, will change his actions. Quantum mechanics is full of dynamic flexibility, thought experiments in which cats in safes with poison vials and unpredictably radioactive atoms propose greater logic problems than Zen koans. Consider again an electron the certainty of which, in terms of speed and position, can only be determined by firing a photon—a tiny quantum of light—at it, and then realize that doing so will alter both.

Such is referred to as the observer effect: observing a system necessarily changes the nature of it. The mere fact that Chance has thought to ask those questions indicates he is aware of them and will continue to seek their answers—

Chance will pick up the Samhain in his father's lab, feeling its heft, and he will chuck both it and the one he is carrying at the wall, destroying both. Chance and the Samhain he carried will flash out of existence even as the one he picked up from the workbench reappears on it.—

and

Chance will use a hammer to smash it, and even as the steel strikes the Samhain, Chance will disappear and the hammer will return to its peg.—

and

Chance will return again and again to Cassie's bedroom, and he will again and again ask her to refuse his request to help him when he proposes returning to the past to save his father's life.—

and on and on, and all the while he will concentrate exclusively on saving the universe, on trying to prevent their time travel in the first place, but just as the question of whether they should use the time machine distracted them from wondering how many times they might have already done so, so too is the idea of preventing a temporal paradox from rending the universe uncertain misdirection. Chance moved back home because he'd felt unable to do anything. Chance beat himself up because he'd felt unable to save the man whose cross he'd carried. Chance got so focused on making a difference he thought that using a time machine to return to the past to save his father was the only way to do so.

Chance will focus so intensely on imploring the girl he loves not to use the time machine that he will forget how it felt to lose her. Until—

Observe (and in so doing, change):

33

Flashflashflash forward, a sea of years and blur of events to his house, his street, and damned if Chance doesn't stand there in the middle of the road, between his house and Cassie's, and think:

You've been here before.

The sky above him flickers like a sputtering fluorescent tube, and he realizes this is more than a handful of timelines intersecting, more than a paradox, more than an endless feedback loop—

You've seen this.

—it's n-dimensional permutations supercolliding. The same thing, over and over and over again. But standing there, holding the time machine, something in him, something visceral, something that has nothing to do with physics and everything to do with life, tells him the only way to fix it, the only way to remerge reality into a single, linear, consistent timeline, the only way to stop time from looping back on itself and bringing him over and over and over again to that very moment, is to convince Cassie not to use it. He knows he has tried and failed before, but he also knows he has to try again, because the flashes have become faster and more erratic, a hyperpulse on a hospital heart monitor, and if one overlaps another, or if that monitor flatlines—

He uses the mailbox spare key to open the door of her house, crosses the foyer and climbs the stairs, seeking her bedroom. He slips through the door and wonders how many times he has stood there, looking at her form in her bed, the moonlight on her white comforter, her black hair like ink spilled on her pillow.

He sits on her bed, just near her waist, and he whispers her name. Again.

Cassie moans, rolled toward him, her arm slipping from under her blanket.

Chance squeezed her fingers. "Cassie."

Her eyelids flutter open, and when she sees him she starts, pulling her arm away as she sits up and pulls her comforter to her chest. "Chance?" She closes her eyes tight and then opens them wide again, as if she thinks they're playing tricks on her. "What're you doing here?"

"I—," Chance says, but his voice cracks. He would've hoped that having been there before, so damned many times, he'd know what to say by then, but nothing comes except desperation. Nothing except everything that had already come over and over again, and Chance tries not to break down but can't help it. He begins to shiver.

Cassie touches his shoulder but jerks her hand back. "You're cold. And wet," she pushes her comforter toward him, wrapping it around him as she pulls him toward her, rubbing his body through the fabric.

"It was raining," Chance says against her neck. But it's not. Beyond her bedroom window, there isn't a single cloud in the clear, moonlit sky.

"Where were you?"

"It's a long story," he says, as she rubs his back and neck, but winces when she touches his injured shoulder. "I got shot earlier. Well. Later, technically," he says. A shudder jogs through his body, and his breath starts to come in fits and starts as though he can't get enough of it. "I guess. I don't fucking know anymore. It's all ass-back—."

"Shhh," she says, pulling back, "You're not making any sense, okay? So let's just start from the beginning and go from there."

But when's the beginning? Which came first, the time machine or the paradox?

They wouldn't have used the time machine if they hadn't found it, and they wouldn't have found it had his father not died. His father might not have died had Chance not interrupted the burglary when he'd come home—

He started there, with driving up to his house that morning, or tomorrow. He didn't know how to explain the chronology because he didn't understand it himself anymore. He only knew what had happened, and once he began with crossing his lawn, the story came easily, and he told her about the break-in, the secret laboratory, and the government agents. He showed her the time machine and told her about the explosion and the no-longer-falling rain, about saving his father. He told her about Jerusalem, and about Jesus, about the arrest and the crucifixion. He told her about Munich and Hitler.

He hesitated, then.

"What is it?"

He looked at her, his stomach tight, and then, his voice strained, he told her about losing her. He told her that Hitler had shot her in the stomach, and he had paused time to get her to a hospital, but that a man from a future they had created had stopped him. "I tried to save you, but it just wouldn't fucking work. You just wouldn't start breathing again. And that was when everything started to—," he told her about the flashing, about the endless temporal loop, about how he thought that everything seemed to be happening and unhappening all at the same time, or at least he did his best to; he wasn't sure, by that point, how much sense he was making. "And I wouldn't even fucking care if I could've just saved you."

She began to rub his back but avoided his injured arm. "You're serious, aren't you?"

"And I can't figure out how to stop it from happening. How many times have I already sat here and told you exactly the same story? I just need to make it stop. Just—promise me you won't do it. I'm going to ask you to help me, but promise me you won't."

"Oh, come on, would that really make any difference, Chance Sowin? You're one of the most stubborn people I've ever known."

He swallowed, holding her gaze. "I wouldn't do it without you, Cass."

Her eyes narrowed curiously. "No? Why not?"

He hesitated: *You've been here before.*

He wondered, then, how many times he had been. He wondered how many times he'd looked into her eyes, and how many times he'd not told her the whole truth. How many times had he risked his life to help Jesus and save his father, risked the whole world to make it a better place, but never, even once, risked his heart to tell her how he felt? To tell her that even after all those years, he still remembered her cherry cola lips; that even after not having seen her for so long, her senior portrait could still take his breath away and knock away every damned thought he had.

"Because I love you, Cassie. I always have, and I wouldn't have done it without you, because the only reason I thought I could start over was that I thought I could do it with you. Kissing you made me feel like anything was possible, and when I thought I had lost you, nothing else mattered."

"You didn't tell me you kissed me." Her lips didn't smile, but her eyes did.

"After I carried the cross," he told her. "It's true, you know."

"That you kissed me? I believe it."

"No. That I love you. That I always have," Chance leaned forward. His lips met hers, soft against his firm desire. Their tongues flickered, and time seemed to wrap around and around them, stretching on and on into eternity, into the universe, and by the time it was over, Chance had ceased to exist.

36

Chance Sowin hoped only for a new beginning. He pulled his rental car up to the curb in front of his house, squeezed the steering wheel as he took a deep breath, and got out of the car. As he stepped up the curb, his neck prickled into electric goosebumps when experience and memory supercollided into hyperspace déjà vu as he crossed his lawn—

You've been here before.

and noticed the busted-in lock on his broken front door. He called 911 as he eased down the stairs and into the basement, where he found a man holding a gun on his father. During a brief altercation, both Chance and his father were shot, and by the time paramedics arrived, Dennis Sowin had pressed into his son's hand a rosary ring—

You've seen this.

before both men fell unconscious.

Chance Sowin survived to wake up in the hospital.

When a doctor came to his room, Chance couldn't decide whether he knew his father had died because of the doctor's sorry eyes and haggard manner or because—

You know this.

of the deep sense of déjà vu that had settled into his bones.

*

You've been here before and seen this and know this: Trisha Lackesis has brought Chance home, where time and again he has been struck dumb by the sight of Cassie's senior portrait, the face he has known for so many years cutting through ages of distance and time to rekindle in him feelings he had thought he grown out of, but no, they fit as they always did: tightly.

When he saw his father's lab, he couldn't explain the dread he felt when he saw the device on the workbench. It looked like a CD player, not much different from any he had seen in the window displays of the high-end electronics stores he'd so often passed on his way around Manhattan, but something about it unnerved him. By the time federal agents Hanley and Geisel arrived, Chance was already unsettled. He and Jerry followed Hanley back across the street to the Lackesis house. It had begun to rain.

*

He sat at the large table while Hanley asked questions, but he was distracted by the feeling of familiarity he couldn't shake. The tiny hairs on the back of his neck seemed to have risen to permanent static attention, and when the front door opened, and Chance found all his attention focused on the dining room doorway, the approaching footsteps, that he didn't gasp—

You'vebeenherebefore. You'veseenthis. Youknowthis.

when he saw Cassie was a miracle. The portrait hadn't done her justice. Hanley began to introduce himself, but Cassie cut him off. "I need to speak to Chance. Alone," she said.

Hanley glanced back toward Chance, then nodded. Chance rose to follow Cassie out of the room. "What is it? Are you—?" he started to ask, but she cut him off, too.

"Did they find your father's lab?" she asked him as they entered the living room.

"Oh, for fuck's sake, am I the only one he never told?" he asked, because on top of the crazy strange feeling he couldn't shake, he also had to deal with secrets his father—

"He didn't tell me, Chance. You did."

Chance's thoughts flashed away before they came to full form. He plunked himself down on the sofa but never looked away from her. "Me?"

"I think—last night. You came into my bedroom—."

"But I was in Jersey City last night. And I didn't even know about it—."

"You certainly seemed to last night."

"So what, I just showed up, in your bedroom? What'd I say to you, Cassie?"

She hesitated, then, "You told me they found a secret room your father built in your basement, and that they found—you told me there was a time machine, and—."

"A time machine? Seriously? I told you my father discovered a way to time travel and hid it in our basement?" Chance asked. Because though he had hoped she might help him understand what was happening, he didn't think wild technological fantasies were the answer.

"You don't believe me."

"No, I believe you fine. I just don't believe me. I mean, a time machine—?"

"I didn't believe it myself. But now . . . everything you told me is coming true. So what'd they find in there? Maybe if we can find out what he was working on—."

"Oh, who gives a great goddamn what he was working on? Fuck, he's dead. What fucking difference does it make?" Chance asked, his voice rising as he spoke.

Cassie sat next to him, put her hand on his knee instead.

"I'm sorry."

*

Chance and Cassie returned to the dining room. More questions. More allegations. Hanley seemed especially eager to recruit Cassie, but she hesitated: "I wasn't actually working with Uncle Dennis. Not until next semester." Ultimately, however, she relented, accepting a notebook she began to skim, asking questions about the government's knowledge. Hanley seemed reluctant to divulge much, but then he began talk of quantum bombs and Anthrax; when Cassie didn't believe the first and Chance argued the second, Hanley brought up the affair.

Cassie rose after both her mother and father had stormed out of the dining room, allowing a brief blast of cold wind and rain through the door as they left the house. She picked up the device that had inspired Chance's moment of dread as she gathered her things to leave, and then, when Hanley reached for her wrist, pulled it back. "If you so much as touch me, I swear to Christ I'll knock you cold," she told him, storming out, and neither agent said a word as Chance followed her out, into the living room, where she sat on the sofa, holding the device in her hands. He was about to ask what it was, but she turned it on, turned a dial, and Chance felt a sudden energy like a soft tingle all over his body—

you'vebeenherebeforeyou'veseenthisyouknowthis

while his persistent feeling of déjà vu increased so much it took his breath away.

"You feel it," she said.

Outside, lightning sizzled open the darkness, and thunder blasted through the rift it left behind. Behind him, the front door opened. The chilly air crept up his neck, but it didn't matter, because he already had a terminal case of goosebumps. Cassie moved, but Chance caught her wrist: "Where's Nick?" he asked Trish.

"He went to your house."

Hanley stiffened, shot a look at Geisel, ticked his head sideways. They hustled out of the dining room, crossed the hall and the foyer, yanking the door open. Outside, the storm was loud and furious. Chance, Cassie, Jerry, and Trish all pounded out after them, into the darkness and the rain. Hard wind bit down the street, where Hanley and Geisel stood, looking up and down it. Jerry caught up to them, and the three began shouting at each other, but Chance couldn't hear them over the rain.

Chance saw Nick emerge from the house, then, and immediately understood what he had been doing. Hanley paused as he crossed the street, drawing his gun. Which made Jerry draw his, and Geisel draw his.

Cassie caught up with Chance. In her hands she held the device—

you'vebeenherebeforeyou'veseenthisyouknowthis—

and she pressed the buttons on it, quickly, like she knew exactly what she was doing, and then Chance's house exploded, a giant, whooshing, percussive fireball that speed-blossomed into the darkness and shroomed into the night and the storm, and he put his hands up against not just the blinding flash but also the hard, hot wave that followed like flaming breath and the shards of glass from exploding windows he heard tinkling against the street, and lightning flashed, too, luminesced the sky electric, and then—

the world wrenchedtwingedcareened around him,
and the inside of his head
>snapped<
and then nothing.

Silence.

He pulled his arm down.

His first thought was that the blast had killed him, that this was the afterlife, that heaven existed forever in the moment of death; the world had

Stopped.

The rain hung in mid-air.

The wind held its breath.

The storm had paused

mid-gasp

on its way to a peal of thunder

that never came.

Even the great, blooming cloud of the explosion had frozen in a lightning-lit instant over his house.

Chance realized he was holding his breath. He let it out.

The world did not.

He looked at Cassie. Looked at the device in her hands. Back into her eyes.

Nothing in the world moved, but a million billion universes, all possible in their own ways, ricocheted through his brain; a billion causes and all their infinite effects coalesced like silver suspended raindrops into one perfect, shimmering, crystalline moment. The fireball and the lightning flash, Jerry and Geisel and Hanley frozen with their guns drawn as if a suspended frame of film.

Chance reached out to touch a raindrop; it burst under his finger. He thought of her dream, and he said: "God, Cassie, what the hell's happening?"

Cassie shook her head. "I don't know."

"Do you think—?" he stopped, because he didn't know what to ask her. He felt like the universe hung on them, that something about its existence, the way it might progress, the very nature of it, depended, right then, on them. "If I really came to your bedroom last night, what else did I tell you?"

"You told me we were going to use it to save your father, and then we were going to do all these other things that we're going to end up messing up."

"But how? Maybe we could do it," he told her, and a sudden sense of the potential blew hard through him. Using the device in her hands, Cassie had stopped the rain in the sky, had frozen lightning and silenced thunder; using the same device they could—

Images filled his head. *A grainy blur of JFK in a convertible. A gaunt, bearded man in a stovepipe hat. "I have a dream."*

The planes crashing into the World Trade Center. The towers falling—

Could they stop it?

you'vebeenherebeforeyou'veseenthisyouknowthis

"But maybe we can't," she told him. "Because it's going to keep happening over and over and over again, and we're just going to come back to right this second, and we're just going to do exactly what you told me we were going to do. And if we do—," she bit her lip.

His jaw was clenched. "Well? What?" he asked. He thought she would say something about how it would disrupt the space-time continuum, or unmake the universe, or create some kind of physical cataclysm that would destroy half the world.

She said none of those things. She looked at him, her eyes frightened. "If we do, I'm going to get killed."

Is that what it came down to? A choice between trying to make a difference or saving her? "You really think all that would happen?"

"I—I think it already did. I can't think of any other explanation."

"And there's no way around it? I mean, we could do something, Cassie. Really do something to make a difference—."

"You made me promise to say no. Because you said you wouldn't do it without me," she told him, but she said it like there was more she didn't say.

He thought of the possibilities again. He thought of JFK and MLK. He thought of running from the billowing dustcloud of the World Trade Center, and of his father pressing the rosary ring into his palm. He thought of the impotence he had felt, the singular desire matched catastrophically with the complete inability to do something, anything. "What, like I'd be scared to do it alone?"

"No, not scared, just—."

"What, Cass?"

"You told me you wouldn't do it without me because you said you loved me, Chance. You said you love me," she said, and as she did so her voice trembled, ever so slightly, as if she were scared of saying it, as if she were worried it wasn't true, as if she were worried it really had all been just a dream.

The only thing in the world that can stop an already-paused world is a great truth, the kind of truth that blows through your soul and takes your breath away, the kind of great truth that changes the universe more completely and more quickly than traveling back in time to save your father does. The kind of great truth from which you can't recover, that changes you too much, after which the only thing you can do is let yourself completely go and find your own rebirth.

The kind of truth, then, that kills you, all the parts of you that count, that destroys your entire life and makes possible a new beginning. The kind of truth that makes you suddenly realize that it's okay that you couldn't do anything, that of course you couldn't stop those planes, of course you couldn't save your father, of course you can't save the world, of course of course of course, but you can do something right now, because even more important than doing something good is doing something you believe in, something that proves that you're suddenly a stronger man than you were a moment before, and so you do:

You take a step forward in that paused, frozen world, you take a single step in a world of suspended raindrops and brilliant lightning, and you put your hands on the cheeks of the person you love, the person you've loved for longer than you can remember, and you bring her face to yours and you kiss her—

You kiss her—

and suddenly you don't need a time machine, suddenly it's not déjà vu. Because suddenly you create an unbreakable link between that day at the lake when you were eleven years old and this very moment and the uncertain future, suddenly all those moments and none of those moments matter because of this one, right now, with your lips on hers, with your finger tips in her hair, and you kiss her and you invest in your kiss everything you have and know and are, and when you feel her kiss you back, when you feel her hands upon your back, *you know this* was the right thing to do and the right moment to do it in, and you clutch her, you clutch her hard and close, and you put your mouth close to her ear and you whisper, softly, surely, "Turn off the time machine, Cassie."

Cassie had told him a great truth, and so all those things were exactly what Chancellor Sowin did in that moment, and suddenly

the world

felt

new—

because this is how the world will end: not with a whimper or bang, but a kiss—

and the rain started again to fall, the lightning flashed itself out of existence and thunder boomed behind it, and the fireball bloomedbloomedbloomed into the night, into the darkness of a brand new world.

37

Time may pause, the world may freeze, but life never stops, and Chance held Cassie for only another moment before he heard Hanley shout for Nick to get down on the ground, now, while Geisel shouted to Hanley that he should be more worried about Chance and Cassie. Hanley turned, then, to squint at Chance and Cassie.

"They seemed to flicker for a second there," Geisel said.

Hanley's eyes ticked from Chance to Cassie, then saw that Cassie was holding the device. He began to approach them, and as he passed Jerry, who had pulled his gun, he shot the detective in the head without looking away from Cassie. "You should put that on the ground, Miss Lackesis," Hanley said.

When she didn't move, Hanley grabbed her wrist. She shouted as he hard-spun her around, and Chance lunged forward, didn't know what he intended to do. Hanley torqued Cassie's forearm severely enough to make her drop the time machine.

Chance caught it. One of its four buttons must activate it, to pause everything; he mashed them just as Geisel barreled into him, driving him to the ground as the world stopped around them. The two men tumbled ass over head over each other as they hit the ground, grunting and cursing, each struggling to punch and kick the other. Chance lost his grip on the time machine, which skittered away, but the world stayed frozen; the raindrops stayed paused, and nothing in the universe moved.

Geisel cursed as he looked around. He'd lost his grip on his gun, but it had suspended in mid-air, several feet away. Chance drove his shoulder into Geisel, pummeling and throttling him with his left fist until Geisel clapped him in the throat.

Chance gasped for breath. He noticed Jerry's gun in the street, and he dove toward it as Geisel reached for his own, plucking it from the air. Chance grasped the pistol, twisting to clutch it with both hands as he squeezed the trigger, again, again.

The gun made a strange, chuffling sound, however, and the bullets, when they came, didn't blast from the barrel but rather emerged slowly, rippling in ordered succession and creating in the air behind them tiny wakes. Geisel slid sideways to watch the bullets pass by, then fired a single shot at Chance.

In the silent, paused world, the sound of the gun's firing stung Chance's ears, and pain like a brick wall exploded in his chest, bashing him backward. The gun slipped from his fingers, suspending in midair, as he fell to his ass, touched his chest where the pain seemed focused, withdrew his hand to find his fingers tacky and red. He didn't want to believe it was blood.

"It was never supposed to go this far, you know," Geisel said. "We thought your dad would cooperate, especially after his only son so narrowly escaped from the World Trade Center attack last month. But he didn't. And then you showed up. But we got it in the end. We always do."

He looked down at the time machine, and one of his fingers twitched, and then the rain began to fall in enormous, cold drops all over Chance's body. Cassie screamed in surprise and pain as she fell, as time began again to move forward, just like it always did.

If Jerry's midair-suspended gun hadn't fallen into his hand, Chance would not have been able to reach for it. But gravity took it over, and the wet stock on his palm surged him adrenaline enough he could raise it, fire it, two shots like a binary thunderclap before the world could get its bearings.

Both Hanley and Geisel sank to the ground.

Cassie screamed Chance's name. She sounded a long way off. Chance wondered where she was. He suddenly realized how heavy Jerry's gun was, which seemed odd; it hadn't felt so heavy a moment before. He let it go, and it clattered to the street.

He felt hands, then, around his neck, around his body.

"Cassie," he whispered as she cradled his head.

"Don't move, okay? We're going to get you help," she started to move sideways. She yelled to her parents to call 911.

"No, wait," Chance reached for her. Because he didn't want her to go. Not yet. His body felt heavy, but his head felt light, as if he were trying to break free from his cumbersome skin. His exhalations came easy and full but his inhalations didn't seem to bring enough air. Sleep seemed a haven.

"What is it?" Cassie asked him.

Chance swallowed, gathering up his energy, which seemed to slip away like sand. "Your dream. It was true."

"But we beat it, Chance. We didn't use it. It's going to be okay."

He shook his head. "No. The other part."

"What?"

He swallowed. It was hard. He almost couldn't do it. "I love you, Cass. Always have."

"Oh, God, Chance, I know. I know. Just stay with me. Stay with me."

The rough surface of the road below him bit into his skin. "So cold," he whispered, and it began to seep up through his skin, into his body and his bones. "So wet."

"It's raining," she told him.

"Make it stop."

She nodded. "Just for me."

Darkness.

38

Chance will wake in a bright white room redolent with disinfectant. Beside him, a heart monitor will beep. A tube will hiss cold air into his nose. Swallowing will feel like a knife, and he will groan.

Just a few feet away, Cassie will hear and will put aside her novel to move to his side. "You're awake," she will say, smiling as she smoothes his hair. "God, I was so worried."

He will swallow again. Cough. She will press a plastic tumbler to his lips, and he will sip cold water.

Cassie will hesitate, then. "I should get the doctor. Hang on," she will tell him, and she will duck her head out the door.

*

In a reality without the NAU, without major advancements in physics related to spacetime, Leonard Kensington will study medicine at Columbia University, then take a position, specializing in emergency medicine, on staff at Princeton-Plainsboro Hospital. He will be satisfied by his career but will feel unfulfilled romantically, as though his life lacks a specific someone who should be in it.

Until September 11th, when he will travel to Manhattan to assist in relief efforts. There he will meet a distressed young temp named Jennifer Masters, one of many people he will treat for smoke inhalation and lung congestion but who will stand out, among his other patients, for a reason he will not be able to fathom. Jennifer, dissatisfied with her career (or lack thereof) as a temp will begin to volunteer at the hospital where Leonard works—

and together they will walk into Chance Sowin's room, where Leonard will introduce himself to the young man who keeps turning up in his care. "First your shoulder, and now your back? You were lucky," Leonard will tell Chance. "But the bullet hit your spine, and we had to operate several hours to remove the slug. There was a lot of damage—."

"What sort of damage?" Chance will ask.

Doctor Kensington will hesitate: "We expect some paralysis—."

"I'm paralyzed?" Chance will only during that moment wonder if he doesn't feel much pain below his navel because he can't feel anything at all below his navel. When he tries to raise a leg, it will feel successful, but neither will actually move.

"We won't be sure until you start physical therapy."

"I thought you said I was lucky."

"You're alive. And you can start your therapy just as soon as you're ready. In the meantime, you should get some rest," Leonard will say, looking at Cassie.

"I'll be going soon," Cassie will say.

Leonard will nod, and Jennifer will follow him out of the room, into the next and the next and the next as Leonard continues his rounds.

Chance will swallow again, his throat tightening.

Cassie will brush a tear away from his cheek with her fingertip. "Hey, it's going to—."

"Please don't tell me it's going to be okay. My father's dead and I'm paralyzed—."

"But you're not dead," Cassie will say. "That's got to count for something."

Chance will fall silent a moment before he thinks of something. "The time machine. You—."

"I used it to get you here. Paused the whole world," Cassie will say, and she will squeeze his hand.

Chance will smile when he feels her fingers on his, because at least he knows that sensation remains. It will give him some hope. He will ask after the others, and Cassie will tell him that Jerry didn't make it, and that the government disavowed any knowledge of Geisel or Hanley or any organizational branch for which either might have worked. She will tell him that she saved as much of his father's research as she was able, and that Princeton has hired her to continue Dennis Sowin's work.

And then she will pause.

"What is it?" Chance will ask.

"Back there," she will say. "Did you mean it?"

Chance won't need to ask her what she means. "Always."

She will bend, then, and she will kiss him, firmly, on the mouth.

Chance will return her kiss, and he will feel some peace, some satisfaction, despite what he has lost. Because he will understand that whoever had said you can never go home again had only been half right: it was really less about going home, and more about new beginnings. That's really all the future is, just the present beginning again, over and over. Which is why you can't change the past, and you shouldn't worry about the future; trying to do either can only ruin the present. All you can do, Chance will realize, is embrace the past, and live in the present while the future arrives one new beginning at a time.

Acknowledgements

This novel wouldn't be what it is without its editrix, Hannah Blum. I wouldn't have met Hannah, nor given her a worthy draft, without the help of USC and the teachers, classmates, and students I met there, including Sid Stebel, Janet Fitch, Rachel Resnick, John Rechy, Shelly Lowenkopf, and Syd Field. Also, in memory of Irvin Kershner, who helped keep this book from becoming gobbledygook. Here I must mention my sister, Nyssa, who drove with me from Jersey to USC. What a journey.

My development as a writer was aided and abetted by family and friends: my folks and siblings, my extended family (including my grandparents, Aunt Wonder Woman and Uncle Bob), Tim Campbell, Brian Beldowicz, Kristen Brownell, Andrea Wilson-Woods, Karri Hayes, Trista Rista, and myriad others. So many friends I haven't yet met have lent support first via MySpace and now via Twitter and Facebook and the social web. Shannon Yarbrough had kindest words, Emma Arnold demanded I fix my ending, Maggie Stewart-Grant encouraged alternate history, Natalie Baird-Yates stuck me on the toilet with Vonnegut, Lisa Sura-Noyes always said keep going, boy-o, Rachel Kreuger believed I had a real book in me, Chrissa King supported my awesome, and if I kept enumerating I'd write another 90,000 words.

Art is never created in a vacuum. It is a product of its society and a result of influences that not only shape but also create whoever commits it. If I have committed art (and I hope this qualifies), it owes to everyone I've known. I thank you.